Subversion of Trust

Also by William T. Close

A Doctor's Life: Unique Stories

Ebola: Through the Eyes of the People

A Novel
by

William T. Close, M.D.

Subversion
of Trust

To Barry with warm
regards + much esteem
Bill

William Stone M.D.
April '02

MEADOWLARK SPRINGS
PRODUCTIONS

Published by:
Meadowlark Springs Productions
P.O. Box 4460
Marbleton, Wyoming 83113

Subversion of Trust
By William T. Close, M.D.

Publisher's Cataloging-in-Publication
(Provided by Quality Books, Inc.)

Close, William T.
   Subversion of trust / by William T. Close. — 1st ed.

   p. cm.
   ISBN 0-9703371-2-4

   1. Health maintenance organizations—Fiction.
2. Physicians—Fiction. 3. Medical ethics—Fiction.
4. Montana—Fiction. I. Title.

PS3553.L587S83 2002   811'.6
                           QBI33–295

Cover design by Peri Poloni, Knockout Design, Cameron Park, California

Book design by Christine Nolt, Cirrus Design, Santa Barbara, California

Edited by Gail M. Kearns, GMK Editorial & Writing Services,
Santa Barbara, California

Book production coordinated by To Press and Beyond,
Santa Barbara, California

Printed in the United States of America

This book is dedicated to Bettine, my friend,

my wife of fifty-nine years.

. . . the secret of the care of the patient

is caring for the patient.

—Francis Peabody, 1927

Chapter 1

THE TELEPHONE'S JANGLE shocked Alex awake. The dispatcher's high-pitched rasp stabbed his ear. "Sheriff's office, Dr. McKinnon. Brawl at the Sagebrush Saloon. Ambulance on its way."

Peggy pulled a pillow over her head.

Alex exploded, "Can't you people keep the lid on the bars for Christ's sake? What time is it?" He reached for the light.

"One A.M., Doctor."

"God Almighty!"

After a heavy pause, "You okay, Doc?" The voice sounded more sympathetic.

"I suppose." He sat up. "Sorry to bark at you."

"It's okay. I know how ya feel."

"Tell the ambulance to call me when they've loaded the patients." He hung up and rolled over to Peggy, put his hand on her hip and kissed the back of her head.

"What," she mumbled.

"The ambulance is on its way to the Sagebrush."

Alex sat on the bench in the cabin's mud room, pulled on his boots and grabbed his duffel coat and tweed cap as Peggy struggled into her parka. They clomped down the back steps to the car shed. The snow showers had eased and stars sparkled between moonlit clouds. A chilly wind reminded them that the warmth of summer was still a couple of months off. He opened the door of the Blazer. Gus, his shaggy black dog, jumped into the back seat and Peggy crawled into the front. Alex backed out, then headed down the lane past the main house of the Morgan

11

Ranch and turned onto the county highway toward
Cicero, fifteen minutes away.

They passed the Collette place where a yard light illu-
minated mud-splashed pickups and the yellow glow from
small barn windows were signs that calving was in full
swing. Alex realized, with little comfort, that during the
mud season in western Montana, a stockman's night work
was even more demanding than a rural doc's.

"It pisses me off to have to get up in the middle of the
night for some meathead drunk," said Alex.

Peggy rubbed the back of his neck. "So, what would
happen if you told them you weren't available?"

"The ambulance crew would drive a hundred miles to
the nearest hospital."

The radio crackled, "MS-One to Dr. McKinnon."

"Go ahead, Donny."

"We have one patient with lacerations of his mouth
and scalp."

"Donald Duck?"

"He's conscious, combative and bleeding . . . " Donny's
voice faded, then returned . . . "and vomiting. Not a happy
Duck."

Saying "drunk" over the air was frowned upon, so the
code for drunk and disorderly was Donald Duck. A happy
Duck was drunk, but not disorderly. It made a huge difference, especially in the middle of the night.

"We're on our way," replied Alex. He gritted his teeth
and set his mind to the ordeal ahead.

They drove by Jolene's modular home on the outskirts
of town. The bedroom light was off. Peggy sighed, closed
her eyes and rested her head on Alex's shoulder. A few
hours ago, the distraught young mother had called. Her
screaming two-year-old's infected ears needed more time
to respond to the antibiotics prescribed earlier. Tylenol
and drops of warm mineral oil in the canals had appar-

ently allowed mother and child to sleep.

Alex turned down Cicero's main street. A sheriff's patrol car, lights flashing, sat outside the Sagebrush Saloon. He drove past the bank, general merchandise store, town hall, post office, drug store and library. The town's six churches of various denominations occupied lots on side streets nestled among garages, oil-field maintenance outfits and tire shops. Off on a site, that could almost be called historical, perched a small log building whose function had changed from a doctor's office to a police station and jail to an answering service at the present time. The only thing that had grown about the building was the number of fancy antennae that sprouted from its roof. These allowed Roxanna and her part-time helper/full-time husband John, the operators of the intelligence service, to keep their radio or telephone ears tuned into the life of the community and many of its inhabitants, especially Doc, whose freedom of movement depended on efficient communications. Roxie could be tough if his phone was accidentally off the hook or his radio battery dead. She treated him like she did her kids, Nebraska-straight but warmhearted. If he teased her, which he often did, her response was always, "Are you messin' with me?"

Main Street ended at the high school football field. Alex turned right and parked next to the ambulance and another sheriff's car at the clinic's emergency entrance. The vehicles' rotating lights swept across the medical building, empty parking lot and a stack of snow-covered hay in an adjacent ranch pasture.

Donny and Deputy Moose Magoo struggled to hold the patient on the table. Peggy drew up local anesthetic and opened a suture set and gloves. Alex cut a wad of blood-soaked hair off the edges of a jagged scalp wound. A spurter splattered his shirt with blood.

"I'll hold his hands, you sit on his legs, Moose," said Donny. The deputy was six-foot-four and weighed two-hundred-eighty pounds.

The patient snarled, "Fugginsonofabish gedoff me. I donwanna haircut. I doneed any fuggin' doctor. Jusneed to kill that fuggin' cowboy."

The patient struggled to sit up. Alex grabbed a fistful of grimy shirt and pushed him down on the table. "Listen, mister, if you don't want to be sewed up I'll let them pack you off to jail and you can bleed to death."

The drunk tried to focus on Alex. "Who're you?"

"I'm the doctor and I'm telling you, when you're in my clinic you watch your language and behave yourself or I'll throw you out."

The drunk's head waggled on a scrawny neck as he took in Alex's size hovering over him. His stomach heaved and a stream of bile-stained alcohol drooled out of the corner of his pulpy mouth. He flopped back onto the table. "Shorry, Doc."

Alex clamped and tied off bleeders, then ran his finger under the flap of scalp to check for a fracture before closing the wound. By the time they got to the man's lips, he was in a drunken stupor and the repair was quickly done. They wrapped a dressing around his head and Moose stuffed him into the back of his patrol car for the ride to the holding pen in the basement of the town hall.

Alex wrote in a chart while Donny helped Peggy clean up. As a young man, Donny rode bucking broncs and worked on oil rigs. He'd started the EMT ambulance program and become the caretaker of their small town. Over the years, he'd delivered more babies in the ambulance on the way to the hospital than Alex had in his whole career. Efficient and reliable, he could also be tough. But even though Donny and Alex were friends, he kept secret his favorite fishing holes.

Outside, the wind had died but the cold penetrated to the bone. The fur around Peggy's hood framed her face and her large dark eyes shone in the starlight.

They headed home. Both were beyond exhaustion. Peggy said, "At the risk of sounding like a cracked record, we can try to keep going forever but unless we get regular breaks I might go bananas and you'll have a heart attack or a stroke."

"We do get some time off. Jenny comes out two weekends a month."

"If she was with us full time we'd have a life."

Twelve years ago when Alex and Peggy had moved to Cicero, Jenny was thirteen. She had puppy-dogged Alex in his office and lugged his black bag on house calls. She'd kneel on the lab stool, bent forward to peer into the microscope, her dark brown hair forming a tent around the lenses. From time to time she'd lean back, shake her head and hook some of the tresses behind her ears, then focus again on the microcosm below. She was unperturbed by blood or festering wounds and a favorite with patients. After some practice, she became sharp with a stethoscope. Now she was in her second year in the emergency room of the regional medical center on the other side of the mountain pass that separated Cicero from the county seat in Big Timber.

Alex pulled into the garage. "Right now we need a shower and some sleep."

It was 2:15 A.M. when they tossed their puke-stained and bloody clothes in the washing machine and stepped into their twin shower to soak away the ache of tired muscles. Under the drenching hot water they rubbed each other's backs and necks. Alex massaged Peg's shoulders then wrapped his arms around her.

"Let's throw a few things in a suitcase and drive to a beach in California."

She rested her head on his chest. "Why not Yuma?"

"Yuma?"

"Yes. I like the name," she added, sleepily. They varied their escape dreams from western deserts to French villages and Nordic fjords.

They dried off with big soft towels then crawled under the comforter and Peggy held him in her arms. He kissed her neck. "The last thing I want is for our work to start driving us apart. I'd rather give up medicine altogether than lose you. Anyway, I love you."

"You're not about to lose me and I love you too."

They were both too tired to sleep but lay still to avoid keeping the other awake. Gus snored away on his couch, his shaggy head resting on a pillow of contentment. His philosophy was simple: "sack it" in the absence of chaseables. The old dog never played catch up on sleep. Sleep was his principle activity day and night. But at the words "walk" or "fish" he became a bounding, high-energy twirling dervish that filled Alex with joy and laughter.

Peggy was right, of course, they needed real time off to get a life beyond the reach of telephones and radios, beyond the demands of patients. But that was hard to do without feeling guilty and wondering what was happening to those they were committed to care for. Younger doctors, especially the women who were mothers and wives, struggled with two full loads of work, family and patients. In a city practice a doctor could sign out from the office and the hospital, but in rural practices the only way to sign out was to leave town.

Peggy went through the exercise of relax your feet, relax your knees, relax thighs, butt, back, neck and relax your shoulders, three times. Especially the shoulders. But sleep was impossible. She thought about the patients they'd seen in the last twenty-four hours and ahead to the ones they would see the next day. In her mind, she listed the supplies used and what she would need to order. She kept a tablet and pencil on her bedside table to note things she needed to remember. She'd once read that if you wrote it down it would clear your mind for sleep. She looked over at Alex and envied his gentle, rhythmic snoring.

At 4:30 A.M. the telephone rang, this time on Peggy's side of the bed. Alex heard her say, "I'll be right over." He went back to sleep until his phone rang. It was Peggy calling from Grandma Ellen's. "She's having a hard time breathing and her lungs are filling up."

"I'll come."

Again he had no choice. But this time the patient was a friend and he wanted to go. Gus opened one eye and elected to stay on his couch. Alex pulled on khakis, a turtleneck and boots, grabbed his bag and coat and drove to Ellen's home in town. Peggy met him at the door.

"It's her heart again."

Alex greeted the family as he walked through the living room into the hall and bedroom. Ellen's daughter Lucy sat on the edge of the bed holding her mother's hand. She got up as he walked in.

"She's plumb out of it. She had two shots of bourbon after dinner. Do you think that might be the trouble?"

"I doubt it." Alex pulled up a chair to the bed. "Having trouble breathing again?"

The old lady smiled weakly and nodded. The oxygen hissed through the prongs in her nose.

"Any chest pain?"

She shook her head.

"No pressure or discomfort?"

"A tad," she whispered.

To Ellen, and others of her ilk, pain was when a horse kicked you in the face or a bull ran over you. Alex called them his TNTs—Total Non-Turkeys. But congestive failure was tough, even for a TNT.

The old lady's heart had become a flabby bag over the past year and she'd been in chronic heart failure with a couple of acute episodes that brought her to the brink of death. Each time, a strong diuretic and more oxygen pushed her through the crisis until the next one.

Peggy had already checked her pressure and pulse and turned up the oxygen to six liters. She took Ellen's hands and eased her up so Alex could listen to her lungs.

"More Lasix should help again," he said. Peggy opened his bag and a moment later handed him a syringe with the diuretic drawn up. After injecting the medicine, Alex fluffed up her pillow and straightened the sheets and comforter.

"Try to sleep, Ellen. We'll sit with you 'til you feel better."

She closed her eyes. Alex sat forward and watched her. She was in her eighties, still as feisty and independent as ever, even when the fluid in her lungs made her speak in short bursts. Her father, one of the earliest settlers in the valley, had scooped out some of the larger irrigation ditches allowing the native grasses to flourish and feed his cattle. On the side, between punching cows, he was the town's undertaker. His advice on sickness was available to those who sought it.

Half an hour later, Ellen's breathing had improved and she slept. Alex talked with the family. They were realistic about her condition yet still sure she was better off at home than in a hospital. And, anyway, that's what Grandma wanted, her daughter reminded them.

The repetitive squeak in his wristwatch woke him at six. Peggy's routine started half an hour later. Maybe he should turn off her alarm clock and let her sleep in. No, she wouldn't like that.

He worked the stiffness out of his back, shuffled into the bathroom and forced a grin at the face in the mirror. Not too bad for sixty. Tummy still flat or flattish. Hair and whiskers going from gray to white, and only a few extra wrinkles around his eyes, mostly sun squint and smile lines. He repeated what a psychiatrist once advised tired doctors to recite on mornings such as these: "Damn it man, you're the handsomest, most energetic and competent doctor in three counties!" At least it made him chuckle. He stretched his upper lip over his teeth and again considered shaving off his mustache. He might look younger without it. He'd ask Peg what she thought. He glanced at his profile in the mirror on the shower door and sucked in his gut. Those thick peanut butter and jam sandwiches he had for lunch all settled between his chest and belly button. He and Peggy shared the chores of cooking and dishes, so half the time he ate normally. She talked to him about diet but didn't nag. He held a hot washcloth to his eyes, then shaved and dressed.

Gus was asleep on the couch. Doc ruffled his long ears. "C'mon, you lazy mutt. Let's go." The long plumed tail wagged twice and an eye opened in the mop of black hair. The shaggy head came off the pillow and, after a wide yawn, the big dog eased off his bed one paw at a time, stretching and licking the long muzzle hair off his teeth. He had the comfortable ears of an otter hound, the deep chest of a setter, the rough coat of a Bouvier. He followed Alex into the kitchen and sat by the door until he was let out. Alex scooped Science Diet—Senior—into Gus' dish, turned on the coffee machine and pushed bread into the toaster. The morning routine was immutable. While listening to National Public Radio news, he drank two cups of coffee and ate the toast with jam. Gus would eat after the walk.

Alex put on his duffel coat and cap, opened the door

and followed the dog up the dirt road through the Morgan Ranch. He glanced at his watch: 6:30. Right on time. Seven-thirty would see him home in the shower, and at 8:00 Peggy and he would climb into the Blazer and be in the clinic at 8:15 to go over the charts for the day. Security and sanity rested in routine so long as night calls left enough energy to function.

The frost on the grass and the willows sparkled as the sun rose from behind the silhouettes of the mountains. A meadowlark on a fence post practiced his mating call and curlews skimmed over soggy glades where an early thaw had swollen the creek that ran through the place. John Morgan, with straight-backed dignity, rode slowly among his pregnant cows. He raised his hand in greeting when he saw Alex.

Gus ranged through the naked willows, their buds chewed off by moose that wintered by the creek. A measured mile up the narrow road, Alex sat on his resting log, stuffed a pinch of burley in his pipe, lit up and thought about last night's three calls. The first had been straight-forward: the kid with infected ears and a desperate young mother. The second call made him wish he worked in an ammunition factory; the third ensured that life as a country doc remained worthwhile although exhausting. Behind him, Gus set up a howl. Alex stood, knocked the dottle out of his pipe and walked over to where the old dog had spotted a porcupine up a tree.

"Leave it, you silly old dog. You'll never learn, will ya."

Gus glanced at him, then up the tree and howled again, his mouth becoming an O like a cartoon dog.

"Gus, come!"

The dog took one more look then padded over to Alex. His eyes said, Aw gee, Doc. Alex squatted down and took his shaggy head between his hands and buried his face in the thick fur between his long ears. "You're such a funny old dog. Now come on, we can't be late."

Alex stood and a cold gust off the mountains made him close the top horn button on his coat. The dull ache in his chest returned and he pulled the nitros from his pocket and popped one under his tongue. He felt the reassuring tingle, the ache in his chest eased and, picking up the cadence, he and Gus strode into another day.

Chapter 2

A LEX EXCHANGED HIS CARDIGAN for a white coat and adjusted the stethoscope in the pocket. He was uncomfortable with it around his neck, unlike the younger doctors. Gus collapsed behind his chair with a bony thud. Peggy walked in with two cups of coffee and sat in the antique chair with its petit point seat and cherry wood arms in front of Alex's desk. His mother had given him this family heirloom when he graduated from medical school. In her view, it added a certain cachet to his office.

"Good morning, Miss Peggy Strong."

"Good morning, Dr. McKinnon."

This first act of the day in the office was a routine established a long time ago in New York when Peg had left the hospital to become his office nurse. And every morning he marveled that she looked so fresh and serene in her neat white pants and colorful blouse, regardless of sleep or not.

Peggy glanced at her to-do and questions list. "Ellen's daughter called to say that her mother was feeling much better. She's talking about going up to her cabin."

"I'll talk to the family. One of them needs to go with her to haul her oxygen around."

"They won't want her to go."

"I think they will. We've talked about letting her do what she wants. They agree it's the best way to keep her happy." He looked up at Peggy. "If we told her no she'd go anyway." Alex reached for the top chart on the stack.

"Will you drive up to see her if she gets into trouble?"

"Sure, we could all go and take a picnic. Gus would

like that." The black tail slapped the floor.

Alex sipped his coffee as Peg ran down her list. She knew the answers to most of the questions but asked them anyway, not for approval but as a partner in their work. In her calm, no-nonsense way she made sure he saw people who needed to be seen whether he was tired or not.

The telephone rang. "Cicero Clinic, Peggy." She covered the mouthpiece. "It's Hugh Drummel, the new administrator from the hospital."

"I don't want to talk to Hugh Drummel. What does he want?"

"How should I know. Here, talk to him."

"No. Ask him what he wants."

"The doctor's busy and asked me to take a message." She listened, then added, "I'll be glad to pass it on. Thank you for calling."

"Well?"

"He wanted to invite you personally to a meeting next week. He hoped you'd call him back. He doesn't sound all that bad."

"Neither did the spider to the fly."

Peggy looked at him across the desk. He thumbed through a chart.

The telephone rang again. "It's Dr. Blanford in Missoula." She passed the receiver to Alex.

"Alex, how's your patient Jim Davis?" asked the oncologist.

"I took his stitches out yesterday. His back is still sore but he's doing fairly well. Has the path report come through yet?"

"That's why I'm calling. The tumor in his back came from his lung. Our x-rays didn't show it any more than yours but the bone scan lit up like a Christmas tree. The biopsy shows an oat cell cancer. I think we should see him as soon as possible to discuss radiation or chemo for palliation."

"What a tough break for the old boy. No wonder he was having so much pain. I'll go over and talk to him and his wife today and call you back when I know more about what they want to do." Alex hung up and said to Peggy, "The tumor in Jim's spine came from his lung. It's probably all over him by now."

"Why didn't it show up in the chest x-ray?"

"It often doesn't until it's too late."

"You'd better see them around noon. We're solid the rest of the day."

Alex had a fleeting sense of helplessness. Sometimes it seemed that the most dangerous diseases were the hardest to diagnose early. He couldn't think of a lung cancer patient that he'd picked up soon enough to cure. He rested his elbows on the desk and rubbed his eyes. "Will you call Shirley?"

"If I call her to say we'll be over, she'll know right away the news is bad. Maybe we should just show up."

"That would really scare her. Call her and tell her we'll drop by to see how Jim's doing. She'll want to get him cleaned up and have her house in order." He looked at the next chart. "Who is Barb Tate?"

"A young woman with some sort of attacks of sweating and dizziness."

"How long has she had her symptoms?"

"Since her brother was killed in a car crash."

"Can't we see her later? It'll take more than half an hour to work her up."

"I know, but you can get started. She needs to see you."

Darrell Adams' rugged face appeared in the doorway. "Howaya, Doc?"

"Okay, what about you?"

"Joints need oilin'. Stiff as a board."

Darrell had worked for the Morgan family for many

years. Now he was retired and lived in a cabin down where the creek ran into the river, using kerosene for light and wood for heat and cooking. He drove into town once a week to take a long hot shower and push his clothes through the laundromat. During his life of "cowboyin'," he'd broken every major bone in his body and most of the smaller ones. Both hips were artificial and one knee had been replaced back when success for that type of surgery was iffy. The stiffness in both knees made it difficult to dress, but he used a piece of laundry line to pull his boots on. His work-worn shoulders were so stiff that threading his arms through the sleeves and tucking his shirt into his jeans was a slow and painful exercise. With all his disabilities, he cherished his independence. He was as dignified as an old Percheron and, in his strong quiet way, made it clear that he could and would take care of himself in his cabin.

Alex checked his blood pressure, listened to his lungs through his denim shirt and felt his knees through the jeans.

"Did that stuff I gave you a month ago help your joints?"

"Sure did, Doc, but I ran out a week ago."

"I gave you some refills."

"You did. But, unless you can refill my wallet, I just can't afford that stuff. It's almost two bucks a pill."

"I'm sorry, Darrell. I should have checked that. It's easy to forget that some of our modern miracles cost an arm and a leg. I can give you a generic that costs less."

"Well, I've been using an ointment the vet gave me for my horse. It's got a bite to it but I figure if it helped him it'll help me."

"Does it leave a taste in your mouth?"

"Sure does. Kinda jazzes up my Copenhagen."

Alex laughed. "Whatever works for you is fine by me."

DMSO (dimethylsulfoxide) was a standard home remedy on many ranches and actually worked. Bag Balm, another home remedy, and an ointment ranchers used on sore cow udders, had proved successful in the treatment of irritated nipples on a sophisticated "dudeen" from Baltimore. He chuckled. Jenny and her modern hospital colleagues would be horrified. Well, not Jen, she was raised on a ranch.

He turned back to Darrell. "Let me see you in a month, sooner if you have more problems." Alex walked the old cowboy over to Emma's desk.

Emma Morgan, Jenny's mother, was a licensed practical nurse and part-time receptionist for the clinic. Her full-time calling was that of John Morgan's ranch wife. Her family had started a grocery store in Cicero. She was a small woman who, at one time or another, had mothered most of the people in the valley, including Alex when he arrived from New York. Her mothering provided a shoulder for comfort or, when needed, a proverbial boot that dealt firmly with self-pity or indolence.

Peggy handed him another chart. "Rusty's ready for you. He's fine." When she said a patient was "fine," it meant that a short visit was probably all that was needed. Rusty Polson was a long-time rancher. His father, known as "The Boss," was one of the original settlers in Cicero. At eighty-nine, Rusty walked with short steps and a gnarled cane thrust out in front of him to help his balance. He came in regularly once a month for a "visit." He was the first and only patient Alex had treated for Shy-Drager Syndrome, an odd disease that required him to take salt every day to keep his pressure up. Five years ago, the conductive system in his heart had "rusted away like my hair," as he put it. A pacemaker now kept his rhythm regular, but had done nothing for his hair. In his younger days he smoked and chewed and his lungs were now scarred and tight, making him puff when he walked.

Rusty was perched on the end of the examining table like a bald parrot when Alex walked in. His bright blue eyes danced under scraggly white eyebrows. "You're lookin' pretty spry, Doc." His fingers opened and closed over his cane. He was bubbling with the anticipation of giving Alex the latest news of goings-on and the cycle of life on his ranch.

"Sure gettin' a fine crop o' calves. Real fine."

Alex sat on the stool.

"I'll tell ya somethin' else, I feel real good. Little wobbly on the way to the barn, but ya know, Doc, I don't have pain in my hip, none at all. Ain't that somethin'?"

Alex laughed. "It sure is somethin', Rusty."

Three months ago the old rancher had called to say that his hip was "kinda sore, not real bad, just sore." It turned out that he'd crawled over the rails into a corral holding several of his angus bulls. One of them had "become too friendly" and crushed him against a pole. His son stretched him out on an old mattress and pile of saddle blankets in the back of his pickup and drove him the thirty miles into the clinic. Rusty's pelvis was cracked in two places with little or no displacement. Bed rest was all that was needed. After ten days, Rusty's wife and children told Alex that they had let the old boy get up and hobble to the barn. It was that or they'd all go crazy.

Alex checked him over and reviewed his medicines.

When he was through, Rusty pumped his arms rapidly over his head in an exercise Alex had given him to increase his heart rate before he stood. He climbed down from the table and headed for the door without collapsing. "Sure means a lot to come in once a month. Look forward to it, Doc." Alex followed him out to his truck.

"It's great for a doctor's morale to see a friend who's so positive and doing so well."

They stood taking in the beauty and zest of an early spring day.

Rusty wiggled his bushy mustache and sniffed the air. "You can almost smell grass gettin' ready to grow on a day like this."

Two patients later, Barb Tate, neatly dressed in jeans and a sweater, sat before him clutching a balled-up handkerchief. She looked at him shyly. "I feel silly bothering you."

"I'm glad you came in, Barb. Tell me what's been going on."

She looked down at her hands. "You'll probably think I'm crazy or something. I've had bowel and stomach problems since I was fourteen."

"What sort of problems?"

"Diarrhea, constipation, cramps, cold sweats and sometimes I feel sick to my stomach."

Alex questioned her about the specifics, jotting notes in her chart. Her repertoire was well rehearsed.

"Have you seen anyone else about these symptoms?"

"I went to Dr. Peterson in Simms. He told me I was anxious and sent me to a psychologist."

Alex waited for more.

"I saw Dr. Peterson once. I wasn't real comfortable with him. He talked too fast and didn't answer my questions."

"And the psychologist?"

"Just once. He was very expensive." She continued, "Sometimes I can go a week without going to the bathroom. About three years ago I got real painful knots in my stomach after eating. I chewed Rolaids but they didn't help. Usually I feel better after a good night's sleep. A year before that I had started going to a . . ." she stumbled over the word, "'chwiropacter', for pain and spasms in my back and pelvis, and charley horses in my neck. He said I was low in calcium."

"Did you take calcium?"

"I did for a couple of months, but it didn't help." She sighed.

"Keep going, Barb, this is important information."

"Well, about a year ago I had what they said were 'anxiety attacks'."

"Who was 'they'?"

"A mental health guy."

"Go on."

"The spells started with breathing trouble. I felt like I was smothering, like I couldn't get enough air, like I was dying, like the sky was falling on me . . . like a terrible panic. Once, when I was tucking my baby in for the night, I was sure I wouldn't make it to her first birthday. A nurse told me that I had a serious sinus infection, so I left it at that." She shrugged and raised her eyebrows.

"Then what?"

She went on to describe what were classic panic attacks caused by sudden discharges of adrenaline in her body. She added, "Then I saw another mental health guy who told me I'd be fine when he got my head straight." She started to cry. "Do you think I'm nuts, Doctor?"

Gus came around the desk and rested his muzzle on her lap. She hugged him and left wet spots on the top of his head. He lay down next to her.

"No, Barb, I don't think you're nuts. You're probably having panic attacks and those are terrifying."

There was a knock on the door and Peggy stepped in. "Sorry to interrupt, but we'd better do our house call."

"Barb, we need to finish your history, do a physical exam and check your blood. We can do that next week and then start you on a program that will help. Can you hang on until we get you worked up properly?"

"Sure, Doctor. I've been hanging on for a long time. A few days more won't make any difference." She ruffled the top of Gus' head before stepping out of the office. Emma scheduled her for a blood draw the next morning and gave her a card with the follow-up appointment.

As Alex and Peggy headed out, Emma told them that Milly Hastings had called to say that Tad, the retired sheepherder who camped out on her place, had returned and wanted to know if Doc could take a look at him before the end of the day.

"What time do we have to be back?" asked Alex.

"Two o'clock."

"Can't that little buzzard come to the clinic?"

"He can, but he won't," replied Emma. She called Roxanna at the answering service to let them know where the doctor would be.

They pulled up to Jim and Shirley Davis' place and walked in through the garage. Jim's workbench stood against the wall, every tool in place. Shirley met them at the back door. "Did you hear from Missoula?"

"Yes," said Alex. "I'm afraid it's not good news."

Peggy put her arm around Shirley. "Let's sit down with Jim so Doc can go over the report and we can talk about what to do." They joined Jim at the kitchen table.

Alex came right to the point. "Dr. Blanford called this morning. He gave me the report on the tumor in your back. It is cancer, Jim. I'm afraid a rather serious one, which seems to have originated in your lung."

Shirley, who was making coffee at the stove, looked at Jim over her shoulder. He stared at his hands. "Is that why I've had pain in my back and been coughing so much?"

"Sure seems to be the reason, though neither we nor

the doctors in Missoula were able to see anything on x-ray, and the studies of your sputum were negative for tumor cells."

Jim hesitated, then asked with a tremor in his voice, "What do you mean by serious?"

"I mean a tumor with primitive cells that are growing very fast. One that has probably spread to other places in your body."

Shirley poured the coffee and sat next to her husband. "Can anything be done?"

"Yes. We think that radiation and chemotherapy may slow the growth for months or even longer. There's no way of knowing without trying."

Jim gripped his coffee mug with both hands and looked squarely at Alex. "What'll happen if I do nothing?"

"You'll have pain and probably more coughing. And you may bleed. We can control your pain, Jim. Chemotherapy with or without radiation might make it easier to keep you comfortable."

"Can you take care of me here at home?"

"Sure, for everything except the radiation. That would have to be done in a big center like Missoula."

Jim ran his hand over his bald head. Alex wondered what he would do, how he would feel if he were in Jim's shoes. Would he go through a month or so of radiation and accept the side effects of chemo or would he accept a quicker end? It's harder for doctors, he thought, they know what it usually adds up to. And yet, if he knew he was going to die, a few more days or months might make all the difference.

"What would you do if you were in my shoes, Doc?"

"I don't know for sure, but I think I'd go to the center and have a frank talk with the radiologist and oncologist about what their treatments would do to the tumor and to the rest of me."

Jim nodded slowly.

Alex continued. "Shirley would go with you and you could talk it over together. When you come back we can sit down with all the cards on the table. You know Peggy and I are available anytime."

"When does he have to make up his mind?" asked Shirley.

"This week. Really, the sooner the better if we want results."

"All right, Doc. We'll let you know tomorrow morning," said Jim.

Shirley stood by the back door and waved good-bye as Alex and Peggy drove away.

"What do you think they'll do?" asked Alex.

"I don't know, but I do know she'll have a hard time adjusting to being alone."

Some couples were pasted together by ceremony and habit. For others, the death of a spouse brought a release of sorts. But not for Jim and Shirley. He reached for Peggy's hand and held it.

He glanced at her. "What?"

"Just thinking about Jim and Shirley." *And you,* she thought. If something happened to Alex, her life would go on, it had to, but it would be like living next to an empty space. What would she do? Go back to Maine and live with her grandmother? At this point only speculation, thank God. Not yet the certainty that Shirley faced.

Two muddy ruts led to Tad Irola's sheep wagon. He'd wintered in the lee of a bare knoll on the Hastings vast south pasture that stretched to the foothills. A week ago Alex sent him to the hospital with pneumonia. His infection responded rapidly to IV antibiotics, but as soon as he felt better he fought the nurses who tried to give him a bath and cut his toenails. That very evening, while the shifts were changing, he pulled on his pants and sheepskin jacket and, carrying his boots, escaped to his rattletrap pickup and drove away. The nurse had notified Alex and was relieved when his only comment was, "He'll show up."

"Do you know what Tad stands for?" asked Peggy as they drove up to the wagon.

"No idea."

"Tadpole, for his big head and small body. He told me that himself. Maybe you can find out where he's been since he left the hospital." A brisk wind whisked away smoke from the rusty stovepipe. "I'll wait here. Call me if you need help."

"I won't be long," said Alex, grabbing his bag. He climbed the wagon's two steps, banged on the door and disappeared under the canvas top.

An ancient border collie with mange on his back growled, then, recognizing the intruder, whined and wagged his tail as Doc adjusted to the dim smoky light.

"Tad, goddamit, where the hell have you been?"

The sheepherder rolled over on his side, propped himself up on an elbow and after a long, chest-rattling cough, spat into a coffee can and cleared his throat.

"Up da mountain with my compadre, Beak Abio. He make medicine for cough." He reached for a brown bottle on the shelf above his bunk, pulled the cork and took a swig. "Powerful . . . ." He hacked up another glob that looked like lemon pudding and egg white.

Alex reached for the bottle and sniffed the contents. "Smells like whiskey and creosote."

"I dunno, but it's sure good stuff for me."

Alex opened his bag and pulled out his stethoscope. "Let me listen to your lungs."

The old Basque peeled back the top of his sleeping bag

and sat up. Alex pulled up the stained thermal undershirt and thumped his bony back. The lower half of his left lung was still dull and, when he listened with his stethoscope, normal breath sounds were muted by low-pitched, soggy rales where phlegm clung to the walls of the larger bronchi. He put his hand on Tad's weathered forehead. If he had a fever, it wasn't very much.

"Have you had any chills, Tad? You know . . ." Alex shivered and chattered his teeth.

"No chills. I keep da stove goin'. It's real nice and warm," he said as he tucked his undershirt into his long johns and lay back.

"It's like a furnace in here, Tad. You need air with that stove going."

"Dis ol' wagon is plum fulla leaks and I sure get air when I go out to pee."

Doc checked the plywood cupboard and counted two cans of baked beans, a can of condensed milk with two gummy stab holes in the top and a half empty can of Spam. In a chipped enamel basin under the cupboard, a coffee mug and plastic plate lay half submerged in greasy water.

"You need more food," said Alex. "You got enough coffee and tea?"

"Grub's good, Doc. One of da boys brings stuff every coupla days. Da boss lady take good care of me, even sends food for Dog."

Alex sat on the edge of the bunk, reached over and scratched Dog behind the ear.

"Well, I guess you two are pretty well taken care of, but that stuff you're bringing up from your lungs is putrid and you still look gaunt to me." He dug into his medical bag and brought out an envelope and a large vial of brightly colored antibiotic capsules. He poured them into his hand, counted out twenty and transferred them to the envelope. "I want you to take one of these four times a day. They'll help clear up the pus in your chest."

The sheepherder took the envelope and looked at the capsules. "Four times in one day?"

"Yes." Alex emphasized the point. "Take one with breakfast, one with lunch, one with supper and another before you go to bed."

"I don't eat but once a day, Doc."

"Well, take one when you first wake up."

"Okay I'm up real early to pee."

"Take one around noon with your meal."

"Yeah."

"Take one just before dark and one when you take your last leak before hitting the sack."

"Dat's real clear, Doc."

"And drink water 'til your tonsils float."

"Just water?"

"You can put some of Abio's concoction in it or a touch of whiskey if you want. You got enough?"

"Yup," replied Tad with a big grin. "Two lamb chops, Doc?"

"Sure, Tad. Whatever."

On the ride back to the office, Peggy asked if he wanted Emma to submit a Medicare claim for Tad.

"Sure, why not?"

"What diagnosis?"

"Pneumonia in a stubborn old sheepherder."

"Any procedures?"

"Sure. A swallow of Beak Abio's elixir of something-or-other."

"I doubt they have a code for that."

"Well, let's not waste time on their forms."

After coffee and a sandwich, Alex removed a potentially malignant mole from a man's back, then saw a variety of patients including a gaggle of elementary school kids who were passing a flu bug around like a basketball. Peggy interrupted Alex's examination of a boy with epilepsy who needed written permission to swim. "Hank Collette just came in with a chain saw injury to his face."

Alex turned to the boy's mother. "He can swim if the coach is there. I'll write it on a prescription for you."

The chain saw had kicked back and chewed up Hank's cheek and forehead, then bounced off the base of his neck and shoulder. Hank had been forty miles up in the foothills tidying up an old cabin. He'd driven himself in.

"Those are nasty looking wounds, Hank. It'll take a while to get you cleaned up and put back together. Do you want a shot for pain?"

"No need for that, Doc. Just numb it up and go to work. Could one of you call Maybelle and tell her I'm having my face redone to make me handsome?"

"I'll get Emma to call her," Peggy replied, as she finished laying out sterile drapes and gloves, surgical instruments and a syringe with local anesthesia.

Alex looked down at Hank's lanky frame and weather-lined face. Luckily his long nose with its Concord-like droop at the tip had escaped injury.

"You can fix me up can't ya, Doc?"

"We do the best we can with what we're given to work with."

The trimming and sewing took almost an hour. It was painstaking work but Alex enjoyed the surgery. It brought back memories from New York and Africa and didn't require anywhere near the mental effort of trying to piece together a history from a monosyllabic patient. And Peg knew what he needed without his asking.

As he worked on Hank's face, Alex whistled under his

breath marching tunes he learned in the Air Corps Cadets. "What's that your whistling?" asked Hank from under the drape. Alex stopped his cutting and sewing and sang: "Texas is a hell of a place. Parlez-vous.

"Texas is a hell of a place. Parlez-vous.

"Sheppard Field is even worse, it's the asshole of the universe."

Hank and Peggy joined in the chorus: "Hinky dinky, parlez-vous."

They laughed. Alex readjusted the drapes and continued his work.

Hank had fought in the Screaming Eagles, the 101st Airborne Division, dropping into Normandy at Saint-Mère-Église the night before D-Day. The trooper whose parachute got hung up on the church steeple was a buddy of his. Hank had been in the Battle of the Bulge when General McAuliff replied "Nuts" to the German demand for surrender. Alex's Troop Carrier group had towed gliders across the Rhine and Hank teased him about doing his fighting sitting in an airplane. The two of them had swapped stories, usually about wine and women after a few drinks, but never about buddies killed or maimed. Hank especially liked Alex's story about Cookie, which could become the source of heavy philosophical ventilation. Alex and Cook had been dropped off during a driving rainstorm on a metal runway in Normandy. They were replacement pilots for those killed during the invasion. They were billeted over the bakery shop in the village of St. André-de-L'Eure. Alex became the Squadron Morale and Booze Officer, and Cookie screwed the baker's wife in the early morning hours when her husband made the best baguettes Alex ever tasted.

As Peggy applied dressings to Hank's wounds, an angry mother burst through the emergency room back door dragging a boy by the arm, his thumb and hand wrapped in a bloody handkerchief.

"He cut his thumb! I've told him a hundred times never to play with his father's knives." The kid was howling in pain, not from his thumb but from his sore bottom.

Peggy took the child over to the sink and replaced the homemade dressing with a sterile pad. "You come and sit with your mother and hold this tight on your thumb. Dr. McKinnon will be right with you."

She parked Hank in the waiting room until Alex could write prescriptions for an antibiotic and pain medication, then returned to the boy.

The front door opened and a man in a business suit walked in. He glanced around the full waiting room and stepped up to the desk.

"I am Hugh Drummel, Administrator of the Western Montana Regional Medical Center in Big Timber. You must be Peggy Strong."

"No. I'm Emma Morgan. Peggy is busy in the emergency room."

"I'd like to talk to Dr. McKinnon, if he has a moment."

Shrieks and loud voices came from the treatment room. Peggy called out, "Emma, we need your help."

"Mr. Drummel, please have a seat in the waiting room. I'll let Dr. McKinnon know you're here."

Drummel squeezed himself between two patients, as discomfited as a whale in a wading pool. The shrieks from the emergency room produced beads of sweat on his forehead.

With the boy's elbow and wrist gripped by his mother, and Emma holding his legs, Alex anesthetized the thumb and the screams became sobs of, "No please, no, no." Peggy washed the wound and Alex had it repaired with three stitches. They dressed the thumb with bandage and tape.

"Hugh Drummel is in the waiting room," said Emma,

releasing her grip on the boy.

"Drummel? He called this morning. Did he say he was coming over?"

"No," replied Peggy. "He just hoped you'd call him back."

"What shall I tell him?" asked Emma.

"Just tell him to wait. He can see we're busy."

A quarter of an hour later, Emma stepped into Alex's office. "You haven't forgotten about Mr. Drummel have you?"

"No. What's he doing?"

"He's telling Hank Collette all about their new services at the hospital and the plastic surgeon who comes down from Missoula twice a month. He told the others what a nice little clinic you have and how his company could help with equipment and more personnel. He . . . "

"Hold on, Emma." Alex strode into the waiting room just as Drummel was handing out business cards to the patients.

"Mr. Drummel."

"Yes. Oh hello, Dr. McKinnon," said the administrator, handing Alex a card. They shook hands.

"What are you doing?"

"A little public relations with these fine people. I . . . I don't mean to intrude. I see you are very busy but I was hoping for a quick word with you."

"You drove an hour and a half for a quick word? Must be a hell of a word."

From the front door Hank called out, "Thanks, Doc. You want to check the stitches in five days, right?"

"Yes, and call if the pain pills aren't strong enough." The door closed and Hugh was about to say something when Hank's bandaged face reappeared in the doorway. "Better watch that guy in the three-piece suit, Doc. He don't quite fit under those shoulder pads. Seems kinda smooooth like a flimflam man." The door closed to the laughter of the people in the waiting room. Hugh's face flushed and his eyes popped. He pulled a blue silk handkerchief from his breast pocket and wiped the sweat from his forehead.

"Come in for a second, Hugh," said Alex, stifling a laugh.

Chapter 3

A SIREN'S WAIL FADED to a moan outside the emergency room of the Regional Medical Center. Seconds later the doors slammed open and the crew rushed in with a screaming, struggling adolescent strapped to a gurney.

The senior EMT walked over to the desk where Dr. Jenny Morgan was finishing a note on a little girl with appendicitis. "Another meth head for you, Dr. Morgan. Pressure's 180/110; pulse 120. The police picked up his supplier."

"Put him in the drug room and start an Ativan drip," Jenny ordered without looking up. Sally, the ER's head nurse, followed the gurney into the room. The door closed behind the patient, muffling the racket. Half a dozen curtained bays with gurneys surrounded a large U-shaped staff desk with monitors and phones. Two small examining rooms off the hall that led to the rest of the hospital were used for obstreperous patients and procedures like colonoscopies.

Jenny pushed herself away from the desk and turned to a wide-eyed, frightened six-year-old girl in a wheelchair, hugging a floppy bear. She put her hand under the child's chin. "Melissa, you and your teddy bear are going to be just fine." She looked up at the girl's mother, a thin young woman with blonde hair pulled back in a ponytail. A baggy Texas A&M sweatshirt stretched over her swollen belly and upper thighs. Her knees showed through threadbare but clean jeans.

Jenny glanced at the chart. "Waynona. Is that your name?"

"Uh-huh."

41

"You live in Simms?" The girl nodded. "How old are you?"

She stuck out her chin. "Twenty-one."

Jenny noticed the dark circles under the girl's defiant brown eyes. She laid her hand gently on Waynona's bulging tummy. "When are you due?"

"Anytime." She backed away and tugged at her sweat-shirt.

"Have you seen a doctor or nurse about your pregnancy?"

"Nope."

"Dr. Peterson is in Simms. Why didn't you check in with him?"

The young woman stared at the doctor. "I did once when I was puking my guts out with morning sickness. He said that was normal and I'd get over it. He was awful. Would you go to him?"

"Well, I don't know . . . but I'm not pregnant."

Waynona shook her head slowly in disbelief. How could a woman, especially a woman doctor, not know about Peterson's wandering hands and pelvic exams. She asked, "What about Melissa's appendix?"

"Go upstairs with her, then come back here and I'll go over you."

Waynona squinted suspiciously. "I've only got two bucks with me, anyway I'm fine."

"Just come back here after Dr. Woodhouse has seen Melissa and we can talk more. Okay? Won't cost you a nickel." Jenny waved over an aide and handed her the chart. "Please take them up to surgery. Dr. Woodhouse is expecting them. The mother is to return here."

The phone rang. Sally picked it up, listened, jotted a note on a pad and hung up. "The Simms Clinic is sending in a ranch hand with a possible forearm fracture and face lacerations."

"Where's Peterson?" asked Jenny.

"They didn't say."

Jenny walked to the drug room. The patient, a scrawny, emaciated Hispanic, moaned softly on the gurney. The Ativan worked fast once the needle was in and running. She checked the boy's vitals and slowed the drip. In an hour he'd walk out in search of another fix unless the police took him away. She looked at him: sixteen, seventeen years old? Where were his folks? This kid would have to be on the wrong side of the law to pay for his drugs. There were no facilities worth the title to deal with these addicts. The prisons were brutal and often young people thrown into the tank were sodomized and introduced to the high life of pushers and pimps. They became prisoners in a pitiless culture, which consumed its members like a malevolent, lethal cancer.

During her training in San Francisco, drugs and violence were constants. She'd hoped that in this Rocky Mountain medical center things would be different. But the gangs and cultures of inner cities on both coasts were taking over the streets of middle America.

The overhead page called her out of her musing. She picked up the phone. "Dr. Morgan."

"Hi, Jenny. Mr. Drummel would like to see you," said Patricia, his secretary.

"Is it important, Pat?"

"He has good news for you."

"More staff for the ER?"

"I don't think so. Can I tell him you're on your way?"

"I'll be there in a few minutes."

Jenny returned to her desk. Sally asked her to see a boy wheezing and coughing in the pediatric bay. His mother had tried their own doctor but was told by voice mail to go to the emergency room. Inhalants through a nebulizer relieved his worst symptoms. By the time she finished writing orders and talking to the parents of the kid with asthma it was time to deal with the discharge instructions for the crack patient, interrupted by a man who'd fallen off a scaffold and needed an x-ray of his ankle. The page called her again. She answered.

Patricia crooned, "Jenny, he's waiting."

Jenny repressed the desire to say "so what," but replied in her own sing-song voice, "I'm coming." She put down the phone and turned to Sally. "I'm off to Mount Olympus. Call me when Peterson's patient comes in."

"Don't get eaten, Jen," said the nurse. She was a handsome woman with neat white pageboy hair, an authoritative chin and a body with comfortable curves that she struggled to reduce. She was one of the few experienced nurses left after the new administration's clean out of "nonessential personnel" for the sake of the bottom line, and efficiency of course.

In the women's locker room, Jenny washed her face, ran a brush through her dark brown hair and redid her ponytail. She covered her green scrubs with a white coat that had her name over the pocket. She smiled at herself in the mirror and tried a serious frown, but laughed. She was pleased with her green eyes and long lashes and proud of her figure. What did Drummel, that gift to corporate medicine, want now, aside from a piece of her body. She was certain she could handle anything he dished out. Jenny rode the elevator up to the administrative floor.

"Have a seat," said Patricia. "He'll be with you in a second."

In the few months since Patricia and her husband, Bob, had joined the staff, the two women had become friends. Bob's job was to insure that the girls in the record room played the Medicare code game to maximum profit. Their computer software guaranteed to milk every penny out of a diagnosis skirting gingerly between possibility and reality, between truth and fiction. He was the chief accountant and made no bones about being in a job that would give his family a pleasant, uptown lifestyle and money to send the kids to college.

Patricia and Jenny were attractive women, comfortable with themselves and thoroughly competent in their professions. They were a generation away from the old type feminists who pounded pulpits at demonstrations or marched to the drums they beat. Their mutual intolerance of what they called "bullshit" had sealed their friendship early on and, although they played the game, both were turned off by corporate antics at the summit of the medical industry. Jenny's preference would have been to shy away from hospital administration but, since being elected chief of staff by her colleagues, she had no choice. As the youngest member of the staff, she considered her election a challenge and she did her best to be diplomatic. Her real goal was to defend the interests of patients rather than coddle hospital egos.

The door opened and a distinguished looking man in a blue pinstripe suit stepped into the anteroom followed by Drummel.

"Ahhh, Jennifer. I'm so glad to see you. Clayton, I want you to meet Dr. Jennifer Morgan. I consider her one of the brightest stars in the medical galaxy shining over the Rocky Mountains. She runs our emergency department. Jenny, this is Dr. Clayton Updike, Head of Public Relations in our Paducah headquarters."

"I'm glad to meet you, Dr. Updike," said Jenny.

"The honor is mine," replied the executive with a wide grin and a nod of his large white-maned head. "Sorry I don't have time to linger, I have a meeting with the chamber of commerce and lunch with the bankers. I look forward to seeing you again soon." Updike turned to shake hands with Drummel. "And I'll see you at lunch."

Hugh turned to Jenny. "Come in, come in. Sorry you weren't able to get here when I called." He stepped behind his desk, resplendent in a dark blue shirt with a white collar. His scarlet nouveau art suspenders matched his tie. He glanced at his watch. "We're both busy so I won't keep you." He sat and waved her to a seat. "Clayton is an important and powerful man in our organization. I wanted him to meet you. He leaves tomorrow morning to visit our hospitals up north, but he will be back a week from today to speak to the hospital staff and our attending physicians and all the outlying providers we can assemble. It doesn't give us much time, but I'm counting on you to exert your influence on the staff to attend his presentation."

"What's he going to talk about?"

"The exciting future of corporate medicine, with emphasis on horizon-of-research technologies."

Hugh's round face under thinning hair reminded Jenny of a religious zealot in Washington whose eyes popped with intensity when he spoke. She couldn't remember his name. Her glance swept over Drummel's desktop with its typical furnishings of importance: a signed baseball, a Tiffany clock, a Moroccan leather blotter and accessories and a picture of corporate headquarters in a silver frame with "Congratulations, Hugh" and a scrawled signature across the bottom. No people pictures. No homey wife and laughing kids.

"He's a businessman I take it."

"He is a visionary, Jenny. He has the heart of a doctor and the . . ." Drummel searched for the word . . . "and the savoir-faire of a businessman."

"So he's coming to give us dumb doctors fixated on our patients his business savvy?"

Hugh blinked and drew in air as if in pain. "I wish you wouldn't put it that way, Jenny. The raison d'être of our corporation is to create synergy between the medical community and the business world."

Jenny sighed theatrically, "So sorry. I forgot. So what do you want me to do?"

"Just talk up the meeting and say how important it is to all of us. But also, I'd like you to contact some of the older providers in our catchment area and invite them."

"You won't get many."

"They'd come if they knew Dr. McKinnon was coming. He's a friend of yours, I believe."

"He's more than a friend, he's family. I can try to get him but I wouldn't bet on it. He's very independent."

"From what I hear, you're the apple of his eye."

"Who told you that?"

"Our personnel files are thorough." He stood. "Gotta gather some data sheets before lunch with the bankers and Clayton and Pete Peterson."

"Peterson?"

"Yes. I'm checking him out on the challenge and responsibilities of managed care."

Jenny stood. "Peterson's sending us a patient he'd be taking care of himself if he wasn't having lunch with you."

"You can handle it, Jen."

"Oh, I'm not worried about that." She was annoyed and uncomfortable that he had a file on her and that Peterson was being courted by Drummel. "It just seems that since he joined your HMO he's less available to his patients."

"I wouldn't put it that way, Jenny. I'd say that since we take care of his billing and staffing he has more time for the big picture. His own quality of life has improved with managed care. Now I really have to go." He stepped around the desk and added, "What about a nice dinner at Rubero's on Monday? I hear they're serving soft-shell crab. Maybe Patricia and her husband could join us."

Jenny looked at him, wondering how he could be so sure of himself. "We'll see." She turned and walked out. As she passed Patricia's desk, she rolled her eyes to the ceiling.

Back in the emergency room Waynona and Sally sat at the nurses' station drinking coffee.

"Another invitation for candlelight sushi?" asked Sally.

"Soft-shelled crab."

"He's really after you, isn't he?"

"No problem. I learned to corral horny little bulls on the ranch."

Sally laughed. Waynona looked surprised. "You mean doctors have to put up with that stuff?"

"Women doctors do," replied Jenny. "Come on, let me take a look at you." She led the way to the examining room.

Waynona's history was the familiar story of camp followers who were part of the hand-to-mouth existence of odd-job workers. Her first man, Melissa's father, had been a plumber in College Station, Texas. A Bible thumping, crew-cut Christian, he drank Tang and sang hymns on Sunday but reverted to a brutish drunk during the rest of the week. One day she saw a public service message on TV urging battered women to report their abuse to county authorities. After a social worker visited their trailer, the plumber beat the hell out of her and threw her and the baby out on the street.

The man she lived with now, who had fathered the child she carried, had picked them up along Highway 6 in a thunderstorm. A day laborer between jobs, he drove them to Houston where they spent a week in a cheap motel before moving into an old school bus they now called home. They got along okay. He always washed before coming to bed. She cooked and did the laundry; he provided food and beer and didn't hit her. He was quirky about his name, Lawrence, never Larry. They lived from job to job and were now plugged into a primitive trailer park on the edge of Simms. They enjoyed the luxury of toilets, showers and a coin-operated laundry. Lawrence had a job fixing fence and cleaning out chicken coops and horse stalls at a dude ranch. He roared off to work in an ancient purple pickup with painted flames along the hood and no muffler. He was a hard worker and proud of his body.

Jenny pulled off her gloves and charted her findings. Waynona pulled on her pants as quickly as she could, using diaper pins to keep them up.

"Did you have any problems or complications when Melissa was born?"

"You don't want to hear about it."

"I do. That's why I ask."

"Well, I was on a stretcher along with a bunch of others in the hallway outside the delivery room. It was hot and dirty and people were rushing around and women were screaming their heads off."

"And the delivery?"

"She came on the stretcher and I was torn real bad and bled a lot. They took me to the operating room to sew me up. It hurt real bad. The doctor showed a medical student how to do it." She paused. "Can I go now?"

"Sure. As soon as Sally gets a little blood for routine tests."

"What tests? You think I have VD or something?"

"No. I want to be sure your blood sugar and kidney functions are normal and that you're not anemic."

"That's all?"

"That is all. I really think you're a healthy young woman."

"I try and eat good."

"You're close to term so I'd like to see you in a week. You don't need an appointment, just show up."

Waynona pulled two one-dollar bills from her pocket.

"What's that for?"

"You."

"Put it away, Waynona, and let me see you again next week. I want to take care of you. That's my privilege as a doctor. Go on upstairs to Melissa. I'm sure they'll arrange for the two of you to share a room."

"Sure never met a doctor like you."

"How many women doctors have you met?"

"You're the first."

"Well, there you are," replied Jenny with a smile.

During the afternoon most of the patients had colds and headaches and tummy pains and other minor ailments. They had no doctors of their own so they used the ER for non-emergency complaints.

Peterson's patient from Simms came and left. He had a laceration on his jaw and a cracked radius in his forearm. His horse had stepped in a badger hole and thrown him. A hundred mile round trip because his doctor had left early for lunch with Drummel and Updike.

Sally and Jenny closed the books and records for the day. Their replacements for the next shift were on their way. Jenny had changed into Levis and a blue cotton mock-turtle sweater. "Any special plans this weekend, Sal?"

"Just rest, yard work and mother."

"How's she doing?"

"Like she was when you saw her last: dying, but comfortable and peaceful."

"She's lucky to have you for a daughter."

"She's lucky to have you for a doctor."

Jenny looked wistful. "Sometimes I feel I'm towing the wrong boat to the wrong harbor. Working with you and the staff is great, but I hate the artificial whoo-ha of people like Drummel and the crass ambition of a guy like Peterson. Then I look at myself in the mirror and think, what the hell makes you such a hot-shot angel of mercy?"

"That's just what you are, Jen. You're a fighter for patients and that's lonely. I'm just glad you have every other weekend off out on the ranch with your folks and Doc and Peggy. You'll work things out."

Jenny shouldered a backpack. "Thanks, Sal. You're a wise old healthcare provider, I mean nurse."

"Nurse for another month maybe," said Sally.

Jenny stopped in her tracks. "What do you mean?"

"This afternoon I got a note from the personnel office that I was being demoted."

"Demoted?"

"Yes, the company is doing another personnel budget reduction exercise. They've offered me a job as a floor nurse at night with a cut in pay."

"What about the ER?"

"They're probably going to replace me with someone younger who doesn't cost as much."

"Not if I have anything to do with it!"

Jenny called Drummel's office. Patricia answered.

"I just heard a rumor that Sally's being fired."

"Let me look on the list," said Patricia. "Well, not fired, just relocated. She still has a job."

"I'm on my way up," shouted Jenny into the phone.

"Wait, Jen. He's not here."

"Where the hell is he?"

"On the golf course. He's polishing his public relations image with a fat cat from the newspaper."

Chapter 4

SATURDAY, AFTER BREAKFAST, Alex and Peggy stopped at the big house and turned the radio and Gus over to Jenny for the weekend.

"We're spending the night at a spa near Missoula," said Peggy. "We'll be completely out of touch."

Gus looked at Jenny and wagged his tail. "Sounds wonderful," she said.

"Yeah, well here's the infernal machine," said Doc, handing her the spare radio. "Tad, the sheepherder on the Hastings place, might need more attention. You can look at his chart. And you might call Hank Collette and check on his pain and swelling. He chewed up his face with a chain saw. We'll be back Sunday afternoon."

Peggy cut in, "Sunday *evening*, Jen. Alex, you gave Jenny the backup radio. Where's yours?"

"In the car."

"You don't really have to take it!"

"I always do. I could name a bunch of people who would've been in real trouble if I hadn't had the radio with me."

"You don't think I can cover your practice?" asked Jenny.

"I'm sure you can. But you don't know all the details on the patients."

"The details are all in their charts, which are as compulsive as you are."

"I'll keep the radio in case the car breaks down and we need some help."

"You're impossible," said Jenny, then she added, "I

almost forgot, Hugh Drummel asked me to invite you to a meeting of the staff and attendings to hear a talk by the company's VP for public relations."

"I know about it. He came to the clinic yesterday to invite me personally."

"He asked me to invite you. He didn't tell me he'd driven over here to see you. That's two hundred miles round trip."

"A long way to see an old codger?"

"No, Doc, a long way for a jerk who tells everybody his time is precious." She paused. "It pisses me off that he would do that behind my back. What did you tell him?"

"I told him no. Too far. Not enough notice."

"But it's not 'til Friday."

"You're at the hospital next weekend. Who would cover the practice?"

Peggy said, "I could for the three or four hours you'd be away."

Doc frowned at her. She smiled.

"What's the talk about?" he asked.

"Advanced technology and the goals of the medical industry. The speaker is sort of a futurist."

"Sounds awful," said Alex. "Drummel sure made an ass of himself in my waiting room. In a couple of days he'll be the new joke in the valley."

"We might all learn something about managed care and its plans."

"I don't give a hoot in hell about managed care and its plans. I think those people are making fortunes subverting our profession. Frankly I'm surprised you're pushing the meeting."

"I'm not pushing the meeting! I'm the chief of staff and the administrator asked me to invite as many of the outlying doctors as possible."

"That's fine, Jen, that's just fine. But I don't want to go."

"You could come to support me like you always have."

"Damn it, Jenny." She looked at him expectantly. "All right, all right. When you look at me that way I can't say no. I'll come, but just to support you."

Jenny gave him a peck on the cheek. "Have a fun weekend, you growly old bear. I love you."

As they drove out of the ranch, Alex mumbled, "Do you two talk about me behind my back?"

"Of course. You'd be impossible if we talked about you in your presence," replied Peggy.

"Well, I don't want to be bossed around by a couple of women."

"Bossed around by a couple of women?" Her voice had an edge to it. "Is that how you see it?"

Alex knew he was on dangerous ground but cutting communications to his practice made him anxious, more than anxious—panicked, like a swimmer cut loose from a life buoy. "Why do we have to take this trip anyway?"

"You don't get it, do you," said Peggy. "You only see it through your own eyes. You're a savior to your patients but in case you haven't noticed, being a savior's helper can be a royal pain in the ass. They call, you jump, I follow. No one worships at my gate!"

They drove in silence, passing the clinic and its empty parking lot, on the way out of town heading for the interstate west.

Peggy said quietly, "This trip was for us as well as for you. I need my batteries charged as much as you do. Probably more. Following can be more exhausting than leading: the follower has less choice."

Alex pulled over in a wide place off the road. "I'm sorry, Peg. I know our patients are my security and that doesn't help them or us. We couldn't practice the way we do without each other. I wouldn't want to practice without you."

"The same is true for me, that's why I want you to take care of yourself." They started down the road again. "I packed a picnic. Where do you want to stop for lunch?"

"There's a river access on the way to Missoula where the fishing is great. We can check it out. We can eat, then you can try out your new spinning rod while I use a fly in the gentlemanly art of angling."

Jenny sat on the porch steps with her arm around Gus. Small puffs of dust from the car hung in the air after it turned onto the highway and disappeared. She sighed. She loved those two but worried about them. Sometimes Doc was like a big farm horse with blinders, pulling his load day after day. Peggy used a loose rein to help guide him from patient to patient, from crisis to crisis. Between times she ordered supplies, dealt with insurance forms and kept the clinic spotless. She did the shopping and most of the cooking. Doc had a gruff bark but a huge, soft heart filled with love for Peggy, and a commanding sense of commitment toward the people he "doctored." Although he would frown and tell her to "knock it off," he was her North Star.

Jenny walked into the kitchen and poured herself another cup of coffee and returned to the swing on the porch. Working with Doc and living at home was a dream she had frequently during her first two years of medical school. And, although she still thought about it, emergency medicine was exciting and the status and money that came with it were pluses. Her huge education debt would be paid off in another year in her present job. That was one positive thing that the HMO had done for her.

Jenny's women friends from her medical school days were proud of her success and the respect she had earned as chief of staff at the hospital. In some medical schools women had to be ten times smarter than the men just to get in. They also had to live through sexism and discrimination, sometimes blatant, sometimes subtle, that still existed in schools catering to the old western macho male image. She'd talked to Doc and Peggy about this cultural anomaly after she graduated. Doc had told her to put a sign on her desk: *What can you expect from a pig but a grunt,* and tell them to go to hell. She laughed at the thought. Only one attending, Dr. Krohl, tried to hassle her because she was a woman with authority. But she could handle him. She had to admit that she felt secure as a corporate employee. Progress in her career and within the company were assured if she could suppress the frustration of being told how to practice by people whose chief aim was to line the stockholders' pockets. She pushed the swing in motion and leaned her head against the back. Of course, being so near to home was the biggest bonus of working for the company. She loved her mom and dad, loved their lifestyle and this big old house that had been the family home for so long.

In 1923, the Morgan's Foursquare Sears and Roebuck frame house had been shipped out to Simms on a railroad freight car. From there, wagons hauled the precut boards, flooring, roofing, windows, doors and other parts of the home up the switchback track to the top of Divide Pass and down through Sage City into the Cicero valley. Daniel Morgan and his bride, Maude, from Connecticut, were the proud owners. A year later, a Blackfoot midwife helped Maude bring her only child, John, into the world.

The two-story home looked like a transplant from New England. A gabled roof and covered porch along the front and one side added warmth and variety to the square, stark lines of the house. Jenny's bedroom on the ground floor off the kitchen had been her nest for as long as she could remember. She loved the smell of old wood and wax and the squeaking of the bird's eye maple floors laid down in different patterns in each room. Large windows, low enough for toddlers to look through, were features of each upstairs room. The leaded windows in the parlor and dining room contained bottle glass panes each with its own, slightly distorted, view of the sheds and barn and the huge old cottonwood tree that shaded the backyard. Downstairs, the parlor, for many years used only for special occasions like weddings or funerals, had become a comfortable living room with deep leather chairs on each side of a native stone hearth. An inviting sofa, with a variety of cushions, ran along the inside wall, separating the living room from the dining room with its bay window. A large kitchen and pantry filled a quarter of the ground floor.

Jenny sat on the old porch swing to finish her coffee. She rocked gently, watching Gus check out his favorite trees and bushes down by the creek that ran between stands of spruce and aspen. A hint of green announced early buds on the cottonwoods. Crocuses would be poking their heads through the neat flower beds next to Alex and Peggy's cabin. They kept the place in immaculate shape in spite of their schedule. Jenny pondered the difference between city and rural practice. Rural would be perfect if you were able to enjoy the country and not dig a rut between your house and the clinic. She stood up and stretched, then called Gus and set off on her morning run.

Jenny jogged to the end of the ranch road and into the pastures past several hundred range cows who eyed her with suspicion and turned to face her if they had already dropped their calves. Several advanced menacingly when Gus ran by. He stayed close to Jenny and, with his tongue lolling out, wondered when she would slow to a dignified pace like Doc.

After a shower, Jenny called Hank Collette. "Hello, Mr. Collette. This is Jenny Morgan. Dr. McKinnon asked me to check on your wounds."

"My wounds? Who did you say you were?"

"Jenny Morgan. John and Emma's daughter."

"Oh yes. Jenny. How've ya been? Where've ya been? Haven't seen you around for a long time."

"Well, I've been in medical school, then residency. Now I'm working at the medical center over in Big Timber."

"Ya don't say. So, you're a doctor. Do you take care of kids and women or what?"

"No, Mr. Collette. I'm an emergency room physician."

"Hey, Jenny. Mr. Collette was my father. My name's Hank, remember? When you were a squirt you used to tag along when your dad and I went fishin', remember?"

"Yes. I'll say I remember. Those were wonderful times."

"Little Jenny Morgan. I'll be damned. I thought you were an insurance agent or somethin' when you first called and wanted to know about my wounds."

"I cover Doc a couple of times a month, and before he left he asked me to call and make sure your face wasn't too swollen and that you had enough medicine for pain."

"Maybelle says I look like I've been in a duel with Zorro, but I'm doin' fine."

"No big swelling or redness around where Doc sewed you up?"

"A little sore when I wrinkle my face. Nothin' bad."

"If you have any questions at all just give me a call."

"I'll do that, Jenny. Imagine that, an emergency room doctor. Wow, that's big time. Hope to see ya around."

"Me too." She hung up. Sure was different calling one of Doc's patients.

After dinner, John, Emma and Jenny sat in the living room reading with occasional conversation about the ranch and valley folk. The phone rang.

"Jenny, this is Roxanna. Stan Cummings got kicked real hard by a cow. One of the boys is driving him to the clinic. They asked me to call."

"We'll meet them there."

Emma and Jenny arrived at the clinic just as a pickup truck pulled up. Stan stepped out gingerly, holding a bloody towel around his thigh. Emma wheeled a gurney out from the ER. They helped Stan lie down and wheeled him in to the operating table.

"Hi, Emma. Jenny, what a surprise seeing you. I'm really sorry to bother you guys on a Saturday. Is Doc around?"

"He's off. I'm covering for him. What happened?"

"I was doing a cesarean on a cow. She bucked out of the squeeze chute and kicked me in the balls, I mean groin." He looked at Jenny. "I can easily drive over to the center. I hate to bother you with this."

"Relax, Stan. Don't be embarrassed. I'm a doctor. I deal with a lot worse things than a cowboy kicked in the balls."

Stan lay back on the table, "Well I guess . . ."

Emma eased off his boots, then she and Jenny unzipped his bloody jeans and pulled them off along with his underpants. Blood oozed from torn muscle and a bruised hoof-shaped laceration in his upper, inner thigh. His scrotum was swollen and blue. Jenny pressed a large gauze pad into the wound and Emma spread a sheet from his waist to his knees.

Jenny pulled on rubber gloves, lifted the sheet, examined the wound and gently felt the tightness in his sack. He tensed up and pulled her hand away.

"You have a gash in your thigh we'll have to clean up and suture. And it looks like you've bled into your scrotum. Do you need something for pain, Stan?"

"Not really, unless you do that again."

"I won't. We'll put an ice pack on it and give you a shot." She nodded to Emma who had the painkiller ready. She gave him the injection, then drew up a large syringe-full of local anesthesia and set out the necessary instruments for the repair. Jenny took her time scrubbing her hands to let the Demerol take effect. Emma placed a towel-covered ice bag over his groin. Jenny draped the wound and numbed the edges and their adjacent tissues, then washed the area with Betadine soap and alcohol.

"You can relax, the worst is over. Want a pillow?"

"Sure."

With his head propped up, he could see Jenny better. Her head bent forward in concentration. An ear peeked out from her shiny brown hair with its copper highlights pulled back in a ponytail with a white scrunchie. He had-n't seen her in a long time and now, as he watched her so near to him, he felt the old excitement in her presence as her hands worked painlessly on his thigh. He closed his eyes as the narcotic settled in.

Their last real time together was during their ten-year high school reunion. They'd talked about careers and the challenge each was meeting in their individual lives and goals. He opened his eyes and stared at her. She'd always been pretty; now she was beautiful. Her track-star body had filled out and the tiny smile lines under her lower lids added humor to her eyes. How could anyone so gorgeous do this kind of work?

"Do you really enjoy this type of thing, Jenny?"

"You mean sewing you up?"

"Yeah."

"Do you enjoy doing a cesarean on a cow?"

"Well, that's different, it's what we do on the ranch."

"This is what I do. I like to put people back together

and help them feel better, and I'm reasonably certain they won't kick me."

He smiled, took a deep breath and dozed.

During their senior year in high school, Stan and Jenny were elected homecoming royalty. After graduation, they spent most of the summer together helping out on their family ranches and driving to the city for dinner and movies. Facing the reality of separate careers with no flexibility on either side tempered thoughts of the future and sometimes left them prickly. Stan respected Jen. He had always been attracted by her strength and looks, and a little reticent to take her on when he disagreed with her views: independent women and liberal politics. Once, when Stan had remarked to John Morgan that Jenny "could sure be set in her ways," her father had replied, "I treat my dog like a dog and my wife like a wife. You'll have to learn to say no to a woman like Jenny." Of course neither Jenny nor her mother were within hearing range.

In the fall, Stan moved to Bozeman to study animal husbandry, grass sciences and agricultural management at Montana State. Jenny did her premed in Missoula, then was one of the few out-of-state women accepted to the University of Utah Medical School in Salt Lake City. They had no claim on each other, but their trust and friendship remained a distant, often comforting, source of stability.

Stan starred on his college basketball team and had dated several girls, but in spite of his popularity he was shy and, in his own way, as independent as Jenny. He avoided serious attachments hoping that Jenny, his first and only real girlfriend, would some day share a life with him.

He woke up while they were wrapping a bandage around his thigh.

"Thanks a lot."

"You need to keep an ice pack under your scrotum

and take the antibiotics Emma will give you—two now,
then one every six hours by the clock."

"I'll do it. How much do I owe you?"

Jenny looked at Emma. "I'm sure we have your insurance information. We'll take care of it," said Emma
helping him sit up and pull on his torn jeans and boots.

After her folks had retired to their room, Jenny sat on
the porch swing with Gus curled up on a pillow beside
her, his head on her lap. She scratched behind his shaggy
ears and he yawned and settled in. Seeing Stan had stirred
up all sorts of memories.

*The homecoming had been a huge success. The Cicero
High School football team was on the way to being state
champions in their division and the presentation at half-time
was spectacular with Stan and Jenny, Homecoming Royalty,
riding around the field on the back seat of a new convertible.
He was the team's quarterback and she the president of the
senior class. The people cheered as they rode by, handsome
and beautiful and obviously in love. Everyone knew they'd
gone steady since the tenth grade. That evening he held her
close and rested his cheek on her hair as they danced to the
music of the Dynamics. Stan drove her home and they kissed
at the foot of the porch steps. He invited her to ride up to an
old cabin in the hills behind the Cummings place for a picnic
the next day. He'd pick her up at noon.*

*In the autumn glow of a fresh Indian summer day, they
rode up a game trail next to a spring that tumbled through
woods of dark green pine and the shimmering gold of quak-
ing aspen. They stopped from time to time to take in the vast
unspoiled panorama and to rest the horses and let them
drink. Continuing their climb, they reached the edge of a lush
glade where a small harem of white-tail does crowded behind
a six-point buck. For an instant they challenged the intru-*

sion, then bounded away through the trees. Beyond the glade, nestled in a grove of quakies, an ancient log cabin sagged on its foundation but seemed to welcome people and critters of all kind under its corrugated roof. Some of the caulking between the logs was missing and the door hung loose on its hinges. They dismounted, removed the saddles and let the horses graze.

Inside the cabin, their footsteps sent puffs of dust into the slashes of light that filtered through gaps between the logs. A smoke-stained enamel coffee pot stood on a wood stove. Shelves of rough timber held tin cups and plates. A square table and two stools occupied the middle of the dirt floor. On the wall opposite the front door, a wooden bunk held an old rubber mattress with its edges nibbled away.

Stan tested the bunk and sat on it. "Do you like it?"

"It sure is cozy. Is this where you bring all your girlfriends?"

Stan laughed. "You're the only girlfriend I've ever had since that day in the fifth grade when we decked the bullies in the bus."

Jenny stood close to him and pressed his head to her breasts. He wrapped his arms around her and his hands caressed her strong round bottom. She pushed her thigh between his legs and felt his hardness. He stood and ran his fingers through her hair, then held her face between his hands and kissed her open lips and the tip of her tongue.

"I love you, Jenny. I love you enough to wait as long as it takes to find a way of being together."

Since then, Jenny and Stan had been together at a few Christmas parties and rare homecomings. When Jenny graduated with honors from medical school, he sat proudly with Emma and John. She'd been on call the day of his graduation and unable to attend. They were friends and each avoided fanning the flames of passion until fate or circumstances played out their hands. They both hated good-byes.

Chapter 5

THE NEXT MORNING after breakfast, Jenny and John took a long ride through the pastures and up into the foothills between remnants of snow pack, while Emma set a Sunday roast in the oven and represented them in church. The family never talked much during meals. They ate Emma's good food with a sense of thanksgiving, enjoying the fruits of their labor. After Jenny and Emma did the dishes, it was nap time. Although John was not much for going to church, he believed that the day of the Lord was one of relaxation and rest.

Jenny called Stan to see how he was doing.

"Sore, real sore and still swollen."

"What about the wound in your thigh? Any drainage?"

"No, it's fine. You sewed me up real' tight. Do you go back to the city this evening?"

"Yes. Doc will want to see you about the middle of the week to check your leg."

"I drive to Big Timber several times a month to pick up ranch supplies. I'd like to see where you work. Maybe I could drop in at the end of a shift and take you out to dinner some evening."

"That would be fun. We could go to Paulette's. I'm on backup call next weekend after 5 P.M."

"Great. Next Saturday at five I'll come to the hospital. Will they let me in?"

"If you're on crutches and have a bloody bandage around your head they'll probably let you in. Look for

65

Sally if I'm busy. She's the good-looking nurse with white hair."

As the sun dropped toward the horizon, Jenny stepped out of the shower. The telephone rang. The sheriff's office patched through a call from the ambulance. Donny told her Milly Hastings had asked them to take Tad to the hospital. He'd just turned into the Hastings Ranch and would call her after he'd seen him.

She pulled on jeans and a sweatshirt and, moments later, Donny reported on the radio. "We have a problem. He doesn't want to go to the hospital."

"What's the matter with him?" asked Jenny.

"I think he has pneumonia. He's coughing up some cruddy stuff and I'm sure he's got a fever but he won't let us check him over. He says the only person he'll talk to is Doc."

"Tell him Doc's not here and that he must follow your advice and go to the hospital. I'll call ahead."

"I've told him that. He says he'll wait 'til tomorrow. I told him you were on call and he . . . well, he just rolled his eyes to the ceiling and said, 'No woman doctor.'"

"Really. No woman doctor?"

"That's what he said."

"I'm on my way!"

Jenny pulled up to the sheep wagon next to the ambulance.

Donny opened the wagon door for her. "Good luck."

"I'll do my best."

She stepped in and closed the door. Tad was lying naked on his cot, stirring the air with a newspaper. He grabbed the blanket and covered himself. The dog growled from under the bed.

"Hi," said Jenny. "I'm Dr. Morgan." The dog snarled. She backed up to the door. "Does he bite?"

Tad stared at her and pulled the blanket up to his chin. "Sometimes."

"Can you hold him?"

"No."

"Can you let him out?"

"He was out."

"Tad, I need to examine you. I've never seen a sheepherder yet who couldn't control his dog."

Tad reached under the bed and hit the dog on the nose. "Shaddup."

"That's better," said Jenny. "Now, let me look at you."

She put her bag on the end of the cot, sat across from him on the bench and pushed a thermometer between his lips.

"Under your tongue."

He mumbled and the thermometer almost fell out. She grabbed it. "Open your mouth," she commanded, placing the thermometer under his tongue. "Now close your lips."

The sheepherder lay like a mummy wrapped in his cover with sweat pouring off his face.

She checked his pulse. His heart was galloping like a runaway horse. She reached for his legs under the blanket; he pushed away from her but she felt the soft swelling in both his legs. His temperature was over 102. She reached under his neck and pulled him up. The mattress was sopping wet and the odor of sweat and sickness in the stifling heat of the wagon made her gag.

"Tad, breathe through your mouth, in and out."

He tried but coughed, spitting phlegm into a soggy rag.

"Let me see that."

He stuffed the rag under his thigh. After a few more breaths, Jenny had heard enough. She stood up. "Your heart is failing and I'm sure you have pneumonia. You need to be in a hospital where we can deal with both."

Tad shook his head slowly from side to side. "No. No way. I stay here with Dog."

"I'll find somebody to take care of your dog, but you have to go to the hospital. I can't take care of you here."

He stared at her.

"You could die here, Tad."

He shrugged a shoulder.

"Would you follow Doc's advice if I bring him?"

"Maybe."

"I'll be back with him as soon as I can."

Donny was at the foot of the stairs.

"He won't budge," said Jenny. "Maybe Doc can get him to listen to reason."

"I'll try him on the radio. Maybe he's on the way home."

Doc answered immediately. Donny handed the microphone to Jenny who explained the situation. Doc would drop Peggy at home, then swing by.

"I'm glad he's on his way, but he's not supposed to have his radio on when he's off."

"Habit," said Donny.

Jenny sat on an upturned log to wait. The thought of Tad lying on that filthy cot and his refusal of help really disturbed her.

"Maybe Doc can get him to the hospital," said Donny.

"I hope so. He can't just die here."

"Maybe that's what he wants. Most of these sheepherders have always lived in their wagons with a dog or two and a horse nearby. It's their home."

They sat and waited and after a while Alex drove up.

"Thanks for coming," said Jenny. "He's so stubborn."

"I know." Alex walked over to the wagon, banged on the door and walked in, followed by Jenny.

Tad lay on his side coughing and desperately short of breath. He acknowledged Alex's presence and Dog came out from under the bed wagging his tail. The two doctors sat on the bench and Jenny handed Alex her stethoscope. He waved it away.

"Dr. Morgan tells me you have pneumonia and your heart's giving out, and you're refusing to go to the hospital."

Tad nodded. "I stay here with Dog."

"If you die, what about Dog?"

Tad pointed to Jenny with his chin. "Da lady said she'd take care of him."

"You said that, Jen?"

"Yes I did, but only if he goes to the hospital."

Alex looked at her with amusement. "A little blackmail?"

"He has to go!"

"Not if he doesn't want to. He's been there before and knows what he's refusing." He turned back to Tad. "You sure you want us to leave you here?"

"For sure."

"Do you have enough to drink?"

"Booze?"

"I mean anything." Alex stood up and looked in the cabinet above the sink. The whiskey bottle was empty and so was Beak's cough medicine. He took a half-pint of Jack Daniels from his pocket and put in on the shelf.

"Where did you get that?" asked Jenny.

"I had it in the Blazer. It's the only medicine he'll take." He turned back to Tad. "Do you want us to sit with you, old friend?"

"No, Doc. Dog and I okay."

Jenny opened the door. Doc patted Tad's hand and they left.

Jenny followed Alex to his Blazer. "I've always been able to get a patient to at least take a step in the right direction, but not Tad. He's so primitive. I can't get over his just giving up."

"Last time I sent him to the hospital he escaped," said Alex. "I don't think refusing medical advice makes him primitive."

"Well, ignorant then, if you like that better."

Alex heard the frustration in her voice. "I'll have a word with Milly on the way out."

"I'll meet you at home."

Jenny sat on the porch steps and waited. She felt strongly the duty and moral obligation to fight for a patient's life. If doctors allowed themselves to do less, they would lose people's trust. When Alex drove up, she met him and asked, "Was Milly annoyed?"

"No. She said if that's what he wants she'd go along with it." Alex joined her on the steps. "I thought about Tad on the way home and his freedom to choose minimal or no treatment. We doctors must keep the freedom to treat or not to treat."

"That's fine, but the thing that makes me mad is that with antibiotics, a diuretic and oxygen, to say nothing of a clean bed and healthy food, I could save his life."

"I'm sure you could, if that's what he wanted."

"His behavior is a challenge to our authority as doctors."

"How?"

"Patients recognize our knowledge and accept our orders and I don't see anything wrong with that."

"I think there's a middle ground, Jen, between 'I always do what the doctor tells me,' which is usually a lie, and 'I never go to doctors,' which is a pain in the ass when you know you could help them."

"But today we can do so much more for patients than we could in the old days. They need to be brought up to date."

Alex chuckled. "Like some ancient doctors we know?"

She faced him, square on. "The other day Hugh asked me when I thought you'd retire."

"What did you tell him?"

"I said I'd ask you if the occasion arose."

"Drummel's hoping I'll fold so he can put his own man over here permanently. Quite frankly, I think about it all the time. When do you think I should retire?"

She looked back down the road and didn't answer right away. She glanced at him. "When you can't keep up anymore?"

"I'll stop practicing when I don't enjoy it or when all my patients have died off. Even more important, I'll stop when I can't count on younger doctors like you to work with me. As far as doing more for patients than we used to, sometimes I think we do too much for the wrong reasons, like money or the fear of being sued." Alex stood and stretched. "Thanks for covering me, Jen. You going back to the city tonight?"

"Yes."

Alex put his hands on her shoulders. "I would want you as my doctor any day."

She gave him a hug. "I'll say it again, Doc. If I'm ever sick, I want you and Peg to take care of me."

Chapter 6

JENNY PULLED into the staff parking lot for her shift in the ER. As she approached the door, she heard her name called. She stopped and looked around. Waynona appeared from behind a car.

"Waynona, what are you doing out here?"

"Waiting for you." She waddled over to Jenny, supporting her bulging abdomen.

"What's the matter?"

"I'm not allowed to see you anymore."

"What? What are you talking about? Who told you that?"

"A man from the business office."

"Tell me what happened."

She pointed to the ER. "A woman at the desk asked me what I wanted. I told her I was seeing you for my baby. She looked for my name in the computer and said I hadn't ever been checked in. She spoke on the telephone to someone and asked me to wait and this man came. He was furious."

"What did he look like?"

"Like an empty suit with a round head and red face."

"Was his name Drummel?"

"Yes. He asked me whether I was on Medicaid and I said no. Then he asked me how much I paid you."

"I don't believe it!"

Waynona frowned. "You think I'm making this up?"

"I'm sure you're not. It's just an expression."

"I told him that I didn't pay you anything, that you refused to take anything. He said the emergency room was

72

not for routine checkups. I told him I was your patient and he said that didn't matter, it wasn't your job to see pregnant women unless there was some sort of emergency."

Jenny was seething. "That son of a bitch."

Waynona looked surprised.

"Then what."

"He sent me to the maternity clinic with an aide. It was ugly, Dr. Morgan. I waited in a tiny cubicle with my heels in the stirrups and only a little paper sheet to cover me. A guy in a white coat stomped in, asked me some dumb questions and examined me."

"Was he a medical student?" asked Jenny.

"I dunno. He had on a white coat. He hurt me. I didn't say anything because I didn't want to piss him off. It was like in Texas when Melissa was born. He treated me like white trash. I saw Sally on the way out and told her. She was upset and said to wait in the truck; you'd be along soon."

"Good girl," said Jenny. "Come in with me and I'll deal with this."

Sally was relieved to see Waynona with Jenny. They sat the young mother in an examining room. Jenny gave her a can of juice from the machine.

"You just wait here, Waynona. You'll be fine. I need to go upstairs, then I'll be back to do your checkup as I promised."

Patricia was on the phone when Jenny marched in.

"Is he there?"

Patricia nodded.

"Is he alone?"

Pat put her hand over the mouthpiece. "Yes, but he's in a bad mood."

Jenny leaned over Pat's desk. "As the politicians say, 'you ain't seen nothin' yet.'" She marched to the door, knocked and strode in.

Hugh looked up from a stat sheet. "Jenny! Come in. Sit down. What can I do for you?"

She stood and glared at him. "How dare you tell a patient of mine that I can't see her."

"What are you talking about?"

"I'm talking about a pregnant woman called Waynona who hasn't a nickel to her name. I've been doing her prenatal checks in the emergency room."

"Oh, yes . . . she wasn't registered in the system. She's Medicaid-eligible but hasn't taken the trouble to apply. I sent her to the OB clinic where they deal with a lot of these little transients."

Jenny stepped forward and, leaning on his desk with her face two feet from his, declared, "That young woman has been through bloody hell. She went to the OB clinic and was hurt and scared by an unsupervised medical student. When she brought in her first child with acute appendicitis a few weeks ago she offered all the money in her pocket, two dollars. She was obviously very pregnant and admitted that she'd had no prenatal care. I told her I'd take care of her for nothing. That is my privilege and duty as a doctor. And take care of her I will whether you like it or not!"

Hugh pushed his chair back to distance himself from her. He sputtered, "It's against hospital regulations to offer straight charity care to indigents."

Jenny stood straight, every inch of her on the attack. "Screw the hospital regulations, *Mister* Drummel. I'm taking care of this patient or you'll have my resignation." She reached for a pad of paper.

Hugh rolled himself back to his desk. "Jenny, Jenny, Jenny, let's cool it. I was only trying to apply the rules that are handed down for me to execute. I don't make the rules, you know that."

Jenny continued to glare at him. "Well?"

"Well, what?" asked Hugh, condescendingly.

"Do I take care of that patient or do I hand in my resignation?"

"You take care of the patient since you have committed to her," said Hugh, with a magnanimous air.

"And another thing, *Mister* Drummel. Sally cannot be transferred out of my department. She's the best ER nurse I've ever worked with and I need her experience."

"We have to make these personnel changes, Jenny. It's a question of money. We can't afford a nurse with her seniority. We're doing our best to reassign these older nurses to other services. They won't earn as much but that's the way it is. The margins are too close to compromise."

"What goddam margins are you talking about?"

"The difference between revenue and what we spend on patient care."

"If you cut down on experienced nurses, patient care will take a dive."

"We're training new nurses to supervise auxiliaries and keep their units within cost effective parameters. We *are* trying Jenny."

"You may be trying but you have no idea what patient care entails."

"I'm sure you'll help educate me. I look forward to it."

"Fine," said Jenny. She turned and walked out, closing the door behind her. As she passed Patricia, she muttered, "Jerk."

Chapter 7

FOR ALEX, the week building up to the meeting at the hospital brought with it a growing deep-seated uneasiness. His practice remained as busy as ever, but echoes of change, reviews in medical journals and press reports about horizon-thinking in the business end of medicine left him restless and apprehensive.

He told himself repeatedly to keep an open mind: change was normal but uncomfortable. He talked things over with Peggy. She reminded him that new approaches to patient care might be healthy for patients and doctors, not to mention nurses. Who knows, she mused, maybe we would get some help to carry the load.

On Wednesday, Hank Collette and Stan Cummings came in. Their wounds were healing well. Alex removed some of the stitches from Hank's face. The rest needed to be left in for another few days. Hank had worked for the Cummings from time to time. The three of them visited and caught up on the status of the cattle market and the state of "roilyness" in the streams and private creeks where big brown trout skulk in deep water along meadow banks.

Alex was welcomed by colleagues milling around a table with coffee and sticky buns.

Timothy Moore greeted him. The chief of cardiology was one of Alex's oldest friends. They were about the same age. Tim's rugged, lined face and short, gray hair projected the knowledge and humor that helped patients and friends enjoy his presence and trust his judgment. "Your protégé is a breath of fresh air."

"I'm here on Jenny's orders. She thinks I need to be modernized," replied Alex. "How are the new bosses treating you?" He helped himself to coffee.

"Frankly, I'm amazed. If you have time after the meeting I'll show you what they've done to update our heart lab."

Five years ago, Tim Moore had checked Alex's heart and talked about bypass surgery. But all the angiogram showed was spasm of his coronary arteries, Prinzmetal's angina. Tim ordered him to be less compulsive and take it easy.

Other friends were greeting Alex when Hugh Drummel pushed into the circle followed by a man wearing a dark gray suit and red paisley tie.

"Dr. McKinnon, I am so pleased you were able to come," said Hugh. "I'd like to introduce Dr. Clayton Updike, our speaker today." The two men shook hands and Hugh added that Dr. McKinnon maintained a longstanding and respected practice on the other side of the mountains in a remote, but picturesque, part of the state.

Updike beamed at Alex. "Men like you have been the backbone of our profession."

"Jenny didn't tell me you were a physician."

Hugh interjected, "Clay has a Ph.D. in Psychology from Southwestern State as well as an MBA from the University of Ohio. American Health uses his expertise in health care forecasting to build teamwork with doctors and community leaders in our catchment areas."

"I look forward to hearing your talk," said Alex. "Some of us who've been around for a while have a hard time thinking of what we do as a business, like selling cars or shoes."

"I understand how you feel, Doctor," replied Updike. "I think you'll see that we are as dedicated to the delivery of quality health care as our providers."

"Some of us also have difficulty being called providers, but then . . ."

Jenny walked up behind him. "We're ready to get things going."

The administrator interrupted, "Dr. Updike, you remember Dr. Morgan, our chief of staff."

"I certainly do. Very nice to see you again."

Drummel stood on his toes and waved toward a man filling a Styrofoam cup with coffee. "Doctor Peterson . . . Pete, come on over." A tall, bald, red-faced man with eyes set close to a beak-like nose made his way to the administrator who turned to the speaker. "Clayton, this is Dr. Pete Peterson, the newest member of our managed care family. A month ago he sold us his highly successful practice in Simms, on this side of the mountains. It's quite a community with real growth potential. A ski area in the winter and a gathering place for backpackers and fishermen in the summer. It's less than an hour from here."

The speaker clasped Peterson's hand and pumped it like a politician at a fundraiser. "Welcome, welcome, welcome."

Alex interrupted, "I heard you sold out to these people!"

Peterson's pate reddened. Avoiding eye contact, he mumbled, "You will too when you learn to recognize a real deal."

Jenny stepped between them. "We'd better get started." She turned to Updike. "Most of us have only a vague idea about where all the changes in the profession are taking us. I'm sure there'll be many questions." With a tight hold on Alex's arm, she led him toward the front row. Under her breath, she said, "This is not the place for you and Pete to get into it."

Alex rasped angrily, "They must have paid Peterson a helluva lot of money for his practice. He clings to his patients like a bulldog to raw meat."

"Oh, come on. You just don't like him."

"I can't stand a doctor who writes threatening letters to patients who go to another doctor without his permission. It's the tyranny of solo practice in the boonies: 'Don't rock his boat, you might need the bastard in the middle of the night.'"

"We'll talk later." She planted him firmly in a seat and turned to face the gathering. "Please sit down. Hugh Drummel will introduce our guest."

Hugh stepped onto the podium. "It is my honor to introduce Dr. Clayton Updike. American Health Corporation is pleased to have him come and share his insights and wisdom with us. Dr. Updike." A smattering of applause.

The presenter clipped a microphone to his lapel, straightened the wire and stepped behind the lectern. He smiled at Hugh, Doc and Jenny.

"Thank you, Hugh. It's a pleasure to be with you. Please feel free, ladies and gentlemen, to ask questions as we go along."

Gripping the lectern, Updike launched into his presentation. "The present environment of medicine is a disorganized conglomeration of private practices, group practices and community hospitals. These are all too often run by boards made up of people of goodwill, but ill informed, unfortunately, in the science of medical management. Many of our large teaching institutions are academic enclaves featuring collections of mini-kingdoms competing for the research dollar with little or no concern for the Big Picture. Look at it this way. If General Motors had no headquarters, and each parts factory, each assembly line, each sales department functioned as independent units, its production of cars would be chaotic and, of course, economically disastrous. The same is true of the medical industry. Some consider socialized medicine the solution. But we all know how government bureaucracies function. What we need is efficient management of resources, close supervision of margins and healthy competition. These are the mainstays of developing managed care systems in our great country. American Health is one of a handful of large corporations applying economic laws and competitive marketing to meet the health care needs of our people." Updike paused for a sip of water, cast his gaze over the audience in the best Carnegie style, and continued.

"In order to apply business efficiency to the system, American Health brings to bear a large reserve of experience and capital with which to affect the environment in which our profit centers operate. We must control and shape that environment, not be subject to it. Let me repeat, we must control and shape that environment, not be subject to it, ladies and gentlemen. Only then can you as providers be on the cutting edge of scientific progress. Only then can we in administration provide you with the best and most up-to-date equipment and a professional life free of hassles with insurance companies and protected from the specters of malpractice and burnout.

"My friends, the whole country is moving into multi-institutional systems. These will dominate health care delivery. We are engaged in a battle between giants, using modern large-scale marketing tactics. You who provide health care know better than I that you have neither the taste for nor the time to deal with complex administrative factors involved in the successful development and growth of a modern regional center. Those of you in private practice, who can't afford extra staff for paperwork, probably spend thirty percent of your time filling out forms. You should not have to waste your time and energy in administration and logistics. That is where we come in. The enormous resources of American Health corporate headquarters stand behind you to facilitate your work, to ensure your just remuneration and to guarantee you a lifestyle worthy of your skills. You are frontline soldiers, assault troops against disease and injury, and will be the architects of preventative medicine."

With his hands on his knees, Alex rocked in his seat like Leo Mazzone, the Atlanta Braves pitching coach. "I can hear the trumpets sounding the charge," he said in a loud whisper.

Updike paused. "Any questions up to this point?" He looked around the room. "Please feel free. I want this to be a dialogue, not a lecture." A beeper went off and a doctor left the room.

Alex raised his hand. "From what I read, General Motors hasn't done too well. Their cars aren't selling." Jenny jabbed him with her elbow.

"Quite true, Dr. McKinnon. Variations in output do occur in all major industries." He smiled down at Alex and continued, "In cardiology, as Dr. Moore knows, medicine is becoming more and more technologized." He mouthed every syllable of that word with relish. "The equipment he now has at his disposal is far superior in efficiency and quality to what he worked with before the renovation of his department. This new technology will allow more quality procedures in less time. His department is therefore cost effective for this center and American Health."

"What about patients who can't afford insurance?" mumbled Doc, under his breath.

Updike pressed on. "Let us consider the future. My projections are based on research presently underway in Silicon Valley and the laboratories of our leading industries. The explosion in bionics will be one of our greatest technological advances. It will completely alter the contours and geography of the health care battlefield. The most significant factor in the future will be the interface between the microchip and the nervous system. Before long, aging won't be quite as bad. We will be in the business of supplementing and extending all sensory modalities. As the body-mind machine fails, we will transistorize it. By 2050, if you drop on the sidewalk, they will not call an ambulance, they'll call a repairman."

Alex whispered in Jenny's ear, "Make sure you have the proper screwdrivers in your bag." She ignored him.

Updike droned on. Alex glanced over his shoulder and saw that, except for Peterson, most of his colleagues had that stunned ox look so common during must-attend lectures. Phrases from Updike floated in and out of his consciousness. "Things are going to become very, very high-tech. Balancing this, of course, will be the so-called high-touch—to ensure that we have financial resources with which to advance."

Chase the money, thought Alex, and you'll find the truth.

Updike: "Competition will become intense. Those hospitals and practices with sound internal management and cost effectiveness will be able to discount price. Doctors' remuneration will be stable because you will have a larger patient pool." He looked down at Alex who blinked back at him. "And, let me stress, discount in price is essential to long-term survival whether you are in solo practice or part of the more modern medical industry."

Alex stirred in his chair and started to raise his hand. Jenny pinned his arm with her elbow.

Updike: "Another change affecting health care is the recognition by major financial markets that large corporations such as American Health are dominating the entire field. We now administer regional medical centers like this one and are moving more and more into primary care. I am sure you are aware of the fact that those who control primary care control everything because that is where the consumers are found." Again he looked down at the front row. Alex was picking his nails with a penknife.

"Vertical growth of centers such as this one will be accomplished by an increase in technological capability. Horizontal growth will follow the acquisition of peripheral clinics and medical groups except, of course, for remote practices, which, I'm afraid, will go the way of the dinosaurs."

Alex guffawed, Jenny stiffened, and Hugh leaned across her and frowned at him. Updike looked annoyed but continued, increasing the volume and speed of his delivery. "Free standing ambulatory care facilities and surgicenters represent means to capture the referral market. Bluntly speaking, we must control the geography. Independent solo doctors will give way to primary care physicians who become gatekeepers in the larger system. This will mean increasing competition in lab, x-rays, CAT scans, MRIs, and out-patient surgery—all moneymakers. The aged, the chronically sick and the poor will be left for community hospitals. Hospitals and doctors will be forced into joint ventures to prevent them from devouring each other. Already, there is a twenty percent increase in anti-trust litigation. That should give you an idea of how fast things are moving."

Alex's hand shot up. "What if the referring doctor sends his patients elsewhere?"

"Good question, Doctor." Updike paused for another sip of water then resumed. "The corporation comes in and sets up artificial competition. Then, with the help of company subsidies, it lowers its prices. The uncooperative doctor will be run out of business. We call it 'market development.'"

There was a stir and rustle of paper in the room, but no one spoke.

Updike relaxed and took on a confidential manner, coming around to the side of the lectern. "Let's be realistic, my friends. We all know that quality is our bottom line. Our challenge is simply to find the safe level of quality versus cost trade-off to be free from litigation." He stepped back to grip the lectern like a sea captain at the helm of his vessel, squared his shoulders and sailed on.

"Now, how do we win? In delivering our health care product, we stick to four basic principles. First, it must be cheap. Secondly, it has to be convenient. Thirdly, it must be *perceived* as high quality by the client. Lastly, it should provide a positive subjective experience for the consumer."

"Wow," muttered Alex under his breath. Jenny poked him again and he folded his arms, slumped in his chair and closed his eyes. What a crock, he thought. Updike hadn't mentioned patients once. A 'positive subjective experience for the consumer.' What the hell was that supposed to mean? Sexy nurses giving massages? Filet mignon and braised endives for dinner served from a gourmet section of the hospital kitchen? He considered his own practice. Did seeing patients on time or offering them a cup of coffee if he was backed up with an emergency constitute a positive subjective experience? What about Gus resting his big black head on a distraught girl's lap? Or fresh banana bread and coffee for the patient who'd skipped breakfast because of lab tests. But these weren't special things to be planned and taught like the canned courtesy of telephone operators. They were the ordinary things you did every day. It would be rude not to do them. He felt like being rude to Updike, but the sight of Jenny out of the corner of his eye kept him silent. The man was expounding on the segmentation of the market that abandoned the elderly and the poor.

He boomed, "They will either get free care from community hospitals who have to accept them or they will get inferior care in some paying hospitals. These people may cause a political backlash in a few years but, since there isn't enough money to take care of everybody in the same way, nothing will happen. The caregivers are under administrative imperatives and pressures to get these people out sooner. A bleak picture? You bet. But that's the way it is. Yes, Dr. Moore, you have a question?"

"Suppose there are not enough patients to justify our new cardiology services, what happens then?"

"We market more aggressively, Dr. Moore."

Alex's hand shot up. "What does that mean, precisely?"

"Another good question, Dr. McKinnon. To be precise, we apply normal business tactics to increase the geography of our catchment area. We make offers to outlying doctors, which they simply cannot refuse. If necessary, we put our own people into satellite offices to wean patients away from other doctors. We convert non-users to users by finding out why people don't go to a particular doctor or hospital service and fix it so they do. We set up birth-to-death services and make the referral market our own. One start-up managed care company in California is seeking contracts among undertakers. Womb to tomb care." He sipped water again, waiting for the effect of this last pearl to sink in.

Alex whispered to Jenny, "Can I ask him whether they've cornered the flower market?"

"No!"

Updike clutched the lectern again and continued, oozing with intimate honesty. "My friends, there is only one way to increase market share and that is to steal someone else's customers."

Alex sat up straight. "I'm feeling sick at my stomach, Jen." He walked out.

Alex let Gus out of the car to run around. He should never have come. Updike's revolting predictions, if true, would make the profession as he knew it as quaint as flaxseed poultices and the Victorian vapors. He kicked the grass. There was nothing he could do to block Updike's entrepreneurs and money men. They were experts at manipulating what they called markets. They studied and computed how to con a gullible public into demanding the best, the latest and the fastest techniques to deal with everything and anything. Lucrative procedures corrected sagging breasts or aspirated fat from thighs and buttocks. Bald pates seeded with tufts of hair from other parts of the body were real moneymakers. Pills and patches were sold to dull appetites, wean smokers from cigarettes and put out the fires of heartburn in the boozers.

Peterson had sold out to them and Alex knew what that meant. They'd probably paid him a fortune and would now send in some of their flunky docs, lower the prices of everything and try to suck patients into their system throughout the area. If any of his patients were dumb enough to fall for that ploy, they would get what they deserved. And yet . . . and yet, Tim Moore was a highly competent cardiologist and a compassionate physician. And Jen . . .

"Oh my God," he cried out. "I've blown it with Jenny." He whistled for Gus. He would go back to the meeting and let Tim show him his new equipment. He could tell Jenny he'd gone to the bathroom . . . he'd only been kidding about Updike. He boosted the dog into the car and knew that Jenny wouldn't believe a word. She would be embarrassed by his rudeness.

"Damn it."

He climbed into the car and headed east for the long, lonely drive home. As he drove out of town, the setting sun cast long shadows across the highway that matched his sense of gloom. Gus circled three times in the passenger seat and lay down with his head on Alex's knee. He scratched him behind the ear. "You're so lucky to be a dog. If you can't eat it or screw it, you piss on it."

An echelon of Canada geese circled a stubble field with tattered remnants of snow huddled against green hummocks left unplowed. A thunder squall pushed over the pass and raindrops spattered the dust on his windshield. He was overcome by a surge of remorse at his self-centered rudeness. How could he be such a smart-ass at his age. Since Jenny's first year in medical school, he'd been proud to be her mentor and cherished her trust. He couldn't remember any long philosophical talks, but he did remember how easy it had been to listen to her and support her.

During her third year, late one evening, she had showed up unexpectedly. He stood to greet her and she threw her arms around him, buried her face in his shoulder and wept. He held her until her crying eased and Peggy led her to the sofa. She was exhausted and seemed to have lost weight.

"Coffee or Ovaltine?"

"Ovaltine, please."

Peggy returned with the drinks and graham crackers.

"Tell us about it, Jen."

She said slowly, "I don't know whether I can stand being a doctor."

They waited for more.

"A young patient of mine just died. The thing that kills me is that I never took the chance to talk to her about dying and her worries about her husband and their infant son." She paused. "I let her down because I couldn't stand seeing the pain and the fear in her eyes. She was bleeding from everywhere . . . end stage leukemia, picked up too late. She was in reverse isolation so that when I went into her room, I was isolated from her by a mask, a gown and gloves. So was her husband. But the baby was there in his arms or on the bed with just a diaper on. Seems silly.

"For the past month I've been drawing blood cultures and blood counts. Her veins were impossible . . . clotted, scarred, her arms black and blue and stiff with pain from all the needles. Every morning she dreaded seeing me. Her husband said nothing, just sat there holding the baby. The day before she died I just couldn't go into her room. I was standing outside crying when the interns and residents walked up to make rounds. I left." Jenny fought back tears. "I can't spend a lifetime doing that, Doc. I may be soft and silly and too female or whatever, but I can't put patients through that sort of torture, and I don't know whether I can ever talk to a young person like that about death.

"You'll never be too female, Jenny," said Alex gently. "Some of us men suppress our feelings and cover them up with science or statistics. Don't knock your feelings and sympathy, they help cross the divide between us and our patients."

"I suppose," said Jenny. "But it hurts so much."

"It's the price we pay to be physicians rather than just technicians."

After the talk, Peggy tucked her into the guest room bed. Jenny left very early the next morning, leaving a note by the coffee pot: "Thanks for being here for me. Love, Jen."

And now he'd walked out on her. What made him think he had a corner on humane medicine? Jenny and Tim Moore were every bit as humane as he was and a hell of a lot smarter. Drummel and Updike might be jerks, but he was a conceited ass and that thought shattered his pride.

Chapter 8

AFTER A RESTLESS NIGHT, Alex and Gus headed out for their morning walk. A chilly wind whistled down the valley and the pressure in Alex's chest made him pop a nitro pill under his tongue and pull up the hood of his duffel coat. He tied a scarf around his neck, covering his mouth and nose, and leaned into the wind, hoping it would blow away the memory of that meeting. Just as he reached the resting log, a crushing pain under his sternum knocked him to his knees. He loosened the scarf and slumped against the log gasping for air. Another nitro made his head tingle. Gus returned and licked the sweat on his face. He pushed the dog away and wiped his face with the back of his hand, the pain a giant fist squeezing his chest.

He pulled the radio from its holster. "Sheriff's office. Dr. McKinnon."

"Go ahead, Doc."

He gasped, "Tell Peggy to call me."

A moment later, "Peggy to Dr. McKinnon."

"My heart, Peg. Oh, God." He doubled up as the pain hit again.

"You on your walk?"

"Yes. Hurry, Peg."

"I'm coming."

The fist tightened its grip and the pain surged into his neck. "Come on, Peggy," he gasped, "get here, get here, get here." He pulled his coat tighter as a drenching sweat sent chills through his body. He closed his eyes and tried to breathe deeply and slowly, forcing himself to relax and wait... for how long? "Oh Peg, I don't want to die, we have so much to do." Breathe in and out slowly, relax, another nitro. Would he wake up if he passed out? Gus barked and ran up the road as the sound of a vehicle reached them.

Peggy jumped out of her car with an emergency bag and small canister of oxygen. She knelt beside him, opened the valve and held the mask to his face.

"Hold it there, Alex, and give me your other hand." She pushed up his sleeve and injected morphine into a vein on the back of his hand.

"Open your mouth," she ordered. She gave him an aspirin and told him to chew it. "Hang in there, Alex. I called the ambulance and Donny's on his way."

Alex breathed in the oxygen deeply and the morphine worked to ease the pain and the terrifying sense of impending doom. "It's better."

Peggy fought back tears of relief and held him to her, rocking gently. "I love you, old bear. You're doing fine."

The ambulance pulled up. Donny and his driver ran to the back and pulled out a stretcher.

"He's had MS and aspirin," said Peggy.

"How's the pain?" asked Donny.

Alex gave him a thumbs up.

They pulled him onto the stretcher and lifted him into the ambulance. Gus jumped in. Rapidly, Peggy had an IV going, the cardiac monitors pasted to his chest, and oxygen at six liters. She drew up Lidocaine in case his heart rhythm went haywire.

"Donny," Peggy said, "see if you can raise the ER at the hospital. Ask for Jenny." She ran a strip from the monitor as the call went through. "How's the pain now?"

"It's coming back. What does the EK show?"

"Ischemia," she said, injecting another 5 mg of morphine into the needle port on the IV. She added with authority, "You'll be fine but you need to cool it and let us do what you've trained us to do."

"Well . . ."

"Well, nothing. Cool it, Alex, and I mean it."

He closed his eyes.

Jenny was on the radio. Donny passed the microphone through the window.

"Peggy here, Jenny. He's having a heart attack. His EKG shows Q waves and elevated ST segments in the anterior leads. His pain is controlled. I gave him morphine IV before we loaded him, and more a moment ago. He's had aspirin and, if you agree, we'll stop by the clinic and pick up some t-PA on the way to you."

"I agree, Peg. Give him a 50 mg bolus stat and the other 50 in his IV at 2 mg a minute."

"I'll do it. We should be there in an hour. I'll call you on the radio to check in."

"Give him 5 mg of MS every fifteen minutes if you need to. You have Lidocaine drawn up if his rhythm becomes a problem?"

"It's all ready."

"I'll have Tim Moore and his cardiology team on standby. Are you okay, Peggy?"

"Yes. I'm fine. But I'll be better when we get to you."

Alex pointed to Gus.

Peggy said, "We'll drop him off at the clinic. Emma can pick him up."

Half an hour out, they were climbing up to Divide Pass. Alex was on cloud eight or nine. The beep of the monitor accompanied the throb in his head. For him, time ceased to exist. At the top of the pass, he made a fist over his heart. "Pain coming back?" asked Peggy. He nodded. She gave him another shot of morphine and he relaxed. He heard snatches of talk.

Donny: "How long before the clot breaks up?"

Peg: "Forty-five minutes or an hour."

"Cicero MS one to Dr. Morgan in ER."

"Go ahead, Peggy."

"He's doing fine. Pressure 100/80. Pulse steady at ninety. He had some return of pain handled well with morphine. No arrhythmias."

They started down the mountain, drove through Simms and onto the interstate heading for the center.

Alex opened his eyes and mumbled, "Peg."

She leaned toward him, "Yes?"

"Am I cool enough yet?"

"Oh, my love, you're very cool and you're doing just fine." Her eyes filled with tears. She looked toward Donny. "He's something else, isn't he."

Donny looked at them in the rearview mirror. "You both are."

She kissed Alex on the forehead.

He reached for her hand and held it.

As they pulled up to the emergency room and opened the back doors, Jenny stepped out to meet them.

"How is he?"

"Pressure's 80/50, pulse a hundred and ten with some skipped beats starting a few minutes ago," replied Peggy. She handed Jenny a rhythm strip. "His last MS was half an hour ago."

The overhead pager called Dr. Timothy Moore to the ER as Alex was wheeled in and attached to monitors and oxygen outlets.

He pulled the oxygen mask away from his face. "Jen, I'm sorry about yesterday."

"Forget about that. Just keep the mask on. How's the pain now?"

"Better."

"Have you had pain like this before?"

A muffled reply, "Not exactly."

"What does that mean?"

"I've had angina for a long time." He pulled the mask up again. "Spastic coronaries according to Tim."

"Doc, please keep the mask on." She adjusted it to his nose. "Have you had more pain recently?"

"Just this morning."

Jenny glanced at the oscilloscope on the monitor. "You're having an MI, Doc."

He pulled at the mask. "I hope my insurance will pay for this."

"It will, so don't even think about it and keep that mask on, damn it!"

"The pain's coming back!" he gasped.

"Give him five more of morphine . . . and the Lidocaine."

Tim Moore put his hand on Alex's shoulder. "I'm taking you up to the cath lab, Alex."

"You're the boss," Alex mumbled sleepily as the morphine took effect again.

Chapter 9

ALEX WOKE UP slowly and looked around the cubicle of the cardiac unit. The gentle rays of the setting sun passing through plastic bags of clear fluid cast angular prisms over the yellow-flowered wallpaper. Drop by measured drop his body received solutions through a collection of tubes connected to his veins. He watched the drops: their monotonous regularity made him drowsy. Tim Moore and a nurse appeared at his bedside.

"How do you feel, Alex?" asked the cardiologist, automatically feeling his pulse.

"Dopey."

"Any pain?"

"None. What time is it?"

"Five P.M."

"You took me to the cath lab, didn't you?"

"Yes, everything went well. We opened up two of your coronaries. You'll do fine."

"I don't remember much after we arrived here."

"The blessings of morphine. You were conscious but real sleepy and amusing a couple of times."

"I hope I didn't say anything to embarrass Jenny."

"You asked her out for dinner with Clayton Updike. You sounded quite sincere."

"Really? What did she say?"

"She just smiled and shook her head. I'll tell you something, Alex, most of us feel he laid it on pretty thick, but we didn't have the guts to say so or walk out."

"Most of you are a hell of a lot more polite than I am."

"Maybe. But I'll bet Jenny will never again pressure

94

the staff to attend a business meeting."

"What a relief!" Alex tried to sit up, but a monitor tab pulled at the shaved stubble on his chest. He sank back into the pillows. "Thank God you were here, Tim."

"Don't get too wild in that bed. You're hooked up to a lot of stuff."

"I feel like the black stallion before he broke loose from the ropes."

"This morning you looked more like a beached manatee."

"Do you abuse all your patients?"

"No, only you. Peggy deserves a lot of credit for doing so well with you on the way over."

"Peg deserves a lot of credit for a lot of things. How long will I be here, Tim?"

"Not long enough, so you might as well make the most of it." The cardiologist said something to the nurse who increased the sedation in the IV. "Don't think about anything except fishing."

The nurse adjusted his pillows, rechecked the rates of his medications and smoothed the sheet.

Alex made a conscious effort to relax and drifted off.

Alex awoke as Jenny and Peggy walked up to the foot of the bed. Peggy pulled up a chair and sat. He reached through the bed rails and took her hand.

"I'm on cloud five, dreaming about when we first met."

"You two must be on the same wavelength," said Jenny. "Peggy was just telling me about your kayak trip in France some years ago. Maybe you should plan to do that again."

"Why not?" said Alex.

Jenny patted Doc's foot. "I have to run. Be back later."

Alex waved and turned to Peggy. "You saved my life, Peg. Thank God you moved so fast."

Peggy drew the curtain across the end of the cubicle, then leaned over and kissed him. "You scared the hell out of me. I'm sure glad Jen was at the other end of the radio."

"Me too. Can you stay?"

"Sure. I called Emma. She rescheduled the patients and everything is under control. She said the phone's been ringing off the hook with people worried about you."

"You spent the day with Jenny?"

"Part of it."

"What are you doing this evening?"

"When Sally gets off, we're going out for dinner somewhere. Jenny has a date with Stan. She said she'd see you in the morning."

Alex kissed her fingers and placed her warm soft palm against his cheek. "You think we're crazy to live the way we do?"

"Yes, I do."

"And there's not much we can do about it?"

"There's not much I can do about it."

"It's up to me?"

"Yes."

Alex mused. "I wish we could go back to France."

"So do I. Let's do it."

"What do you remember best?" he asked.

"I remember the Dordogne, that beautiful river, with chateaus clinging from steep cliffs."

"Anything else?"

"Of course. A lot else."

"Like what?"

"Like Sarlat's narrow cobbled streets and La Boétie's house and *Mme Mathieu's Maison Périgord* where we had dinner and spent the night."

"And . . . ?"

"And what do you remember best, Dr. McKinnon?"

"I remember that big old four-poster with the dark red

damask curtains and gold tassels."

"And?"

"And you. And the way you . . . " Peggy put her finger on his lips.

"Wait," she whispered. She went to the curtain and peeked out at the nurses' station.

"Need something, Peggy?" asked the nurse at the computer.

"No, no thank you. We're fine." She returned to the bedside. "We have to whisper. They can hear everything."

Alex chuckled. "We'll whisper. Where were we?"

"You were about to get into bed with me."

He laughed out loud. "Oh yes, that was the first time. I remember it so well."

Peggy slapped him lightly. "You're so bad."

"I know. It's the company I keep."

"Oh, Alex, it's so good to hear you laugh." She leaned over the bed rail and kissed him again.

An aide brought in a light dinner. Alex picked up the dish cover to expose a white alien-looking glob next to a miniature carton of skim milk. "Hold on, I think I'll go with you and Sally."

An ambulance and two police cars with their lights rotating blocked the entrance to the emergency room. Stan drove around to the front of the hospital, parked, then, following the signs in the halls, made his way to the ER.

A stern-looking woman at a desk held up her hand like a traffic cop. "May I help you?"

"I'm looking for Dr. Jenny Morgan."

"She's busy."

Just beyond the nurses' U-shaped station, police officers stood outside a door. A sergeant spoke into his radio, and a burley man in civvies pushed past him and barged into a room. A moment later he came out. "He's on his way to surgery—got a gut wound. Don't mess with the doc, she kicked me out."

The guardian of the door asked Stan, "Are you an emergency?"

"Not that I know of. I'll wait."

"Not here. Go back to the front. I'll tell Dr. Morgan you're waiting for her when she's free. What's the name?"

"Stan."

She looked him over as she might a side of beef and nodded her approval. "Very well, Stan."

He was about to turn away when a statuesque nurse with white hair came out of a room pushing a dressing cart and scattering cops.

"Sally!"

The nurse stopped and called back. "Stan?"

"Yes."

"Come in, come in. Jenny will be with you in a minute."

She led him away from the guardian to a chair in the nurses' station. "This place will settle down in a moment. I'll be back."

From behind a row of monitors with heartbeats snaking across the screen and blinking lights on ready to alert, he saw Sally lead two orderlies wheeling a gurney past a curtain. A moment later a loud wail, "Oh no!" and the nurse led a distraught woman out of the cubicle to a chair in an empty bay. Stan looked away and wished he was somewhere else. He stood and was about to leave when Jenny appeared with another doctor wearing OR greens and a stethoscope around his neck.

"Hi, Stan. This is John. He's just come on duty." The two men shook hands, then Jenny led Stan out of the ER and across the parking lot to a block of apartments used for staff doctors. "Do you mind waiting while I take a quick shower?"

"Not a bit."

Jenny's apartment was a one-bedroom flat with a kitchenette and living room. It was simply furnished with a pull-out couch, stuffed chair and a desk under a picture window with a view of the city park. Homemade bookcases overflowed with medical journals and texts. Wall shelves opposite the couch held a mini Sony CD player, two speakers and the smallest TV Stan had ever seen.

"Have a seat," said Jen. "There's beer in the fridge and a bottle of Chardonnay. I won't be a sec."

"Take your time. It's fun being with you and seeing your pad."

Jenny disappeared into the bedroom.

Stan sat in the easy chair and glanced around the room. The main wall decorations were three posters: an elephant standing on one foot entitled "Balance;" in another, a young woman running up a forest path was back-lit by the yellow light of dawn—its title, "Perseverance." The third poster showed a downhill racer almost hidden by fluffy snow advertising Alta's powder in Utah's Wasatch mountains. Stan got up and stepped over to the desk and looked at two framed photographs, one of Jenny, John and Emma standing in front of a Swiss chalet. The other of Jenny holding a black child on her lap. He checked out her CDs and saw a mixture of Garth Brooks and Reba McIntyre, the Vienna Boys Choir, music from Broadway, Fats Waller, the Sibelius symphonies and a large selection of Dvořák's works.

The bedroom door opened and Jenny stepped out in a denim skirt, white shirt and a bolero jacket, still toweling her hair.

"These are great pictures of you in Switzerland and Africa."

"Yes. Dad was interested in Swiss charlais. The picture of the boy and me was taken during my second year in medical school. I went over to Ghana for a month with a couple of doctors from the university. They operated on people with leg ulcers."

"You sure have a varied taste in music."

"I listen to it all depending on the mood and the weather. If you need to use the bathroom before we go, help yourself," she said as she hung the towel on a chair by the kitchen counter.

Stan walked through the bedroom and into the bathroom and closed the door. A long T-shirt hung from a hook. He spread it out. It celebrated a "Ten Kilometer Run for Life in Support of Breast Cancer." A drying rack over the tub held red running pants and an athletic bra. As he washed his hands he bent forward and took a sniff of a small vial of perfume called Jessica McClintock. He dried his hands and rejoined Jenny in the front room.

They walked back to the parking lot, climbed into Jenny's Miata and headed for Paulette's.

"How are your wounds?"

"Healing up nicely. I rode most of the day thanks to you. Doc will take the stitches out next week."

"You're a fast healer."

Paulette was delighted to see them. "Nice to see you. You don't look any older than you did when you used to come here during high school." A dozen tables in a dark wood and rustic dining room provided a cozy ambiance for the best food in the county. The owner, a dignified and warmhearted French lady, was a friend.

Jenny gave her a big hug. "You're the one who's timeless, Paulette. I love it that your place is still homey and French provincial."

Stan gave her a hug and she showed them to a table by the window overlooking the garden. "A drink before dinner?" They ordered a bottle of Chardonnay.

Stan said, "I guess the ER can be an exciting place with all the cops and sirens."

"Well, it is for a while," replied Jenny, "then you get used to it. It's certainly a challenge when you have to make a quick diagnosis and intervene to save a life. Sometimes it's heartbreaking, especially when one little kid brings in another because their parents can't be found."

"Don't you miss following up on patients?"

"I do. When I can, I go upstairs to see how they're doing. A lot of times they don't remember me because I was just a cog in their care."

"Do you ever think of practicing like Doc?"

"Sometimes, but not really. He's on call twenty-four hours a day. He's part of the old school: 'This one thing I do.' He has no family life except for us and Peggy. His only recreation is fishing. Even then he usually stays within radio range in case he's needed."

"Can't he hire somebody to hold down the practice while he goes on a trip?"

"He can, and has. Peggy told me the last time they left he couldn't sleep and certainly couldn't enjoy himself because he was thinking about what was happening in his practice. He's driven."

"By what?"

"Mom and I think he's driven by guilt."

"Guilt! Doc guilty? That's hard to figure."

"Well, once when Peggy was away visiting her grandmother in Maine, Doc went into a real slump. Mom finally dragged him out of the cabin. She told him it was morbid to keep to himself. He snapped back at her and said he didn't want to burden other people when he was depressed. He perked up some at dinner, and Dad, who hardly drinks at all, joined him in several shots of bourbon. That's when Doc told us that he would never get over his wife's suicide."

"I didn't know Doc had been married," said Stan.

"Yeah, when he was a young surgeon in New York, very successful, and as you can imagine, very handsome. He married the catch of the year and apparently she was thrilled to be involved with a surgeon in a New York medical center. The social columnists went nuts over them in the papers. They were the ideal couple made for each other in heaven and all that sort of stuff. The reality was that although she was very rich and stunningly beautiful, their intimate life was as dry as the Sahara. He spent more and more time at the hospital mostly because he enjoyed the company of his fellow doctors and the nurses and patients more than the company of his wife and her friends. She blew up and he left."

"He told you all that?"

"He did. He was embarrassed by the whole thing the next day."

They sat silently for a little while thinking about Doc.

"He really seems to have found his place in life practicing in Cicero," remarked Stan.

"He has, and I think part of his obsession is fed by his fear of losing what he's found."

"What about Peggy?"

"She's a great lady who got out of a bad situation. She was married to an electrical engineer who did everything by the numbers, including sex, and he turned out to have a boyfriend in his office."

"A boyfriend?"

"Yes, a boyfriend. He was a bisexual."

Stan leaned back. "Yow. What you don't know about people."

Jenny added, ". . . is a good thing. But Peggy is a wonderful nurse and friend. She can't have kids so she says there's no point in getting married. Anyway, she would never again be just a bed, buttons and breakfast housewife. She loves old Doc but neither of them treats the other as a possession."

Stan looked at her and chuckled. "Another glass of wine?"

"Sure. Why not."

"But what about you, Jen? Can you go on being an ER doc for the rest of your life? Is there a happy medium between being an independent doctor and having a nine to five job?"

"I think there is," said Jenny, thoughtfully. "It takes a partnership so that the responsibilities can be shared. Some of us younger docs want more than just patient care and being on call all the time. We want time to read and run and ski. We want time to climb mountains and go on pack trips. We want to fall in love and have time for all of that and kids." She looked up at Stan. He smiled at her, waiting for her to continue. "But if that is to be a reality then I, for one, would need a working partner."

"You mean marrying a doctor?"

"No way! One in the house would be more than enough. I mean marrying a partner whose work would help bring in revenue and who could help raise great kids."

"Do you think a rancher would fill that bill?"

"Yes. I think he might."

Stan looked quizzical. "Really?"

Jenny smiled at him. "Well, he might."

Paulette walked up. "Are you ready to order?"

"I'll say," said Stan.

After ordering prime rib, well done, Jenny asked, "Is the old cabin still up?"

"Sure is but it needs work. Two people could get it back in shape real fast . . . slick as a whisker on a puppy's nose."

They enjoyed the prime rib. Over apple pie à la mode and coffee Jenny and Stan talked about Cicero and ranching and medicine and their families. As they finished their coffee Jenny's beeper, loud and imperious, went off. She glanced at the number. "Call from home. Probably Mom."

Paulette walked over with the phone.

Emma answered. "Your dad is very sick and he won't do anything about it."

John interrupted, "I'm on the other phone, Jen. It's not *won't*, it's *can't* do anything about it. We're right in the middle of calving."

Emma cut in. "I can handle the calving, you know I can, Jenny."

"Hold on. Let's start from the beginning," said Jenny firmly. "What's going on, Dad?"

"Just a little more constipated than usual."

"Any pain?"

"Yeah. In my gut."

"Where in your gut?"

"Down low on the left."

"Does it hurt to push on it?"

"Yeah, sure does."

"Is the pain getting worse? Does it hurt anywhere else?"

"Well, it hurts all over but worse where I told you."

"Dad, you may have a real problem like an abscess in your colon. We need to see you now. I'm here at Paulette's with Stan. I'll ask if he can help with calving tonight and tomorrow."

Stan nodded "yes."

"He can come out now, Dad."

"Listen, Jen, I'll call you first thing in the morning and

let you know how things are going."

Stubborn old coot, thought Jenny. "Okay, Dad. Stan will be there."

Chapter 10

THE MORNING AFTER his angioplasty Alex was transferred to a private room. Shortly thereafter, Emma arrived and, in a few minutes, Alex's room was filled with get well cards, flowers and a bottle of Chivas with a yellow bow around its neck. Emma handed him a note from Hank Collette. "He made me promise to give you this personally. It goes with the bottle," she said, pulling a chair up to the bed.

The card was a picture of a bear with a paw in a cast and a bandage around his head. Alex read aloud, "Ya shoulda come fishin'." He chuckled. "He's probably right. No new problems?"

"No. Ellen's granddaughter took her up to the cabin for a week. Shirley and Jim have an appointment to talk with the oncologist in Missoula. That big bunch of tulips is from them. Barb Tate had diarrhea when she heard you'd had a heart attack. I called in some Lomotil and she's better."

"How's Gus?"

"He was mopey yesterday, but I took him for a walk this morning and brought him along for the ride. He misses you, but he's fine. Honestly, Doc, everything's fine except for John."

"John Polson?"

"No, John Morgan—our John."

"What's the matter with him?"

"He's had abdominal pains and passed blood last night."

"Why didn't anybody tell me about this?"

"It only happened last night. I called Jenny. She wanted him to come in but he refused. This morning he was worse so he came with me. Jenny thinks he might have diverticulitis."

"Is the pain in his left lower quadrant?" asked Alex.

"Yes. But it hurt him all over his abdomen just to move. Jenny put him in observation as soon as we got here. They're doing blood work and I guess they may scan him. Jenny's worried about an abscess and peritonitis."

"Why didn't she let me know?" Alex asked, raising his voice.

"Maybe she didn't want to worry you."

"Dammit, Emma, I don't want to be treated like some neurotic who can't take bad news."

"That's not fair."

Alex lay back against the pillows. "John's my friend. He's like a brother. I should have been told."

"Well, you know now, so relax. Getting angry doesn't help any of us."

Jenny walked in.

"I just told him about your dad."

"Good. Joe Woodhouse, our surgeon, thinks he has an abscess from a perforated diverticulum. He certainly has all the signs of an acute peritonitis. We're loading him with IV antibiotics. He's being scanned now and, if our suspicions are confirmed, Joe will have to operate on him."

"Does John know what's going on?" asked Alex.

"Yes," said Jenny, "but we haven't told him that he may need part of his colon removed and a temporary colostomy."

"He'd object to that," said Emma. "He's often talked about Joe Hanson and his colostomy and the way the insurance company dropped him like a hotcake."

"I'd better go down and talk to him," said Alex.

"I don't think you need to right now," said Jenny. "I

pumped him about his symptoms and found out that he's had a change in bowel habits, constipation and some diarrhea over the past couple of months and didn't tell anyone. But this morning, the pain got his attention. You had your heart attack and he didn't want to bother us with what he still thought was constipation. In a way, Doc, you're more like family than family to him, so I think it would be better to let Joe Woodhouse deal with him objectively."

"He's never been sick for as long as I've known him," said Alex.

Jenny agreed. "I just hope it isn't anything else. An abscess and peritonitis are bad enough, but we can't forget that his father died of colon cancer."

"I was thinking about that too," said Emma.

"He's in the middle of calving. Who's covering the ranch?" Alex asked.

Jenny answered, "Stan Cummings. He and Dad have the same routines when it comes to calving."

"If it weren't for Stan I doubt whether John would have left the ranch, pain or not," said Emma.

Jenny headed for the door. "I'll come back as soon as I know what's up with Dad."

After a moment, Emma sighed. "I just hope it's not cancer."

"Has he lost weight?" asked Alex.

"Judging by his belt, I wouldn't be surprised if he's lost some."

"Well, we'll know soon."

Moments later the telephone rang. "Doc, this is Jenny. The scan confirms that he has a diverticular abscess with fluid and gas in his abdominal cavity. We're taking him to the operating room. Tell Mom to stay with you. I'll come up as soon as we're through."

An hour and a half later, Jenny, pale and tense, came in with Peggy.

"He had a ruptured diverticulum and peritonitis. A real mess. Joe took out most of his left colon and gave him a colostomy." Jenny put her arm around her mom. "There's no way that he could do a primary closure of his bowel with all the infection."

"But he'll be fine, won't he?"

Alex looked at Jenny's face. "There's more to it, isn't there."

"Joe found an annular cancer adjacent to the abscess. It came out with the bowel he resected. We'll have to wait for the path report on how malignant the tumor is and whether it has spread to lymph nodes. There was so much pus and fecal matter in his belly that Joe did a minimum of exploration."

A tense silence followed interrupted by the phone. Alex picked it up.

"It's for you, Jen."

She answered then put down the phone. "Dad's in surgical ICU. Joe wants to go over things with me. I'll bring him up here."

Jenny and Joe Woodhouse stepped into the room. She introduced the surgeon to her mother and Alex.

"Jenny tells me you know what we found in John. I think his abscess and peritonitis should respond promptly to the surgery and IV antibiotics. As far as the tumor is concerned, it looked and felt like an annular adenocarcinoma." He explained to Emma, "It's a glandular cancer that wraps itself around the colon like a ring and causes some constipation before it becomes obstructive. I didn't explore his abdomen and certainly didn't look at his liver. With so much raw infection around I didn't want to risk spreading it. We'll have to see what the path report shows and we'll get the usual chemistries and tumor markers to help clarify the situation."

"How long do you think he'll have to keep the colostomy?" asked Emma.

"Certainly a few months. He has a lot of healing to do and we still have to answer questions about the tumor."

Alex said, "I'm sure you know he's been a friend for a long time. I've taken care of him over the years—nothing big—the usual ranching injuries and occasional flu and community bugs. He's never really been sick before. I'll do anything I can to help. Maybe we should talk to him together when he's recovered from the anesthesia."

"I would appreciate your help," said Woodhouse. "And I'm glad you're doing well. I'll be back this afternoon to report on John."

After everyone left, Alex turned on his side and gazed out of the window. It seemed like yesterday that he and John rode out together at sunrise to push cows to greener pastures or mend fence or "doctor" calves. John was short on words but exceptional in the way he could help heal a deep wound in a man's heart. Alex sighed and closed his eyes.

Jenny pulled down the top of her Miata and headed out of town toward the mountains, away from the setting sun into the magic twilight of the Rockies. The wind helped blow away the immediacy of questions about her dad and Doc. She pushed in a CD of Dvořák's *New World Symphony* and scrolled forward to the Largo with its solitary English horn floating a haunting melody across rolling plains and distant mountains. She slowed down and stopped and put her arms across the steering wheel and let the tears flow. The anguish she'd felt when the young mother died horribly of leukemia returned in full measure as she considered the future of two people she loved deeply. The symphony played on: the crescendos of French horns and tympani reminded her that sunrise follows the night. She dried her tears and drove on.

At the outskirts of Simms, she remembered Waynona. She saw a scruffy sign pointing to a trailer park and turned in. The yellow school bus was parked on the edge of the campground and plugged into a power post under a cottonwood tree. Waynona sat on a folding chair drawing pictures in the dusty soil with a long stick. Melissa added decorations of pebbles and twigs. Jenny waved to them and parked.

"Dr. Morgan. What a surprise," said Waynona, waddling over to the car. "What's up?"

"I was just driving around getting a little fresh air and thought I'd drop in to say hello." She leaned down and gave Melissa a hug.

"You just dropped in?"

"Yeah, but I also wanted to see where you live."

Waynona led her to the front door of the bus. "Go on in. There's not much to see." She pointed to a cinder block building with a tin roof and two doors: *Cowboys* and *Cowgirls*. "That's our bathroom and shower. They keep it nice."

Jenny stepped into Waynona's home. All the seats had been removed. At the far end, a mattress on a rough wooden frame was squeezed between the walls of the bus. Waynona stood at the bottom of the steps. "All the comforts of home. We have to carry water and heat it up on the hot plate to do dishes. The icebox works and so does the TV. Melissa sleeps on the couch. I'm fixing up a nice little crib with foam rubber in a box for when the baby comes."

Jenny was impressed. Waynona told her she had sewn the green curtains for the windows and covered the floor with a piece of carpet that added a certain flair to the interior decor. The young mother was clearly a good "bus-keeper".

"I've got some Diet Coke or one of Lawrence's Bud-weisers."

"No thanks. I just dropped in for a minute."

"Do ya mind if I ask ya something? A doctor in Texas told me that with my sort of future I oughtta get my tubes tied."

"That's a typical male bullshit thing unless there's a serious medical reason. You're only twenty-one. There are all sorts of options."

"Well, we all know about rubbers. I even bought Lawrence some colored ones with French ticklers on the tip, but he won't use 'em. Says it's like taking a bath with your socks on. We've had real fights about it, especially when he's drunk. I get pissed off when he starts bitching because I'm pregnant. The last time, I threw my coffee at him and yelled, 'I'm pregnant because you won't use a rubber when you screw me.'"

"You shouldn't have to put up with that crap. After you have this baby, we'll see about other possibilities," said Jenny.

"They all cost money; that's the problem."

"We'll work something out."

They heard the purple truck before it turned into the campground. Lawrence stepped out and slammed the door. "Somethin' wrong?"

Jenny got up. "No. I was driving through Simms any-way and stopped off to see how Waynona was doing."

"And check out the dump we live in?" he said, sway-ing as he approached.

"You stopped at the bar again," snapped Waynona.

He threw her four cans of a six-pack held together with plastic. "Put 'em in the icebox. You can have one if you want."

"I can't when I'm pregnant and you know it."

He laughed in an exaggerated, vulgar way.

"See the shit I have to put up with," said Waynona in disgust.

Jenny walked to her car.

From the door of the bus, Lawrence shouted, "Pretty fancy wheels there, Doc."

Jenny suppressed the urge to give him the finger.

Chapter 11

THE DOOR OPENED a crack and Jenny peeked in. "You asleep?"

"Just dozing," replied Alex.

Jenny and Joe Woodhouse came in. "Peggy and Mom are sitting with Dad. I think you and Joe could go down and talk to him and I'll take Peg and Mom out for supper."

"Are you ready, Dr. McKinnon?" asked the surgeon.

"I will be as soon as I change this gown for a shirt and pair of pants, and I'd appreciate 'Alex' rather than 'Dr. McKinnon.'"

The two doctors approached John's bed in the SICU cubicle and Alex thought how weird that only yesterday he was in a similar cubicle in cardiology hooked up to tubes and monitors like his friend.

"Hey, Doc. I thought you were having a heart attack."

"I was. But, thanks to your daughter, I'm over that."

Woodhouse said, "Earlier today I started to explain to you what we did in the operating room, but you went to sleep on me. I brought your friend and doctor so the three of us could have a chat."

"Go ahead," said John.

"The immediate problem, when you came in early this morning, was a perforation, a blow-out of one of the small tubular pouches most of us have to some degree in our large bowels after we're sixty. They're called diverticula. Usually they don't cause problems, but occasionally fecal material is pushed into the dead-end pouch, obstructing its outlet. This sets up an infection. Most of the time, when we catch it early, antibiotics will deal with it. Rarely, the diverticulum ruptures and releases stool and pus into the abdominal cavity. That's what happened to you in the early hours of the morning. Luckily, you came in fast enough so we could deal with the problem."

"Luck had nothing to do with it. Jenny gave orders to Emma."

The surgeon continued. "What we did find, in addition to the ruptured abscess, was a tumor partially wrapped around your colon. That was totally unexpected. The tumor came out with the part of your left colon I removed. There is a chance, a real chance, we got it out early enough for a cure. Sometimes we don't pick up those tumors until it's too late to prevent spread."

John lay on his pillow looking up at the ceiling, taking in the surgeon's words. "So if I hadn't had an abscess we wouldn't have found the tumor?"

"Not until later, maybe too late."

"That's amazing. Don't you think?"

"Yes," replied Alex. "Very amazing, but there's one more thing. Because of the infection and spillage in your abdomen, Joe could not safely sew up the ends of your large bowel after he took out the abscess and the tumor. If a primary closure is done with that much infection around, the reconnection of your bowel would certainly break down and leak into your belly. So, you have a colostomy coming out of your left side."

John felt the dressing over his abdomen and frowned. "A colostomy?"

"Yes. A temporary one," said Joe. "In two or three months, after everything has settled down and after we have assurance about the tumor, we'll hook you up again."

"Two or three months? There was no other way to deal with it?"

"There was no other way to deal with it, believe me," said Alex.

John faced the doctors. "I believe you. Thanks for all you've done, Dr. Woodhouse." He stuck out his hand and Joe took it.

The surgeon added, "Tomorrow one of our home health nurses will meet with you and start making arrangements for your care after discharge. She'll help you with your dressings and the colostomy."

Alex said firmly, "We won't need that, Joe. Peggy and I will do his follow-up care."

"Well, that's up to you, of course," replied the surgeon. "But one of the things American Health does best is package pre-op, operative and post-op care. Our home health people are part of the company and can ensure continuity of care."

Alex said firmly, "In Cicero, our continuity of care is over ten years old with complete, legible records on all our patients. What you call home health care has been house calls to us. They've always been an important part of our practice and we stay in touch with our consultants and specialists on a regular basis."

"I understand," said Joe. "I'll ask John's case manager to discuss the matter with you, Dr. McKinnon. Now I'll leave you two together. I'm sure you'll want to visit. I'll be back later this evening."

Alex followed the surgeon out of the room and stopped him in the hall. "Joe. Let me be clear. There is no discussion on John's follow-up. I will do it."

"Fine, Alex. Let's not make a problem of it."

"It won't be a problem if, when you discharge John, he is discharged to my care, period."

"Consider it done. I'm sure they'll agree to make an exception to normal routine. Thanks for your help. See you later."

Alex was still uncomfortable when he returned to John's room.

"What was that all about?" asked John.

"It's about money. For-profit HMOs, like the one running this hospital, want patients discharged as fast as possible so they can minimize what they spend on patient care. When they have their own home care department, the hospital stands to make more money because home services are profitable."

"That doesn't sound right," said John.

"It isn't. Top management people make anywhere from five to thirty million dollars a year to say nothing of what the companies pay the stockholders. All that money is taken out of medical services."

"Too complicated for me," said John.

"It's complicated, confusing and time consuming to everyone. That's why doctors like Woodhouse just go along with it. He does his surgery, gets paid well, everything else is taken care of."

Alex strolled into the garden and trees around the back of the hospital. His mind was in a jumble with questions about his own future and John's. So many what-ifs, so few easy answers. He agreed with Peggy that only he could do something about their crazy exhausting practice. How did you say no to patients when they called? Most didn't call when they should. They couldn't take the time to come in or they didn't want to bother him with something they hoped would get better anyway. He'd have to get help, good help, and that was almost impossible. Most young doctors, even in family practice, took jobs in the medical industry with companies like American Health that would guarantee a monthly paycheck, cover malpractice insurance and, hopefully, help pay off school debts in the hundred thousand dollar range. He would have to look for the exception, but that would take time and money and he was short of both. Was Peterson right to go with the flow? He hated that gutless cliché. What if John had cancer and couldn't do his ranch work? He'd go crazy.

Alex sat on a bench hoping that with some reflection he could think rationally about his heart attack and what it might mean to his future as a rural doc. The thought of not being able to work as he had in a busy practice filled with challenges and variety depressed him. He dreaded being unoccupied—un-needed, if he were brutally honest. Had the heart attack been a warning? All those superstitions about warnings, omens, supra-natural factors playing into an organized and committed life turned him off.

Back in his room, he stood by the window, letting his meal grow cold. Could they ever be sure that John's tumor cells hadn't spread? If the cells were mature, almost normal looking, then the fortuitous excision of the tumor would have saved his life. If the pathology slides revealed young, wild, rapidly-growing cells, the chances of spread were horrific. He crawled back into bed wondering how much pain and anxiety lurked around the corner for John. Only a few days ago, his friend, rugged and indestructible, rode proudly among his herd. The man was a prime example of an independent non-patient. If he had cancer he'd become dependent on doctors and surgeons and nurses and insurance companies. Alex thanked God that his trouble had only been a blocked coronary artery. He could do a lot to help himself—John might not be able to do as much.

Chapter 12

E ARLY THE NEXT MORNING, Tim Moore pulled a chair up
to the bed. "Now Alex, let's talk. I need to go over
some things that you already know but need to hear, officially, from me."

"Shoot."

"Your father died of a heart attack when he was fifty-
eight. Your cholesterol is 360, which is way too high. Your
triglycerides are even higher at 450. You must cut out animal fats and dairy products and cut down on calories too.
Our dietitian will go over things with you."

"I suppose I'll have to stock up on celery, carrots, V-8
juice, all the vegetables I despise, and eat non-meat like
chicken breasts and fish."

"Alex, we've been friends for a long time, but now you
will listen to me as a physician. You're wonderful with the
people you take care of, but you're an idiot when it comes
to taking care of yourself and that's just plain dumb."

"Sorry, Tim. Go ahead."

"Aside from your diet, I want you to continue one
aspirin a day. You are to continue to use nitros as prevention for angina when you go outside. We'll recheck your
blood fats in three months and if they're not better I'll
have you take one of the statins until we get the levels
down to normal. I know you walk two miles every day
with that big dog of yours. That's probably what's kept you
alive in spite of bad eating habits. But now, because it's still
cold in the morning and because of your heart attack, I
want you to shorten your walk to a quarter mile and slowly build it back over the next few months. I hope that

119

artery doesn't plug up again. As you know, ten percent of patients who have angioplasty will need another one within six months. Any questions?"

"Not one. Crystal clear and I'll do it."

"Finally, and just as important, you have to get some help in your practice. Neither of us can stay up all night and work all day like we used to."

Alex said, "Jenny volunteered to help out, but that's only for a short time and I feel guilty taking her away from her work here. It's damn hard to find young doctors who have the training and desire to work in a rural practice where the hours are longer and the pay less than in the cities."

"I know that's a real problem and I've taken the liberty of talking to Hugh Drummel to see if he can come up with a solution."

"Hugh Drummel! You mean, American Health take over my practice?"

"No, I do *not* mean that. I'm sure we can find ways to combine the best of both worlds."

"Just be sure you don't commit me to anything with American Health until I've checked with Peggy, my lawyer, Emma and St. Luke the Divine Physician."

"Alex, knock it off. Your prejudices can be irritating. I know a lot about you and your practice and I respect what you represent in our profession, but you have never worked in an HMO hospital and I have. There are a lot of good things that have happened as far as I'm concerned."

"It's easy for you to say that," growled Alex. "Every patient you see gets a high cost procedure. No wonder they treasure you. You're a revenue center for the HMO. My practice will always be a cost center to them. Peggy was told by a Medicare clerk that if I did more procedures, shoved more things up or down a patient, I'd make more money."

"I understand all that, but an HMO might help in a practice like yours by making ancillary services like physiotherapy, endoscopy and packaged lab work increase your efficiency and income."

"You're not suggesting that I sell out like Peterson are you?"

"No, I'm not. You and Peterson are totally different. I know. His referral workups are nowhere near as detailed as yours. There must be a happy medium somewhere. I'm not sure what it is, but I'm determined to help you find it."

"Well, I'm grateful for that," said Alex. "But, from what I've heard, the HMO will take over a rural practice with lots of promises and a fat check, but as soon as they've swallowed and digested all the doctor has to offer they'll spit him out for some young member of their staff who costs less and will follow their orders."

"All that may be true, but I look at you as an individual and I think we should try and find a young doctor who will do the routine stuff so you can do what you do so well, which is spend time with patients when they need it."

"God, I wish Jenny would come to Cicero."

"She's certainly an extraordinary young woman," said the cardiologist. "She's extremely competent and I know she enjoys the regular hours and decent pay here. Technically she's outstanding and she has a clear sense of responsibility for patients and the staff teamwork needed to take care of them. You should hear her talk to the nurses. They love her as well as respect her."

"I'm very proud of her," said Alex. "I hope some day she may want to have longer, deeper involvement with patients. In the meantime, I'm sure she'll stick where she is unless something happens that would be against her judgment or principles."

The door opened. "Am I interrupting something?" asked Peggy.

"Not at all," said Tim. "I could use your help in trying to convince our much-loved friend here that he needs to ease off in his practice."

"I think he will," she said, walking over to the bed. "We have too much fun in our life to blow it." She pulled up a chair.

Alex looked at them. "You may find this hard to believe but over the last few years I've wished for an obvious, objective reason to slow down so I wouldn't have to meet every demand of my patients."

"Understandable in your situation," said Tim. "But why do you feel you have to jump every time they call?"

Alex shrugged. "Well, they may need me. And even if they don't, some of them will sue me if I don't jump."

"Come on, Alex. Of all the practices I work with, your patients are the least likely to sue. You've told me that yourself."

"I suppose that's true."

Tim continued. "You know about the two grannies walking past the graveyard? One complained to the other that the new young doctor spent too much time with his family and even went fishing on weekends. Can you imagine! The other, pointing to a fresh headstone under a weeping willow, replied, 'Sure not like ol' Doc, dead before his time. But he sure was dedicated.'"

"That's about the way it is," agreed Alex. "But let me be just as blunt with you. Here in a hospital you have all sorts of help. You have two partners and a retinue of people who jump every time you lift your pinky. Even Jenny has regular hours. When she's on, she's on, but when she's off, she's off. In my sort of practice the only way to be off is to go away far enough that even Emma can't find me. Do you remember that talk we had a few years ago when you did my first heart cath?"

"When I told you your coronaries were as open as

Paris sewers but as spastic as your anal sphincter? How could I forget." They laughed.

"I felt like such a turkey," added Alex.

"We also talked about you being a slave to your practice and as dependent on their approval as they are on yours. You'd lost control of your own life and expected everyone to feel sorry for you because you were so tired all the time."

"Okay, Timothy Moore, so nothing has changed. So, what's the answer? Where do you draw the line between jumping and goofing off?"

"The answer is for me to continue my rounds and for you to tie some flies, read a book or do anything but mull over the past. You're one of the best doctors in the area and a real friend to many of us and we want to keep you around to liven up our meetings." Tim stood. "Anyway, Dr. McKinnon, I'm delighted you've responded well to our excellent clot busting and ballooning of your coronary arteries. In the meantime, without committing you to anything, I have planned lunch for the three of us with Drummel and Jenny in the staff dining room. We can discuss options."

At 8:00 A.M., a knock on the door and another visitor entered, a young woman with long red hair down the back of her white lab coat. She looked eager, like a first year medical student. She stood at the foot of the bed hugging a clipboard. "Good morning, Mr. McKinnon. I'm Heather, your patient advocate from customer relations. We are very happy that you have done so well since your heart attack and hope that you have been satisfied with our resources. We are rather proud of our new cardiac laboratory."

"Nice to meet you, Heather. This is the first time I've met a patient advocate. What exactly do you do?"

"We are intermediaries between the administrative office and the consumer. We pick up complaints early so that we can correct them. We feel that by doing so we can prevent problems in the future."

Alex thought, how smart to have a suing-prevention team. "I can assure you that I'm doing very well and that I have no complaints."

Heather made some checkmarks on her clipboard. "Your case manager will be in soon to help coordinate your discharge and rehabilitation plans."

"I'm sure Dr. Moore has taken care of all that. I've known him for a long time. We've worked on many patients together."

"You have?" The advocate checked her form. "What do you do, Mr. McKinnon?"

"I'm a physician, a doctor."

Heather's blush did honor to her red hair. "How silly of me not to know that. I'm sorry. I guess you don't really need a patient advocate do you."

"I wouldn't be too sure, Heather. Doctors are terrible patients and probably need more advocacy and common sense than most. I appreciate your coming in."

At 8:30 A.M., a sharp, authoritative rap on the door announced the next member of the parade. A middle-aged woman with a variation of a Dorothy Hamill haircut—half modern male crewcut below a circular thatch of brown hair—walked over to the bed and shook hands. "Good morning, Doctor. I am Lucille Karanovsky, your case manager."

"Good morning, Ms. Karanovsky. Is it Ms. or Mrs.?"

"Either." She pulled the chair to the foot of the bed and sat with the ubiquitous clipboard clasped to her ample bosom. She wore a dark blue blazer and well-filled blue pants.

"I hope you will forgive my ignorance, but what exactly are the responsibilities of a case manager, Ms. Karanovsky?"

"Lucille, would be fine, Doctor. I'm an R.N."

"That helps me relax. We're sort of in the same boat aren't we?"

"I doubt it, Doctor. I haven't nursed for eight years. I was recruited by American Health a year ago to work in administration."

"So what does a case manager do?"

Lucille recited: "We work under the managed care department and act as liaisons between hospital services, home health care agencies and outlying providers. We monitor a patient's overall therapeutic plan to ensure that recommended clinical pathways are followed. We are the essential part of a care provider team made up of a case manager, a social worker and a non-professional clerk who deals with the forms and paperwork relevant to each patient's DRG, diagnosis related group and hospital course. The team's goal is to assure the patient utilizes the hospital's systems and resources in the best possible manner, keeping an eye on cost. American Health also has us monitor therapeutic lines of care, also known as TLCs, dictated by ICD-9 codes and standard of care paradigms."

"Wow, well done! But I thought TLC stood for tender loving care."

"Not any more."

"Complicated stuff! It must add a lot to the cost of care."

"On the contrary, Doctor, our new systems make care more cost effective. With proper monitoring of inpatients and close follow-up with our outpatient services, we are able to shorten patients' hospital days by significant percentages. When American Health Corporation took over this hospital they assumed the debts and extravagances so typical of community hospitals. In just a year, we've been able to turn that around and make the hospital into a profit center. Now, I think we should talk about you."

"By all means," said Alex.

"I assume you will be followed in our cardiac rehabilitation program."

"I guess that depends on orders from Dr. Moore," replied Alex. "We haven't covered the point yet."

"Dr. Moore is on the panel of doctors who set up the cardiac rehabilitation program so I am sure he'll want you registered and scheduled before you leave."

"Does that mean you expect me to drive over here to get rehabilitated?"

"Of course." She glanced at her form. "You're from Cicero."

"Yes, and I don't think it would be at all practical to follow up with you."

"Practical or not, our rehab programs are important parts of our accreditation as well as for our patients. There's a certain fellowship created among patients recovering from similar diseases, which has long-term value."

"Financial value?"

"Well, that's not our first consideration, of course."

"I'll talk to Dr. Moore and follow his advice. We're old friends."

Lucille lectured, "Doctors who take care of themselves or each other don't always do what they should. If you're honest, you'll agree with that, Dr. McKinnon. We'll be glad to help in any way—objectively and professionally."

"Thank you."

"Now, Doctor, a word with you as the local provider for Mr. John Morgan. I have spoken with Dr. Woodhouse and he tells me that you are thoroughly familiar with this case."

"Lucille, I have to tell you that I never refer to a patient of mine as a 'case' with its connotation of something either impossible or terribly interesting."

The veteran nurse puckered her lips and frowned. "Whatever."

"Hasn't Dr. Woodhouse called you about Mr. Morgan's follow-up?" asked Alex.

"No. He has no reason to. Our procedures are clear-cut. He has been registered with our oncologist and radiologist so that these services are available for his total care."

"Have you talked to the patient about this?"

"Not yet. We think it courteous to speak to the local provider first."

"Is registration in your follow-up programs also part of the accreditation requirements?" asked Alex, innocently.

"Our whole provider performance is part of our National Quality Care Package."

"Oh, of course," replied Alex. Lucille could have been a programmed matron in charge of student robots. "Well, Lucille, thank you very much for coming in. Maybe after I've had a chance to talk to John and Dr. Woodhouse, we can put our heads together and come up with a provider/consumer follow-up strategy that will help in his recovery and keep your ship afloat, so to speak."

Ms. Karanovsky stood up and held out her hand. "We shall be in touch, Doctor."

The new managed care jargon and layers of administrative worker bees confused and angered Alex. No wonder these people spent so much time running from one meeting to another. Maybe they were as confused as he was.

A short time later, a trim young woman with short blonde hair and the inevitable clipboard stepped up to his bed.

"Hello, Dr. McKinnon, I'm Athena, your dietitian. Dr. Moore asked me to go over a low cholesterol, low calorie diet with you and answer questions."

"Athena? Like the goddess?"

"Yes. My father was a professor of ancient history and mythology."

"And you ended up pushing celery sticks and zucchini?"

"And broccoli and spinach and carrots."

"Well, pull up a chair and give me the bad news. Athena was the goddess of what?"

"Wisdom, skills and warfare," she replied, handing him a printed page from her clipboard.

He sat up wishing he had on something other than a hospital gown, and she launched into her presentation of his new eating habits: the bounties of fiber, veggies, pasta, fruit and carrot sticks . . . daily menus, calories and exercise . . . graduated of course. Clearly, peanut butter and jam sandwiches, hard salami and Irish coffee were out. He was sure that Athena and Peggy would have already discussed his diet.

"Dr. McKinnon, are you paying attention?"

"Of course, haven't missed a word."

"Any questions?"

"None that you could answer, I'm afraid."

"Try me."

"Not today. Thank you for your help. I'll do my best to eat properly."

She smiled as a mother does to a child after a lecture on manners or dirty hands and left the room.

Alex lowered the back of the bed and, turning on his side, stared out of the window seeing nothing but the stupidity of his flippant attitude with Athena . . . with everybody who was trying to help. He wanted to be seen as strong and independent, but he felt his years for the first time and knew that he was thoroughly replaceable: he felt himself sinking in despair. Thank God for Peggy.

Chapter 13

A T NOON, Jenny led Alex and Peggy to a corner table in the dining room on which linen napkins, a tablecloth and flowers announced something special.

Hugh Drummel and Tim Moore joined them.

"It's great to see you up and around, Dr. McKinnon," said Hugh.

As if on cue, Athena approached pushing a cart loaded with covered dishes. She greeted Alex and the others as she passed around plates with swordfish steak, spinach pasta and grilled tomatoes. A salad of chopped chives, celery, lettuce and peppers added color to the healthful entrée.

"Looks wonderful," said Jenny. "Thanks, Athena."

"*Bon appétit,*" said the dietitian. "Call if you need anything."

"Quite a lady," said Alex.

"Yes, she is," agreed Jenny. "She and I run together. She's an Olympic-class skier and really puts out for our patients. She wanted to do this dinner especially for you."

"I'm impressed and . . . moved."

As they started their meal, Tim said, "I thought we should get together to celebrate your rapid improvement and imminent discharge, but also to talk seriously about your long hours and the stress of constant call." Alex was about to say something but Tim raised his hand. "Wait. None of us can or will impose anything on you."

Hugh spoke. "At Dr. Moore's request, we've been going over recent applications from family physicians and physician's assistants to see whether we can recruit some help for you."

Alex frowned at Jenny who cocked her head in a don't-give-me-a-hard-time way.

Hugh caught her expression and, encouraged, continued. "We have two recent applications from young doctors who want to work in this area. Our home office has already done the routine screening, so we know they have valid medical degrees and are not wanted by the law in their home states. I interviewed them last week. You met them, Jenny. What did you think?"

"The one from Illinois wanted a job out here so he could hunt and fish. He would cover one weekend a month and required a huge salary, malpractice insurance, health insurance and retirement benefits. The other is a young woman out of the Denver primary care internal medicine program. Well-trained but weak on trauma. She's married to a geologist who works for an oil company. They have one child, which limits her availability. She'll probably end up in a group practice."

"Not very promising yet," commented Hugh, "but as a critical care hospital we concentrate on specialists rather than primary care providers. That may change now that Dr. Peterson and his practice are on board. But rest assured, Dr. McKinnon, we will keep looking for ways to support you."

"Let me tell you what I need," said Alex with conviction. "A well-trained emergency room doctor like Jenny, who'll do house calls and sit with families when their old folk are dying. She, or he, must do in-depth work-ups for patients who need long-term care and others who have a strong family history of cancer, heart disease, nervous disorders, etcetera, etcetera. I need someone who'll take call every other night and every other weekend."

"Are there still such people around?" asked Tim.

The administrator said, "Very rare. An obsolescent species."

Jenny cut in, "Here comes Joe Woodhouse."

"I just dropped by to tell you that John Morgan, the other VIP from Cicero, is doing well. It will take a few days for his bowel to start up again, but I don't foresee any trouble."

"I dread to think about what John may have to go through if that tumor has spread," said Alex.

"I can assure you he will get the best of care," said Hugh. "Our surgery and radiology departments compete with Missoula."

Alex looked directly at Hugh. "I'm not worried about the mechanics of his care. I'm much more worried about how he'll react when limitations are put on what he can do."

Woodhouse said, "Please excuse me, I have to run. See you later."

Hugh persisted. "We have a new psychologist for our drug and abuse program. I am sure she could help."

Tim caught the flash of anger in Alex's eyes and quickly added, "John Morgan will need much more than he can get from a catalogue of available services, Hugh."

Mystified, the administrator raised his eyebrows and shut up.

The cardiologist cleared the air with, "Alex, let's get back to your needs."

Alex visibly switched gears and turned to Tim. "I've been thinking about the subjects you raised about my practice. The problem with most family practice residents I've had for preceptorships is a lack of hands-on experience with emergencies, especially surgical emergencies and trauma. Some of them from big medical schools seem to be trained as gatekeepers for the medical industry. In the past, they were called triage officers."

"That's true," Tim agreed. "A couple of our better family physicians recognize that. Last week one of them told me he'd rather not be on call in the emergency room because he doesn't see enough trauma and acute hearts to be comfortable with them. That particular doctor is as compulsive and thorough as you are, Alex. His patients come in with competent work-ups. But I agree with Hugh, we are evolving into a critical care hospital. Hopefully in a couple of years our staff will all be hospitalists and intensivists."

"What about people who are chronically critical, if you know what I mean?" asked Alex. He turned to the administrator. "Tim and I have played Ping-Pong with some of our chronic patients who are in and out of heart failure. I send them in for fine tuning. Sometimes Tim will suggest a change in treatment or he'll tell us we're on the right track. The family gets a few days rest and can catch up on their own needs."

"A very reasonable and civilized way to go," said Hugh. "But government rules won't let us do that anymore and, anyway, that type of patient doesn't produce enough revenue to meet expenses. Even emergency care is becoming more difficult and less remunerative. Medicare has a list of procedures we must follow. If we admit someone for pneumonia and hope to get reimbursed we must have two positive blood cultures, a fever over a certain amount for a specific number of days, a positive chest x-ray and a sputum test. If the patient doesn't meet these criteria the care will be uncompensated. It's just that simple. It's the system."

"Screw the system, Hugh. It stinks," snapped Alex. "What would you do if an eighty-year-old comes in with a cough and is too feeble to have much of a fever?"

"I would . . . I would refer the question to the attending physician," replied Hugh.

"I'll tell you what would happen," said Tim. "The

admitting resident would have to explain to the family that he can admit gran'dad but they'll have to pay for it out of their own pockets."

"Does the same thing happen in cardiology?" asked Alex.

"No. Most of our patients undergo some sort of procedure: treadmills, echoes, cardiac cath, thallium scans and all the rest. Uncle Sam and the insurance companies pay very well for these. They're magic high-tech. The government considers them much more important than a complete history and physical exam. But, again, let's get back to your needs, Alex."

Hugh suggested, "If your practice was part of our system, our staff would help cover."

"You're true to form, Hugh. Updike's horizontal acquisition of the referral market," said Alex, struggling with his temper. "Why don't I just work for you as a paid flunky like Pete Peterson?"

"Dr. Peterson will continue to practice as he always has, but he'll be free of insurance and financial hassles. I'm sure I don't have to tell you that Medicare and the insurance industry are becoming more and more difficult to deal with."

"Bullshit, Hugh. Your company is owned by the biggest insurance outfit in the country. You have people and computers who make money manipulating and exploiting the bloody system."

Peggy put her hand on Alex's arm. "Let's cool it and enjoy our lunch."

"Good idea," said Tim. "We can think about these things over the next few days."

Chapter 14

Dr. Moore discharged Alex the next morning. Alex objected to being made to sit in a wheelchair, but "regulations were regulations" according to the aide. Nobody was allowed to walk out. They either sat in a wheelchair or were pushed out feet first on a gurney. Alex grudgingly accepted and asked her to wheel him into the surgery unit to see John. He was sitting next to his bed.

"What's the matter with you, Doc?"

"Not a thing. I feel fine. I'm about to be sprung," replied Alex. "The wheelchair's just for show, I guess. How's it going?"

"Kinda sore and crampy, but not too bad. Joe tells me he'll be very glad when I pass gas. Sure doesn't take much to make a surgeon happy. What about you? Peggy and Emma said you have to take it easy. I can't see you sitting around, you'll go nuts."

"We're trying to find more help. I won't be sitting around quite yet. Is there anything I can do for you?"

"Not for the moment. But when the time comes I want your support to get my gut hooked back together. I don't want a lot of fancy, expensive things done—whatever is going on inside. Is that clear?"

"It's clear, John. You won't be put through anything you don't agree to."

"Fine. See you at home soon. And take care of yourself, Doc. I want you around."

Alex waved good-bye and the aide wheeled him out to the front hall where Peggy and Emma were waiting.

135

The city yielded to vast potato and wheat fields that produced the wealth of the region and Emma picked up speed as they headed home. Peggy sat between Emma and Alex.

"I'm impressed with that hospital," said Emma.

"They do have good people," said Peggy. "But I think they've fired too many senior nurses who gave the place a reputation for real bedside care. You should hear Sally on the subject. The hours she works in the ER plus her administrative responsibilities and paperwork are inhuman. The satisfaction and pride in patient care are stifled by exhaustion and pressure to do more with less."

"What they're doing to nursing is a crime," said Alex.

"Is Sally going to stick it out?" asked Emma.

"She's toying with the idea of just doing night shifts. Apparently the night nurses aren't hassled by statistical geeks and nosy supervisors slinking around the halls."

Alex said, "I was exposed to new administrative types, each with a form to fill out on a clipboard. The older one, my case manager, was quite formidable."

"What was her name?" asked Peggy.

"Lucille."

"Lucille Karanovsky?"

"That's the one."

Peggy chuckled. "Sally has some funny stories about Lucille. She imitates her to perfection. She can talk for two minutes nonstop using all the new administrative jargon and make no sense at all."

"The only thing I got out of her visit," continued Alex, "was her fixation on getting John and me registered in their follow-up clinics. I guess she gets brownie points for that. Like after-sales service when you buy a car."

"It's part of their strategy to make themselves indispensable so long as a patient is a source of income," said Peggy. "Jenny's struggling to understand the managed care approach. Attempts to increase efficiency and cut costs make sense to her, but she's getting fed up with Drummel."

"What's he been up to?" asked Emma.

"Every time he has a visitor, especially one from headquarters, he shows her off and introduces her as 'his chief of staff.' But what's really getting to her is that he's demoted Sally from being head nurse of the emergency room to a staff nurse that does procedures and sits on the new ER management committee. Apparently Drummel is pushing what he calls 'Shared Governance Committees' to give the nurses and some of the other staff the impression they have policy-making responsibilities. The result is that Sally has to go to meetings, often on her time off. She's spending more time on admin and less on real nursing. So I guess Jenny feels her territory is being invaded by newfangled management ideas that aren't useful for patient care."

Emma honked the horn as they drove into the ranch. Gus came barreling out of the barn and jumped up on Alex, barking and pulling at his coat. Stan joined them and helped Peggy and Emma with the boxes of groceries she'd picked up in town. They agreed to meet for lunch to catch up on the news and plan the days ahead.

Emma clanged the dinner bell and, like an echo, the phone rang in the kitchen.

"Hi, Mom. It's me," said Jenny. "Joe and I just reviewed the path report on Dad's tumor."

"Hang on, Jenny. Doc and Peggy are here. I'll put Doc on the other line."

"What did they find?" asked Alex.

"The tumor is an adenocarcinoma. The proximal margin of the specimen is apparently clear of tumor cells."

"That's good news. How's he doing?"

"He's coming along well. He was up and around twice today and is on a soft diet. If he continues to improve, Joe will discharge him the day after tomorrow, especially since I'm coming home with him."

"Has Joe explained to him that we can't be sure about any spread of the tumor to his regional lymph nodes or elsewhere?"

"No. He and I don't think that's necessary. We'll rescan him just before he leaves the hospital and take it from there."

"I agree with that," said Alex. "But you'd better talk to Lucille, the case manager, and be sure she doesn't schedule John for chemo or radiation consults until we're all clear about what he needs and wants."

"I'll take care of that," said Jenny. "Lucille's not a bad egg, she's just a formaholic."

Emma added, "Tell John the calving is going well. Stan's almost as good with 'the girls' as he is."

After lunch, Alex and Peggy drove to the clinic and caught up with the mail, lab reports and a large stack of forms from Medicare and insurance companies. Flowers were delivered from two families who expressed gratitude that Alex was back, and the telephone rang every few minutes with the same messages of relief—that they were home and at the office. The only patient on the schedule was Hank Collette, who needed the rest of his sutures removed.

"Say, Doc, ya know somethin', there's sure a hell of a lotta rumors around town."

"About what, Hank?"

"'Bout you. Ya wanta hear 'em?"

"You'll tell me whether I want to hear them or not, so shoot."

"Well, I was down at the Sagebrush last night havin' a few beers with the boys and seems like people are worried you're about to be taken over by the same outfit that bought out Doc Peterson."

"What do they say about Peterson's deal?"

"Well, ya know how people talk, they say they wouldn't go to Peterson if he was the only doctor around. They sure don't wanna lose you."

"Peterson's still running his clinic, Hank."

"If he is he sure ain't there very much accordin' to my sources."

"What sources?"

"D'you know Horny Mills?"

"Only by reputation."

"Well, he came in the bar with his face all bunged up and his arm in a cast. Told us he'd been thrown from a horse he was workin', a big ol' rogue called Dusty 'cuz he threwed a lot of cowboys in the dust. He busted his arm and his face was sure a mess with an eye all swolled up and cut from an encounter with a fence post. Drove himself into Simms and ran into Peterson in the parking lot. Peterson was all duded up and heading into town and told his gal to send Horny to the hospital in the ambulance. Can't see you runnin' out on a patient, Doc, even if you had a hot date in the city."

"I wouldn't conclude that he's never there with just one story."

"I ain't concludin' nothin', just makin' an observation. Ya know Durant Smith who works for road and bridges?"

"Sure. His wife Nancy is the mayor's secretary."

"Well, Durant told us, confidentially o' course 'cuz he got it from Nance, that some big shot from American

Health was callin' Phil about a deal over here. We figure they're hatchin' up some sort of scheme to take you over, unless of course you want to be taken over, which I told them you didn't. I'm right about that, ain't I Doc?"

"Absolutely right, Hank."

"So I gotta ask ya. Ain't there some truth to the fact that your heart attack means you've gotta slow down?"

"I needed to slow down before the heart attack. It won't make all that much difference, Hank. But we are looking for some help with the practice. Someone who'll be part of our team and the community, not some company flunky. But I'll tell you something, my friend, a lot depends on what the people around here want. Some of them may be persuaded by sweet talk from the center that their medical needs will be better dealt with and cheaper if they sign on with outsiders."

"Like the guy in the fancy suit who passed his cards around in your waiting room. He's one smooth and snakey dude. Like I told ya before, you gotta watch him."

"I am watching him. Like a hawk watches a critter."

Hank guffawed. "I knew I had ya pegged, Doc. We sure 'preciate ya." He stood up. "Sure glad you're home."

Alex walked him to the door. "Keep your eye on the birds and your ear to the rail, old friend. You can warn me when an unscheduled train pulls into town."

Before heading home, Alex put in a call to Bill Blanford and the radiologist in Missoula to discuss options for Jim Davis.

After supper, Emma and Stan rode among John's first-calf heifers close to the calving barn. Almost a hundred had already calved, eighteen during John's first days in the hospital. Stan had only lost one calf: a stillborn. Throughout the day they worked together feeding the stock, pulling calves when necessary, vaccinating them with C & D, cleaning out the pens, and from time to time herding the cows and calves ready to return to life in the open into the large pasture across the road. One cow had been unable to expel her calf and after all the usual measures failed, Stan performed a cesarean, saving the cow and calf as well as a hefty fee from the veterinarian.

John and Emma had always liked Stan. He was a big man but gentle and soft-spoken like many men who know their strength. He wore size 34/38 blue jeans, slim and long enough to touch just his spurs. His Pendleton shirts showed off his muscular shoulders and huge hands. Miraculously, a large black Stetson he wore in all seasons always looked new. He kept his hair neat and short and had not been spoilt by the knowledge he'd picked up in college.

Emma worried that Stan would be missed by his brothers on his own ranch, but he reassured her that they could take care of everything.

"You know them, they think the world of you all and encouraged me to stay as long as I don't get in the way. Besides," Stan added, "it's always a treat to see Jenny."

That evening, Alex and Peggy sat on their back porch enjoying the soft light which, like a curtsy, bowed to the end of the day.

Alex put his arm around her and she rested her head on his shoulder and looked up at him. "Were you serious about returning to France?"

"Yes."

"Is that an unconditional yes, regardless of the practice?"

"It has to be."

"Where would we go?"

"First to the place where we let ourselves fall in love. The Dordogne country and Sarlat."

"I hope things haven't changed too much."

"I bet they haven't. We might spend days in that old four-poster."

"Wonderful. And what do we do when we're all rested up?"

"We'll charter a river boat and spend time alone, bicycling along the tow paths and into rustic villages for dinner."

"And have fresh crispy croissants and café-au-lait in our bunks," added Peggy. "Then what?"

"Then to the chateau country and Coudray and old friends from another life."

"It has to happen, Alex."

"It will."

The temperature dropped rapidly when the sun dipped behind the hills and they moved inside. Alex lit the fire and Peggy opened up the futon couch in front of the hearth. They undressed and headed for the bathroom.

Alex stood under the twin shower heads he'd ordered from France, reveling in the wet heat. Peggy peeked in. "Do you want me to do your back?"

"Of course."

She stepped in, let the water soak her for a moment, then inspected him. "One would never guess you'd had a heart attack and an angioplasty."

Alex stroked her wet hair and rested his hands on her shoulders. "I feel fine except for a minor ache in my groin where Tim threaded in the catheter."

"I wasn't going to do your front anyway. Might get you all riled up," said Peggy reaching for the loofah. She glanced down and saw the riled up had already started. She turned him around and kissed his back. "You have to be good, Dr. McKinnon. We mustn't strain our heart." She sponged his back with long slow strokes from his shoulders to below his bottom.

"Good? How can I be good when you do that?" He turned to face her and locked his hands behind her waist. She closed her eyes and threw her head back, letting the water splash on her face. He bent over and kissed her on each eye and on her lips and her tongue.

Peggy leaned away. "Are you sure we should be doing this so soon after your heart attack?"

"I checked with Tim."

With his foot he pulled over the small plastic footstool they kept in the shower. She stood on it and he pressed his hands into her firm, smooth buttocks. He was hard between her thighs and, with her help, he entered her and they came together, long and deep.

Stepping out of the shower, they wrapped themselves in soft terrycloth robes. They dried their heads and sat on the futon in front of the fire.

"Did you really ask Tim about romping?" asked Peggy.

"How can you doubt me?"

"Easily when it comes to medical advice about yourself. What did he say?"

"He said, 'My policy,' and I'm quoting him, 'is to avoid telling patients after they've had a heart attack that they can't drive and they can't have sex because it just throws them into a depression and there's enough of that anyway after a heart attack.'"

"Is that all he said?"

"No. He pointed out that a few years ago research showed that cardiac demand during an orgasm was about equal to a jog up a flight of stairs. He said they both take about the same amount of time and energy."

"How romantic," said Peggy. "I guess we'd better find a flight of stairs somewhere."

"Seriously, that's what he said and furthermore there

are some adventurous researchers who measured cardiac output, I'm not sure how, in men that romped with their wives and others that romped with their girlfriends. It turned out that a romp with your girlfriend produced ten times the cardiac demand as with your wife."

"Where does that put me?" asked Peggy.

"On a pedestal, where you belong."

"So, having just had a great romp, we can assume you can run up a flight of stairs."

"Assume nothing. Five minutes after Tim gave me that pearl, I put on a bathrobe and ran up and down a flight of stairs in the hospital and felt fine."

"You're impossible, but don't change. I get excited when you put me on a pedestal in the shower. I suppose I should tell you that I spoke to Lucille Karanovsky about physical activities after a heart attack."

"I don't believe for a second that you would speak to Lucille about anything." He pulled her down on the futon and she rolled over on top of him and kissed his nose.

"What did Lucille say?" he asked.

"She said that continuity of care was the *in thing*. But I like your *in thing* better."

"Now who's so bad." He smacked her bottom. "You're a terrible liar Peggy Strong. But I love you with all my heart now that it's repaired."

Alex wrapped his arms around her and kissed her neck. "Mmmmm. What's the perfume?"

"Curve," she mumbled.

"Curve? Just Curve? Who makes it?"

"I don't know, it comes in a green bottle. Tell me more about your friends in France. They're like storybook characters to me."

"Auguste and Kati. He's an artist in pastry—has a shop next to a café in a twelfth century village called Coudray. And Kati is his Russian lady friend."

"Is Coudray like Sarlat?"

"Maybe even nicer. It's next to a small river called the Indre and there's an old mill house we'll stay in."

The phone jangled. "Oh, not now," protested Peggy. She reached for the receiver. "Hi, Teri. Yes, we're both here. Doc's doing fine. What's up?" Peg listened. "Hang on, here's Doc. Howard Lindsey's babbling," she explained, handing him the phone.

"Hi, Teri. Problems with Howie?"

"We had a power outage for about an hour and I walked over to his trailer to see whether or not his electricity had come back on. When I asked him how he was, he just babbled. He seemed to understand my questions, but couldn't answer properly."

"I'll come," said Alex. He handed the phone back to Peggy. "Sounds like he might be having a stroke." He glanced at the fire and at Peggy all warm and delectable. "What a time for Howard to babble!"

Alex's feet were on the floor. "I'll be back as soon as I can."

She grabbed his arm and pulled him down. "Hold on Dr. McKinnon, sir." She locked her arms around his neck and kissed him hard. "I'll race you to the car."

Alex threw off his bathrobe and climbed into Skivvies, a T-shirt, pants and a sweater. Peggy pulled on her sweats and reached the back door behind Alex, who looked around for Gus. He was on the futon with his big muzzle between his paws, gazing at the fire. "Come on, you shaggy mutt. When I work, you work, remember?"

Peggy shouted, "Don't forget your bag!" He stepped back into the kitchen and she ran to the car and opened the door. Gus jumped in and she followed with a shout of victory.

Howard Lindsey was a seventy-nine-year-old rancher. Alex and Peggy had done many house calls on his wife, who had died of a tumor that caused large amounts of fluid to accumulate around her left lung. She had refused to go to a hospital, so two or three times a week they aspirated her chest to help free her from the agony of suffocating in her own fluid.

A half hour later, Teri met them at Howie's door. His Norwegian elk hound Ike barked at Gus, who growled softly from the car, yawned and went back to sleep.

Howard had quit babbling, but was clearly worried.

"Don't know what come over me. I could hear her question about the power, but when I tried to answer the words were all garbled, didn't make sense."

"How long did the babbling last?" asked Doc.

"'Bout ten or fifteen minutes."

Peggy wrapped a blood pressure cuff around Howard's arm while Doc continued, "Have you ever had one of these before that you didn't tell us about?"

"No, Doc, sure haven't."

"Are you dizzy? Do you have a headache?"

"No."

"Appetite okay? Bowels working normally?"

"Yeah, I feel fine. I just don't know what come over me."

Peggy said, "Pressure's 110/60, pulse seventy, regular." She clipped the probe of an oximeter on his finger. After a short pause she said, "Ninety percent."

Alex asked Howard to stand and checked his heart and lungs, then felt both sides of his neck for the pulse of carotid arteries. The left seemed slightly less prominent than the right. He listened with his stethoscope and could hear no swishing sound that might indicate a narrowing or a sclerotic plaque inside an artery. He checked Howard's cranial nerves, his reflexes and his ability to keep his balance with his eyes closed. All were normal.

"I think you've had a TIA, Howie. That's a transient ischemic attack, which means something caused an interruption of blood supply to the part of your brain that deals with speech."

"What do we do about it?"

"At this point, we'll give you an aspirin a day to help prevent blood clots from forming around an irregular spot in your neck arteries. This is a warning that tells us to do what's necessary to prevent a real stroke. Tomorrow we'll get on the phone and arrange for an ultrasound examination of your neck arteries. We'll have to do that in the center. That will give us a better picture of whether we can treat you with medicines or whether you might need surgery to prevent a serious stroke."

"If that's what it'll take, Doc."

"Then we'll see you tomorrow afternoon around two."

"Sorry you had to come out all this way. How're you doin' anyway?"

"Fine. Just fine."

The fire had burned down to embers by the time they returned home. Peggy snuggled behind Alex under the cozy warmth of the comforter. They played spoons, like the colonel and his wife in MASH.

Chapter 15

THE NEXT MORNING Alex and Peggy slept in and had a leisurely breakfast. Peg headed for the office and Alex called Gus and the two of them wandered among the cottonwoods enjoying a peaceful morning. Peggy returned and made fruit salad for lunch. After a nap, they drove to the clinic.

Howard showed up promptly at two. After Peggy checked his vitals, Alex took him into his office for a chat.

"Can you go anytime we can get an appointment for you, Howie?"

"Yup."

"Fine. Now, my friend, over all the years that we've known each other, the only things I've ever treated you for were broken bones and arthritis. After that spell last night, we must concentrate on stroke prevention. We can reduce your chances of getting into trouble but with no complete guarantee. We need to discuss what you want me to do if you get a big-time stroke."

"I guess we can cross that bridge when we get to it, Doc."

"It would be better to look beyond the bridge now when you're feeling fine and we have time to look at the options."

"That makes sense."

"A lot would also depend on how severe the stroke was. It would be important for us to know that you've thought about these things and have made certain decisions about what sort of life support you would want or not want. You know, tubes down your throat and pumps to keep you alive or the sort of care that keeps you comfortable and pain-free."

"It's hard to think about all that when you don't know what's going to happen. But one thing is sure, I don't want to be a veggie."

"So, if it looks like you're going to be a veggie, you would not want us to resuscitate you?"

"I suppose not, Doc. I'd kinda leave that up to you."

"That helps some," said Alex.

The two men walked out of the office and Peggy handed Howard a piece of paper with an appointment for a duplex examination of his carotids. She gave him a return appointment to discuss the results with Doc at the end of the week.

The phone rang and Peggy picked it up. It was Lucille calling to schedule Alex for cardiac rehab and to talk to him about John Morgan's follow-up treatment. Peggy asked her to hold the line for a moment while she checked with the doctor.

"Tell her that I'm doing fine. I do not need her services and, as far as John Morgan is concerned, she is to wait until she receives orders from Dr. Woodhouse or me."

Peggy relayed Alex's message. Lucille pushed on. "We are required to follow-up on our patients," she pointed out testily.

"Who requires you to follow-up?"

"The administration."

Peggy put her hand over the mouthpiece. "You deal with her, Alex."

He grabbed the phone. "Lucille, what . . . is . . . your . . . problem?"

"I do not have a problem, Dr. McKinnon. I am just trying to be responsible and follow-up on you and Mr. Morgan."

"Thank you for your efforts. Please do not do anything

about either of us until you have written medical orders from me, Dr. Moore or Dr. Woodhouse. Have a good day."

Alex put in two hours with some of his older patients who just dropped by with a card or a homemade something-or-other to welcome him back. Grandma Ellen had returned from her cabin and needed her heart and potassium checked. Jim and Shirley Davis were the last patients on the schedule.

"Sure glad you're okay, Doc," said Shirley.

"It's nice to be back. How was the time in Missoula?"

"We met with the cancer man and the radiologist," said Jim. "The first doctor offered chemo, which might slow things down some, and the x-ray man thought that radiation to the tumor in my back would help with the pain."

"Neither of them offered any cure," added Shirley. "They were both sympathetic and the radiologist honest enough to say that the amount of radiation necessary to help might give Jim some serious side effects."

"The cancer man suggested that I take one course of chemotherapy and then we could see what happens," said Jim.

Shirley asked, "I know you've just returned home, but have you talked to them, Doc?"

"Yes. I spoke with both yesterday. How is the pain in your back, Jim?"

"Not too bad. The Tylenol and codeine you gave me seems to take care of most of it."

"That's fine. We have plenty of stuff we can use if the pain gets worse. You just have to let me know about it."

He looked at this couple he had known for a long time and wished, as he had so often, for a magic wand to wave over patients and chase away their suffering and bleak futures. He could deal with their pain and some of the anxiety, but the day-by-day, week-by-week knowledge that their life together was ending was impossible to treat with medicines. Only an *act de présence*—being there— would help support and comfort them.

Alex stressed, "The most important thing is to keep you comfortable and pain free."

"And you can do that here at home?" asked Shirley.

"Sure can," replied Alex.

"Because that's where I want to be, at home," said Jim unequivocally.

"Peggy and I and Shirley will stick with you, Jim. You know that."

"Yes and I appreciate it." He paused. "You have no plans to leave do you, Doc?"

"No. Certainly not in the immediate future. Why?"

Shirley said, "There was talk at our quilting class that you're going to be taken over by American Health."

"I won't be taken over unless the people want me out of here."

"That's the last thing anybody wants," said Shirley.

"That may be true. We'll have to see how people will react if American Health makes a move."

Jim asked, "Have you any idea of how long I have, Doc?"

"Honestly, I don't know. The chemo may give you more time. But it's impossible to say for sure."

Jim looked at Shirley, then turned to Alex. "I guess we'd better go for the chemo. I suppose I'll lose more hair."

Shirley's eyes filled with tears. She reached over and gave him a hug. "There aren't that many more hairs to lose."

Back in the hospital emergency room, Sally and Jenny were doing their paperwork and keeping an eye on a patient with chest pain in one of the bays. He was comfortable and had responded well to aspirin, nitro and oxygen. The monitor showed old and possibly new indications of coronary artery disease. Dr. Moore was on his way in.

The calm was shattered by the sudden roar of an unmuffled exhaust, squealing tires and frantic honking of a horn. The ER door flew open and Lawrence ran in shouting, "She's having it in my truck!"

Jenny ran out. Waynona let out a howl and shouted, "It's coming. I can't hold on." Jenny opened the door and Sally wheeled a gurney up to the purple truck.

Waynona's water had broken, soaking her jeans and the front seat. Jenny put an arm around her shoulder and felt the tightness of her cramping uterus.

"Take some big deep breaths and try not to push." After a moment the contraction eased. "Now wiggle over and I'll help you onto the stretcher."

As they headed into the ER another contraction started. Waynona cried out, "I can't stop it coming."

From the driver's side, Lawrence stared with horror at his front seat. "Jeezus Chrrrist, what a fucking mess."

Jenny and Sally lifted Waynona onto the table and quickly removed her jeans. Jenny pulled on a pair of gloves and checked below. The baby's head was crowning.

"Perfect timing," said Jenny. "Another few contractions and we'll have a brand new baby. When did you go into labor?"

"'bout an hour ago, just before Lawrence came back from work. He wanted to take a shower but I told him *no*, we have to go now."

"Where is Melissa?"

"With a neighbor lady."

"When did your water break?"

"'bout halfway here."

Sally checked Waynona's pressure, placed her heels in stirrups and did a quick pour prep.

Waynona gasped, "Here comes another." She tightened up and pushed with all her might. "It's coming, it's coming." The contraction eased and she lay back taking deep breaths. Three more hard, long contractions with Jenny easing the baby's head and shoulders gently from the birth canal and a new person entered the world. The baby cried and she passed him to Sally who wiped him off, cleaned out his nose and weighed him.

"A six-pound boy," she announced.

Jenny took the child, wrapped him in a baby blanket and laid him at his mother's breast. Waynona kissed the top of his head, then turned away and took a deep breath, closing her eyes tight to hold back the tears. Her whole body shook with muffled sobs.

Jenny leaned over. "It's okay, Waynona. He's a big strong boy with all his fingers and toes. It's all over."

A long, desperate moan escaped from deep within her. "Noooo, it's not all over. What will happen to him?" She let go and cried uncontrollably between great gulps of air. "The son of a bitch tried to make me have an abortion." The baby whimpered and she held him close and stroked his back. She wiped the tears off the top of his head with a corner of the blanket. She hugged him and her sobs became less violent, like echoes from the depths of a passing storm. "We'll make it, little one." She tucked the blanket around him and gathered her resolve. "You and Melissa and me, we'll make it." She sighed, then asked, "Can I have a towel to wipe my face?"

Jenny stepped over to the sink, relieved to be able to hide her own tears. She ran water until it was warm and tried to think beyond the pathos of the moment. Options?

So few for a girl with no schooling or family support. Going from man to man was the only means she had of feeding herself and her kids. She handed Waynona the wet towel, then a dry one, and thought to herself, *We'll find a way to make you free.*

"I was gonna call her Jenny if it was a girl. Guess I'll just hafta settle for Morgan. That's a strong name for a boy."

"Sure is. He can be anything from a buccaneer to a banker. You rest a little, I'm going to clean up and catch up with the other patients."

In the women's dressing room, Jenny lay on the couch staring up at the ceiling. She'd taken care of so many of society's derelicts in Salt Lake and San Francisco. Yet, her knowledge of their lives was flitting at best. They came and they went, and when the weather turned bad they returned with imaginative excuses to be admitted for at least one night between clean sheets. They were beyond self-help, their suffering momentarily deadened only by rot gut booze and street drugs. Waynona's cry, "What will happen to him?" was a plea broadcast to humanity. She had two kids, for whatever reasons, with little hope of escaping from the prison of poverty. Even in this western paradise the poor were becoming desperate and some kids ate only once a day, at school. The rich escaped to ostentatious trophy homes within gated communities with walls thick enough and high enough to keep out the sounds and desperate acts of the *hoi polloi*. She was profoundly moved that Waynona, a girl she hardly knew, would name her son Morgan. How starved some people are for simple kindness.

An hour later, Jenny walked out with Waynona dressed in green scrubs and Morgan wrapped in his blanket.

"I'll get the public health nurse to do a home visit on you tomorrow evening."

"You don't need to do that," said Waynona. "Ma's coming over to help. She's parked her trailer in Sage City."

"That's fine," said Jenny. "But don't forget I want to see you in ten days—sooner if you or Morgan are having problems."

Lawrence, Waynona and the new baby drove off—a struggling ménage facing an uncertain future.

A heated discussion between Sally and the ER clerk at the admitting desk was in progress but stopped abruptly when Jenny returned.

"Has she reported us to Drummel yet?" asked Jenny.

"The second you walked out with Waynona and the baby."

"To hell with Drummel and his spies. What's next?"

"A boy with a fractured finger, x-rays are hanging. A nasty little girl pulled her dog's ears and got bitten on the arm. A seventy-five-year-old with pneumonia, x-rays on the way, sputum sent to lab, white count low. He has a huge hernia in his groin. You may want to give him a bath more than anything else."

Chapter 16

A WEEK AFTER Joyce moved in with Waynona and her children, Lawrence turned real nasty. He objected to sleeping in his truck so that Joyce could sleep in the bed with Waynona, and the baby's wailing got on his nerves. He turned up the volume on their TV to drown out the infant's crying, but the owner of the campground told him he'd have to turn it down if he wanted to stay.

On the morning Lawrence told them that other living arrangements had to be made, Joyce slipped on the bus steps and fell hard on her rear end. She couldn't get up and was too heavy for Waynona to lift. A woman in a trailer nearby called the Simms ambulance. After much heaving and pushing and cries of pain from Joyce, Waynona and her mother found themselves in a corner of Dr. Peterson's emergency room. They were separated from the rest of the world by two white curtains on overhead rails and two walls filled with medical paraphernalia. Melissa and the baby had been banished to the waiting room.

Within this narrow rectangular space, Joyce lay on a gurney with the back raised. Waynona sat next to her on a stool. A long counter with a stainless steel sink ran along a wall under glass cabinets filled with vials of medicines and boxes of sutures and instrument packs used in emergencies. Under a narrow window behind them, a shelf ran the length of the back wall holding various monitors and pumps and suction machines. Above these, special needles, trochars, laryngoscopes and tracheotomy tubes of various sizes and shapes, large volume syringes and irrigators, all sterilized in plastic envelopes, were fixed to a pegboard ready for immediate use. Two large oxygen tanks and trays of tubing stood ready for use next to an EKG console and oscilloscope.

A short, plump nurse walked in, closing the curtain behind her and introduced herself. "I'm Irene. The doctor is finishing with another patient. He'll be in shortly. In the meantime, I'll check you over and ask a few questions. Okay?"

"Okay," replied Joyce, forcing a smile.

Waynona spoke up, "Joyce is my ma. Can you give her something for pain? She's hurting real bad."

"We'll give her something as soon as we've done these preliminaries and the doctor's seen her."

A purple stethoscope snuggled around the folds of Irene's chin. She had the tight lips and frown of a nurse under pressure. With clipped efficiency, she started down a list of questions on an admitting form. "Your name?"

"Joyce Jefferson."

"Age?"

"Fifty-nine, almost sixty."

"Address?"

"Sage City, Montana. Got there a little over a week ago. I came from Kentucky to give Nonie a hand with her new baby."

"That's nice. Nearest relative to be notified in case of emergency?"

"Waynona Jefferson. Right here. We're the only two grownups left in the family."

"Where do you live, Waynona?"

"In the campground south of town."

"Telephone?"

"Not really. They don't like us to use their phone."

The nurse turned back to Joyce. "Do you have any insurance?"

"Just car insurance."

"No health insurance? And you're not on Medicare."

"That's right," replied Joyce. "One of the great unin-sured, but not part of 'the great unwashed.'" She brushed off her grey sweatshirt and pants. "Sorry I didn't have a chance to clean up before coming here."

Irene put down the clipboard and reached for a blood pressure cuff. "What happened?"

"I fell coming out of the bus and landed hard on my butt."

"So you hurt your butt?"

"It's a little sore but I really hurt in my chest."

Irene pumped up the cuff and let it deflate. "We'll have to use the wide cuff. You've got a big arm."

"I've got a big body, but we've done okay together 'til recently."

Joyce's blood pressure was fine. "Can you tell me how much you weigh?"

"I avoid scales."

"So do I," said the nurse, warmly. "Just give it a guess, might be important later."

"Put down 270 pounds. That's with shoes on."

"Of course. Any other medical problems?"

"About a month ago the toilet bowl was filled with bright red blood. Looked like someone had dumped a bot-tle of red ink in it."

"Any pain or burning or frequency with that?"

"None. It scared me because I had no warning. I was feeling okay, just tired."

"And you've had no more bleeding since then?"

"No."

The nurse examined Joyce's hands and fingers. The tips were flattened and enlarged and the nails brittle and curved. The tips of her index and middle fingers were stained with nicotine. "How long have you been smok-ing?"

"Ever since I was old enough to light a match. My granddaddy was a tobacco farmer."

"Anything else we should know about, Joyce?"

"Only a cough and I'm short of breath if I have to do very much, but I guess that's because of the weight I carry around."

"And the cigarettes," added Irene.

"I know. I've tried to stop smoking so often I've given up trying. But since I've been here I've been real tired, I mean more tired than I've ever been. At first, I put that down to the drive from Kentucky. But now I think something else must be wrong."

Irene asked Waynona to stand at her mother's feet and take her hands and pull her up so she could listen to her lungs. But, with even a light pull, Joyce shouted with pain and they let her down.

Waynona pleaded, "Please give her a shot."

"I will," said the nurse. "Where did that hurt?"

Waynona wiped the sweat off her ma's face. "Please, Irene?"

Joyce gasped, "In my breastbone and back, between my shoulder blades."

"You may have cracked something in your spine when you fell. I'll have a word with the doctor and be back with a shot."

Moments later, she returned with a syringe. "We need to get x-rays of your thoracic spine and ribs after this shot takes effect." She injected the medicine into Joyce's upper arm.

Waynona asked, "Do you mind if I bring my kids in from the waiting room? The baby can be quite a handful for Melissa."

"I'll get 'em," said the nurse. "You stay with your mom."

For half an hour Joyce dozed and her little family sat

quietly behind the curtains. Waynona gave the baby her breast and after he was full he slept in her arms. Footsteps passed by on the other side of the curtains. Phones rang, people spoke and from somewhere came a raucous laugh and a door slammed. Waynona was relieved that her mother and the baby slept but as the clock on the wall behind them ticked away she grew apprehensive that the effect of the pain medicine would wear off before they were seen again. She wondered, over and over, how much it would all cost and how they would pay. Health insurance was a farce unless you had a job with benefits or a lot of money. A friend of hers in Texas died in an ambulance while being shuttled from one hospital to another because she had no health insurance or other means of paying for care.

Irene returned and they wheeled Joyce into the x-ray room across the hall. Eugene, the x-ray tech, built like a wrestler, put his arm around Joyce and helped her stand for the x-rays. She cried with pain and had to be supported and kept still by Waynona and Irene.

Suddenly, the sliding door of the x-ray room slammed open and Dr. Peterson strode in. Waynona looked at him and felt sick to her stomach. While Irene, Waynona and Eugene struggled to get Joyce back on the gurney, the doctor read the sheet Irene handed him, then followed them back into the emergency room.

"So you fell on your bottom and have pain in your sternum and upper back."

"Yes."

"You've had some shortness of breath, fatigue and one episode of painless bleeding from your bladder."

"Yes."

"And I gather you started smoking right after you were weaned."

"Not that early."

"I presume you know that smoking gives people lung cancer," said the doctor, in a condescending self-righteous tone.

"Of course. It's a chance you take if you choose to enjoy tobacco."

"A stupid choice that costs our country millions and millions of dollars every year."

"In lawyers' fees?" asked Waynona.

"No, in heath care," snapped the doctor. He looked at Waynona. "Haven't I seen you before?"

"Once, when I was puking my guts out."

"I remember. You were pregnant—not married but pregnant for the second time." He looked at her closely. "Did you keep it?"

"Of course."

"Where did you have it?"

"It's not an *it*," said Waynona sharply. "He's a boy and I had him in the hospital."

"With old Krohl?"

"No. With Dr. Morgan, Jenny Morgan."

"Oh my, the ER queen!"

"The woman doctor who gives a shit about patients."

He turned his attention back to Joyce. "Let's have a look."

He pushed his stethoscope between her back and the mat on the gurney and asked her to take a deep breath. She did and triggered paroxysms of coughing. "Oh, my chest. Oh God, my chest."

"I'm sorry. We won't do that again." Gently he felt the tightness in the muscles on either side of her thoracic spine and thought there might be some loss of the normal curvature. Her sternum was exquisitely tender. "I'll go check the x-rays and be back in a minute." He glanced at the clock on the wall and walked out leaving the curtain open.

Waynona closed the curtain, walked over to the sink and ran cold water on a paper towel. She laid it gently across her mother's forehead. "You okay, Ma?"

"I will be when we're out of here."

In the x-ray room, Peterson and Irene looked at the films on the viewing box. "Looks like a compression fracture of T7 and maybe T8. I've never seen a fracture of the sternum but she may have one. She's very tender there so something must be going on."

"Just sitting down hard can cause all that?" asked the nurse.

"We see it in old ladies with osteoporosis."

"Her other vertebral bodies don't look like osteoporosis, do they? And she's not that old."

He looked at the x-rays again. "I suppose if you weigh as much as she does, sitting down hard on your rear end would put a lot of stress on the spinal column. We'll settle for that."

"What are you going to do?" asked the nurse.

"They don't have insurance so let's keep it simple. We'll put her in a plaster corset."

They walked back to the ER and Peterson reported his x-ray findings to Joyce.

She nodded her understanding, then said, "I've been so tired and weak way before today. You don't think there's something else, do you?"

"Like what? Like lung cancer? You've smoked enough to be a prime candidate for that disease."

Waynona started to object but her mother cut her off. "Okay, Doctor, so what do we do?"

"We'll get you sitting up and Irene will bring a basin of water and some six-inch rolls of plaster and we'll make you a corset that will reduce the pain until the bones heal."

"I wish I could clean up before that."

"If you'll step out for a second, Doctor," said Irene, "I'll give her a sponge bath and put a body stocking over her chest then you can do the cast."

Peterson looked at his watch. "Okay. Call me as soon as you're ready."

Irene brought the necessary wash cloth and towels and helped Joyce give herself a good wash. She dried her off, being careful to put as little pressure as possible on her breastbone and spine. Then, with Waynona's help, they dressed her in a large body stocking and wrapped padding around where the cast would go.

Peterson returned and, insisting that Joyce sit straight with her shoulders back and hands above her head, he started wrapping plaster around her chest and heavy breasts. The cast went from just under her armpits to below the bulge of her abdomen. He worked the plaster into the gauze until it hardened and Joyce was finally allowed to lower her arms.

"How are you all going to get home?" asked Irene.

"I guess I'll thumb my way home, get Ma's car and drive back and pick her and the kids up. Can you keep an eye on Melissa and the baby?"

"I have a better idea," said the nurse. "I'm off in five minutes and I have a Dodge Caravan and can run you all home."

Peterson said, "Let me see you in two weeks. Irene will give you an appointment on the way out and sample pills for pain."

With the cast on, Joyce had less pain when she stood up and walked. Irene loaded them into her car and headed toward the campground on the edge of town.

"How can a nurse like you work for a son of a bitch like Peterson?" asked Waynona.

"I don't work for Dr. Peterson, dear. I work for the hospital. I used to be head nurse in surgery before they downgraded most of us with seniority. Now I'm in the nursing pool and jump whenever they call, at least for another year. Then, as you kids would say, I'm 'outta here.'"

Chapter 17

PEGGY JOINED Alex and Gus for the morning walk, which was more of a stroll down the lane and a time for the old dog to run after gophers. The only animal he'd ever brought back to Alex was a flattened, desiccated road-killed gopher. Gus never killed anything—he even wanted to play with the coyotes.

After breakfast, they headed for the clinic and a schedule that was almost back to normal. Peg drew routine blood work on Barb Tate, followed by Annie Taylor who needed her liver chemistries monitored every three months.

At twenty-three, Annie was a physical education teacher in the Cicero High School and an example to Alex of someone who lived an active, constructive life in spite of having almost constant pain from ankylosing spondylitis, an inflammatory arthritis. Following consultations with a senior rheumatologist, she was started on Methotrexate, a powerful drug used in some cancers. This medicine had dealt with her joint pains to a point where she could coach sports. The main requirement was that she come in for blood counts and liver screens regularly.

After Annie's blood draw, Peggy gave her a tray with two cups of coffee and banana bread for herself and Doc, who was in his office going over charts.

Alex looked up. "Thanks, young lady. Peggy's got you well-trained. How's it going?"

"Just a little stiff in the morning, otherwise fine."

"Have a seat, at least while you finish your coffee." Alex was always amazed and humbled by this young

165

woman whose pain had sometimes been almost impossible to tame without risking toxic doses of her potent medicines. She had often been reduced to tears but only when she was alone or, occasionally, here in the office. And yet she persevered.

"I hear your volleyball team might end up at state," said Alex.

"Yeah. They're a lively bunch of kids and they're finally getting their act together."

"That's so funny," said Alex.

"What's so funny?"

"You're only a few years older and a lot smaller than most of the players you coach, yet your teams are winners. How do you do it?"

"I'm feistier than they are."

"I'll vouch for that. I'll bet they don't know how much pain you have sometimes."

"Of course not! It's none of their business." She drained her cup and stood. "Thanks for the coffee."

Peggy handed Alex the mail with a letter from American Health Corporation on top of the stack.

American Health Corporation
Western Montana Regional Medical Center

Alexander McKinnon, M.D.
Cicero Clinic
Cicero, Montana

Dear Dr. McKinnon,

I have asked Dr. Lester Leavitt, family physician, and contract member of our locum tenens staff to call you for an appointment at your convenience.

Since his graduation from the Western Kentucky

Family Practice program affiliated with the University of Kentucky Health Care Center in Paducah he has worked in emergency rooms and as a locum in two of our Insta-Qual-Care facilities.

Dr. Leavitt is married and without children. His wife is a nurse who, unfortunately, has a serious kidney disease and is a patient in our renal dialysis unit in Paducah. She awaits a donor kidney.

He is available to you for an initial period of three months all expenses paid. We hope that you can find suitable lodging for him at our expense.

If at any time you find his presence unhelpful please feel under no obligation to keep him. My hope is that he will be a valuable asset to you and help bring some relief to the heavy burdens of your practice.

With best regards,

G. Hugh Drummel, III
Administrator

"That's a smooth letter from G. Hugh himself," said Alex, handing the letter to Peggy.

The telephone rang and Peggy took it in the outer office. A moment later she told Alex, "That was Nancy, the mayor's secretary. She called to say that someone in the regional center's administration office had called to make an appointment with the mayor to discuss a plot of land next to the football field for ancillary medical services from the center. She wondered if we knew anything about the center's plans."

"Call her back and tell her that Drummel is acting on his own and that whatever he's doing she shouldn't trust him any more than she does her boss. Find out if the mayor has any intention of discussing these developments with us."

The next two patients were quickies for blood pressure, weight checks and prescriptions. They visited with Peggy and she gave one patient another appointment for a follow-up on his blood fats.

Peggy handed Alex the prescriptions and insurance forms that needed his signature. "We need to stop in and see Gerald. Shelly will be there servicing the oxygen concentrator and wants a word with you. Also, his daughter from the east arrived last night. It would mean a lot to her if she could talk to you about her dad."

"How is he?"

"I saw him yesterday morning. His emphysema is about as bad as it can get. Edna is scared he's going to fall when he goes to the bathroom. He's so big and she's just a wisp of a thing."

"Having their daughter there will help," said Alex.

Peggy added, "He's very short of breath when he does anything. Going to the bathroom is agony even with the oxygen way up."

"We'll stop in on the way home. Any other calls?"

"Yes. A lawyer called from Missoula. He says he represents a burn patient from an oil rig accident you took care of last year."

"What did he want?"

"He wanted to talk to you. Do you want his number?"

"No, but I'll take it."

Alex dialed Missoula, identified himself and said he was returning a call from their office. A moment later he was put through.

"This is Tom Burgess, thank you for returning my call, Doctor."

"What can I do for you, Mr. Burgess?"

Alex heard a rustling of paper, then, "Do you remember a patient of yours called Henry . . . Henry something-or-other . . . here it is, Henry Randquist?"

"No, I don't."

"You saw him a year ago. He was involved in a rig accident and sustained a fifteen percent total body burn, mostly on his back and chest."

"We've had a number of rig accidents over the past few years, but I don't remember the patient. Why are you calling? Did he have a bad result?"

"No. Not at all. You took excellent care of him and he's very grateful for that. He knows and appreciates the fact that your prompt actions and his evacuation to the burn center probably saved his life."

"So why are you calling me? Who are you suing?"

"That's just it, Doctor. He has outstanding expenses and fees so we're trying to raise money for him. We thought the company that sold him the nylon shirt he was wearing that day should be held liable for the extent of his burns."

"What?!"

"If he hadn't been wearing a nylon shirt his burns would have been nowhere near as serious. We are seeking redress for Mr. Randquist."

"You must be kidding!" exploded Alex, slamming down the phone.

Peggy came running in. "What's the matter?"

"Another lawyer trying to make money out of someone's misery."

During the rest of the day, Alex and Peggy saw a half dozen patients with sore throats and runny noses and other minor ailments. He spent time with a family dealing with having their mother's driving license revoked while the old lady sat at home by her kitchen window struggling for her independence. The discussion had been poignant but peaceful. Already Doc had received calls from friendly neighbors about grandma weaving down the road. Her speed was greater than her control. Most of the people in the county knew about her erratic driving and they sort of ran herd on her as they did on old range cows ambling down the highway to fresh pastures. If you could keep the cars on the road strictly local, the problem would not be as acute. Unfortunately heavy tank-like traffic from the oilfields made grandma's unpredictable perambulations a real hazard. The family, understandably, did not want the old lady hurting herself or anyone else. They would set up a rotation of older grandchildren and others in the family to drive her wherever she wanted to go, even to the gambling casino, a long day's drive from Cicero.

The telephone rang. "Cicero Clinic, Peggy."

"Hello, Peggy, this is Joe Woodhouse."

"Nice to hear you, Doctor. Would you like to speak with Alex?" She handed him the phone.

"Hello, Joe. What's up?"

"Just called to say that John Morgan is doing well and looking forward to coming home tomorrow."

"We're expecting him."

"There's another thing if you have a moment, Alex."

"Go ahead."

"Hugh Drummel and I were wondering if we could come for a short visit and see how we could increase our collaboration with you."

"I think we collaborate very well. What do you have in mind?"

"Well, nothing specific yet. We were just thinking that although most of the Cicero patients come from your practice, a few self-refer here to the center directly. We were thinking that our home health service could help in their follow-up care and, of course, help with your patients too, starting with our patient John Morgan."

Alex felt a tightening in his chest like an alarm. None

of the other offers of help that Drummel had made had really bothered him. The surgeon's proposition reminded him of an octopus exploring cracks in a rock with the tips of its sucker-bearing arms ready to grab a prey and devour it. His rational mind told him not to exaggerate.

"Alex, are you still there?"

"Yes. I was just thinking it's a long drive from the center to Cicero. Give me time to catch up after being away. We can be in touch next week."

"We'll do that."

Alex hung up. "I wouldn't be surprised if Drummel is using Joe to scout out our territory. Come to think of it, I wonder if that's his strategy with this . . . rent-a-doc." He put his arm around Peggy. "I really don't trust the son of a bitch in spite of his smooth letter. I just wish we could sign out to someone and have guaranteed peace for the rest of the day and night."

"As soon as Jenny gets here she'll take the night calls." Alex looked surprised. "That's what she told me. She'll cover at night and on weekends when she's here. During the day she wants to help Stan and have unhurried time with Emma and John. If the stuff hits the fan, she'll help whenever we need her."

"That's what she wants to do?"

"Yes, and I wouldn't argue with her if I were you."

"I won't. I can't imagine having uninterrupted dinners and nights with you." He looked at Peggy with suspicion. "Did you and Jen hatch this plot?"

"No, Dr. McKinnon. There is no conspiracy. Only happy coincidence. She looks forward to being with Stan and will do her part with you as she's planned. I think it's heaven-sent. If she has a big emergency at night, we'll help her. Are you ready to go home?"

Alex reached for his bag and Gus stretched and yawned. They walked out to the car.

It was a short drive to Gerald's home. Shelly's oxygen truck was parked in the driveway. They went in through the kitchen where the coffee was always on with Twinkies and sugar donuts in a porcelain bowl. Edna came out of the front room to meet them.

"Thanks for coming. His feet are swollen and he's having a hard time breathing, even sitting up."

In the living room, Nichole sat in an armchair facing her dad. She shook hands with Peggy and Doc. "Nice to meet you," said Alex. "We're all glad you could come. It's a big help."

Shelly was checking the oxygen tubes and greeted Alex with a wave of her hand. She and her two friends, Penny, a respiratory therapist, and Debbie, the secretary/bookkeeper, worked for a private company out of Missoula—Home Oxygen, Inc. They supplied patients in the Cicero valley with oxygen and with hospital beds, commodes, crutches and all the other medical hardware known as durable medical equipment. The three women were all natives of Cicero with families involved with the school, the roping club and Shelly's quilting group.

Gerald's face was pale and puffy and a glance at his feet showed a lot of swelling.

"Pressure 100/70, pulse 120 and irregular," said Peggy, jotting on a pad.

In spite of his labored breathing, he looked up at them with a wide grin. "I was just . . . telling Nichole . . . about the ol' Swede . . . who cut off his thumb. Have I ever . . . told you that one . . . Doc?"

"No, Gerald. Never heard it."

Edna started to interrupt and Doc held up his hand. "Go ahead."

"Old Ed Johnson, the Swede . . . was a rancher who lived up the road. One day my dad and I stopped at his place . . . on the way to get groceries. He was chasing the cat around the house. 'What the hell are you doin'?' asked my dad. Ed replied, 'I was choppin' vood and chopped m'damn thumb off . . . so I stuck him up on the vindow . . . til I'd time to sew him back on . . . and dat gutdamn cat, he ate him.'"

The room was filled with laughter.

Nichole wiped her eyes. "You never heard that one, Doc?"

"Maybe once or twice, but it gets better with each telling."

Gerald had an indwelling catheter in his bladder, but the bag contained only a few drops of dark brown liquid.

"Have you been able to eat or drink anything, Gerald?"

"Not much."

Edna added anxiously, "He hasn't eaten anything since yesterday's breakfast of bacon and eggs and he's only had two cans of Sprite all day."

"I'll get him to drink," said Nichole.

"Just a couple of swallows at a time, frequently." Alex looked at Gerald. "Would a nip of Scotch brighten up your soda?"

"It'd have to be bourbon. But not today."

Alex leaned over with his stethoscope. "Let me listen."

The old boy's lungs were filled with fluid and his heartbeat was racing and irregular. Alex had Peggy give him another shot of Lasix. "That'll make you pass more water and help your breathing," he explained.

Peg packed up the bag.

Alex turned to Nichole and Edna. "Call if you need anything."

"We will," replied Nichole. "And thanks."

Shelly was waiting in the kitchen for Alex and Peggy.

"We're doing all we can," said Alex.

"I'm sure we are," replied Shelly. "What I really want-ed to ask you is whether you know what's going on at the regional center? They're sending someone over to talk to us about working with them. They even hinted that they would like to hire us away from our Missoula company. Have you heard anything about their coming over here?"

"I'm hearing all sorts of things, Shelly. Dr. Woodhouse called just before we left the office, wanting to come over with their administrator. I'm sure they're up to something, and I don't like it. All these HMOs want to expand what they call their geography and catchment areas. When they come over don't commit yourself to anything, just be friendly and they might tell you more about their plans."

Alex turned to Edna to review Gerald's medicines, then wished her a good night and left.

"What a horrible disease," said Peg when they started home.

Alex fed Gus and stoked up the charcoal grill on the porch for the elk steaks, courtesy of a patient, and French style green beans and baked potatoes without butter, courtesy of Peggy. She nursed her glass of sherry, and Alex his long Scotch and soda, as they relaxed and enjoyed the twilight. Half an hour later, when the charcoal had burnt down to gray bricks with scarlet halos, Alex dropped the steaks on the grill. Smoke rose up and watered his eyes. Peggy came over and wiped his face with her hands and put her arms around his neck. "How long?"

"How long for what, our trip to Europe?"

"No. How long before the meat is ready?"

"Say five minutes."

The steaks were perfect and the meal cozy and peaceful out on the deck.

After dinner, the phone rang. Peg answered.

"Are you ready for us?" asked Jenny. "We'll be home tomorrow after lunch."

"Great. How's John?"

"Amazing. He's walking straight and eating a normal diet but without jalapeño peppers or cowboy beans. Is Alex there? I need to cover a point before seeing Hugh."

Alex took the phone. "Hello, Jenny. It'll be wonderful to have you and your dad back home."

"We can't wait. Doc, I have to ask you something. Did you get a letter from Hugh Drummel about a doctor who could help you in your practice?"

"Yes. I just got it today."

"I met him and he seems like a pretty good guy. Are you going to give him a try?"

"I don't know yet. We've been getting all sorts of reports about American Health trying to move into Cicero. I'll tell you all I know when you get here tomorrow. At this point I'm not keen on getting hooked up with Drummel in any way. I'd rather try and find someone myself."

"You know how hard it is to recruit someone for a rural practice. Do you have the money to pay a recruiter or a locum?"

"I just don't trust Drummel. If a young doctor is paid by him he'll have to follow his orders. He'll probably be a nice guy, but he'll be a company employee. I'll interview him, but whether he comes into my practice or not depends on me, not on Drummel."

"I understand. When do you want to meet him?"

"Whenever. How long can you stay, Jen?"

"Ten days, then I'll come Friday, Saturday and Sunday for a month or so. I want to be with Dad and I want to help cover the practice. Peg and I have talked about it, I'm sure she's told you."

"And you can do that with your job at the hospital?"

"You bet."

Chapter 18

THE NEXT MORNING, Sally handed Jenny an envelope bearing the logo of the American Health Corporation. "Patricia brought this down from the front office."

Jenny tore open the envelope and read:

American Health Corporation
Western Montana Regional Medical Center

Jennifer Morgan, M.D.
Emergency Department

Dear Dr. Morgan:

It is my duty to inform you that we have received a complaint from the chief of the department of OB/GYN, Dr. Augustus Krohl, concerning your delivery, this morning, of an indigent patient in the emergency room. In his letter he recognizes your competence as an emergency room physician and appreciates the extra responsibilities that are yours as president of the staff council. However, Dr. Krohl feels that the delivery of this patient was not an emergency and that, furthermore, you had blocked or, at the very least, not encouraged the patient's attendance to the appropriate prenatal clinic.

Recently you expressed to me your feelings about this particular patient and, you will recall, I appreciated your point of view for the care given her in the past. I never imagined, after our meeting, that you would continue providing her with uncompensated care ending with her delivery in your department.

*Unfortunately, Dr. Krohl sent a copy of his letter to me
on this matter to corporate headquarters. It is my reluc-
tant duty to hand deliver this letter of reprimand, which
will be part of your personnel file, and request that you
write a letter of apology to Dr. Krohl.*

Trusting in your understanding, I am sincerely yours,

G. Hugh Drummel III
Administrator

The phone rang. Sally answered.

Jenny stuffed the letter into her pocket.

Sally put her hand over the phone. "Bad news?"

"Just more shit from Drummel. He objects to our
delivering Waynona's baby in the ER. Hell, she almost had
it in the truck. There was no way she could have made it
to OB even if she'd wanted to."

"The doctors are looking at your dad's scan in x-ray.
Go ahead. I'll take care of things here."

John's x-rays were spread over three rows of viewing
boxes. The two doctors were focusing on cuts through the
liver. The radiologist summarized the findings: "Both
these three-centimeter areas of decreased density in the
liver could be anything, like cysts or metastatic tumor.
They're deep but you might reach them with a long biopsy needle. Further down, there appears to be a three- or
four-centimeter, ill-defined mass proximal to the colostomy stoma. Did you feel anything when you examined his
colostomy?"

Woodhouse replied, "Nothing within three centimeters of the opening. I didn't scope him. Maybe I should."

"Any abnormal lymph nodes?" asked Jenny.

"None big enough to see. They have to be around two centimeters or more to show up. The rest of the films are okay."

At the end of the review, the radiologist left Jenny and the surgeon to discuss further steps in her father's care.

"What do you think, Joe?"

"I examined John before his scan. He says he's feeling okay, but tired. His colostomy was fine. His blood work shows he's slightly anemic, his liver enzymes are slightly elevated and his CEA is seven. Since we don't have a CEA prior to his surgery the elevation may or may not be relevant." Woodhouse paused and looked up at the collection of x-rays. "If everything was completely negative, I'd say we could let him go for another month or so, then plan to get rid of the colostomy and hook him up again."

"But everything is not negative," said Jenny.

"That's right. I'm worried about the ill-defined mass not far from his stoma as well as a possible or probable spread to his liver."

"That's what I'm afraid of," said Jenny. "So what do we do?"

"We open him up and see what's going on and deal with what we can surgically. We'd have to wait until his present wound heals before doing that."

"Wouldn't it be too late to do much if the tumor is in his liver?" she asked.

"It depends on whether the lesions are resectable."

The two doctors stood in silence looking at the scan films, which showed so much, yet not quite enough to be sure. Joe wondered if the ill-defined mass below the colostomy opening was a new, synchronous tumor he could excise. His surgical instinct pushed him to find out as soon as possible and deal with it. A faint non-surgical voice whispered that more surgery meant repeated procedures with mounting risks of complications and major miseries for patient and surgeon.

Jenny found it almost impossible to be objective. The letter from Drummel was burning a hole in her pocket. She knew her dad had no tolerance for uncertainty. If a problem arose, he thought about it and made up his mind how to act and did it. Waffling or spending time on what-ifs had no place in his nature. He'd told her more than once, "There are so many unknowns and luck involved in any decision, especially if you're dealing with critters and the weather, that you'd better make up your mind and go for it." He would want all the facts and options, then he would decide.

"I guess we'd better go see him," she said.

John was sitting in the radiology waiting room. Jenny borrowed an empty office and the three of them sat down together.

"Well, Joe, what's the verdict?" asked John.

"From a clinical standpoint, except for some fatigue, you've recovered from your emergency operation. The colostomy seems to be working well. Your liver tests are slightly abnormal and you're a little anemic. That could still be from your surgery. What does concern us is that you have two spots on your liver. They could be cysts or they might represent a spread of your tumor. In the pre-op scan we didn't see these spots, but the x-rays were not focused on the liver and all we can say is that they may or may not have been there at that time. Today's scan also shows a worrisome, ill-defined area near your colostomy. We can't tell what it is at this point. We can't tell without looking further."

John interrupted. "So you suspect more cancer in my liver and colon?"

"These are possibilities we need to address," replied the surgeon.

John looked at Jenny. "The answer to your question is yes, Dad."

He turned back to Woodhouse. "Keep going."

"I should go back into your abdomen and be sure of what's there and what isn't so we can deal with it surgically, if possible."

"And if you can't deal with it surgically?"

"Then we would have more accurate knowledge, which would help the oncologists in prescribing appropriate chemotherapy."

John's expression was noncommittal. "Well, that's clear. When do I have to give you my answer?"

"Whenever you're ready, Dad," said Jenny quickly.

John thanked the surgeon. "I'll call you when I've talked to my family and Dr. McKinnon."

Jenny wheeled John out to the front hall. "I have to check out in the ER, make a couple of phone calls and get the car. I'll be back in a few minutes."

She walked to the women's locker room, found it empty and sat heavily in a chair. After a moment she dialed Peggy and summarized the time with Woodhouse. "Tell Mom I'll fill her in when we get home. There's one more thing, Peg. I delivered Waynona's baby. Everything went well. But Drummel just sent me an official letter of reprimand and a demand for a letter of apology to Krohl in OB. As soon as I've talked with Mom I'll come over to you and Alex. I'll call Stan and ask him to join us. Right now I'm so worried about Dad and so furious about Drummel that I can't think straight."

"Why don't you all come for dinner? I'll tell Emma we'll have a family welcoming party and she doesn't need to cook tonight. I'll brief Alex and we can spend all the time we need together."

"I'll pick up some salad and a bottle of wine—red or white?"

"Red. We'll grill some steaks. See you soon."

Jenny called Stan and told him about her dad and

Drummel. He'd meet her at Doc and Peg's.

"You okay, Jenny?"

"Of course I'm okay. Why shouldn't I be?" she snapped.

"Well . . ."

"I'm fine. Just mad. See you soon."

On the way out of town, Jenny and John stopped at the IGA and bought groceries and two bottles of California Merlot.

For Jenny, the drive home was usually a journey toward peace and security, but this time her mind raced from one option to another. One thing was certain, she would never write a letter of apology to Krohl. He would want her to crawl just because she was a woman. As far as Drummel was concerned, she would not let him or his bosses tell her who she could and couldn't see. If she was not allowed to intervene in the care of a patient who'd been abused, then they could take their managed care and ram it. If this meant that she was fired, so be it. Maybe she should resign before they fired her. The main thing now was to take care of her dad.

John glanced at her. "You have the same look on your face I remember when you climbed back on a horse that had thrown you. Anything wrong?"

"Yeah, that jerk Drummel is pissing me off." She handed him the letter.

John read it. "Stuffy little prick."

"That's not the half of it." She told him about Waynona and sketched for him a portrait of G. Hugh and summarized the whole political imbroglio and financial ambitions of American Health. Her portrait and summary were as unflattering as they were colorful. "And the last straw is what they're doing with Sally, my indispensable

ER nurse. They're going to save the stockholders money by demoting her to a general duty nurse. God, she has a sick mother she takes care of at night on top of her work in the ER. 'Orders from above,' is all Drummel could tell me when I objected."

"What about the patients?" asked John. "I could write a testimonial about the nurses that took care of me."

"The business wonks consider patients 'cost centers.' Whatever they spend on patient care is money taken from the investors. So cut down on qualified and experienced nurses and replace them with cheaper staff, and cut down or cheapen the medicines, dressings, food and laundry that patients unfortunately need to survive a profit-centered, all too short stay in the hospital."

They drove through Simms and started up the pass. John said, "Sometimes I wonder how you can work for such an outfit. You're so great at what you do. They should let you be. All the nurses and the doctors I met have real confidence and affection for you as a person as well as a doctor. Business politics don't belong in a hospital. I hope they won't get ornery with you, Jen."

"They might, but don't forget I carry your fight and perseverance genes."

"So what are you going to do?" asked John.

"As soon as we get home I'll give Mom a rundown on our meeting with Joe. We'll put all the cards on the table. We're all invited for supper with Peggy and Alex, if you're not too tired. Stan will be there too. We can have an old-fashioned, tribal war council."

John sat up and his jaw squared off. "I'm not tired at all." As they turned into the home ranch, John added, "Anyway, just because you're my daughter is no reason I can't thank you for being such a good doctor to me. Your no-bull approach makes my situation easier to understand. I need time to sort things out and to talk with

Emma and our lawyer, Art Bigelow."

Emma waved from the top of the porch stairs. John opened the door. "I'll come to some sort of decision in a couple of weeks. Is that time enough?"

"Take however long you need to be comfortable with whatever decision you make. I'll back you all the way, and I know Mom will."

"Amazing!" said John. "You sound more like a pussycat than a medical tigress." They walked up the steps to Emma. John gave her a hug. "Jen will give you the official word. I'm going to the barn for a minute. Alex and Peggy are expecting us all for dinner."

Jenny and her folks walked over to the cabin. Stan met her on the path, relieved her of the box of groceries and gave her a kiss.

Jenny waved at Alex who was hovering over his barbecue and joined Peggy in the kitchen.

Over steak, salad, biscuits and wine at the picnic table, Jenny, with her father's permission, covered the results of his examination and scan and reviewed the options. She concluded, "It all boils down to what Dad chooses. He knows as much as we do. I told him we'd back his decisions all the way."

"I need time to think about things and talk with Emma before I decide what to do." said John. "Now we need to concentrate on Jenny."

After Jenny cleared the dishes and Peggy poured coffee they sat around the table.

"Now, what about you?" asked Peggy.

Jenny pulled Hugh's letter from her shoulder bag and handed it to Peggy, who read it and passed it to Stan and Emma. When Alex finished reading he returned it to Jenny. They waited for her reaction.

"I will not apologize to Krohl, period. Waynona was manhandled by a med student in Krohl's clinic. There was no way she'd go back."

"Quite right," said Peggy. They waited for more.

"I honestly don't know if I'll be fired and I'm not sure whether or not I should just resign."

Alex said, "You're very valuable to that hospital, Jenny. I can't see Drummel firing you."

"You may be right. I'm sure Drummel wouldn't have the guts to fire me himself, but I'm also sure that his bosses in Paducah will not stand for what they'll consider insubordination from a member of their medical staff. As far as they're concerned, ER doctors come a dime a dozen."

"So being fired is a reality?" asked Peggy.

"Yes."

"Resigning over a medical principle would be better for you, wouldn't it?" suggested John.

"Maybe."

Alex said, "What about standing up and fighting?"

"For principle or her job?" asked her dad.

"For principle," said Jenny. "I wouldn't want the job if it meant knuckling under to Drummel and the company on medical decisions. The latest thing they've done is move Sally out of the ER. I'm the head of the department and chief of staff and they didn't even ask me about it."

"Sally called this morning," said Peggy. "She's more upset about you than about herself. She can retire in sixteen months, so she'll stick it out. She says that the admin people will do whatever they want with the personnel regardless of what the doctors think. They didn't ask you about Sally because when it comes to the bottom line and budget items like nurses and patient care the heads of departments are token heads, especially if they're women."

"I didn't realize until now how true that is," said Jenny.

"Do you want to resign?" asked Stan.

"No. I like the work and the people I work with. The hours and the money are good. But if I have the responsibility of running a department and taking care of patients I need the authority to do just that."

Peggy added, "Sally told me that in some HMO hospitals, doctors and nurses that don't do as they're told by the money people are considered troublemakers. A friend of hers, a senior ICU nurse and teacher, fought hard to maintain standards of care in her department and insisted on the need for continuous training of the personnel. She was told that this would cost too much. When she did the teaching herself, on her own time, she was hauled in front of a human resource committee and told she had to follow the orders of the money people or she'd be out on her ear."

Alex said, "From everything I've been reading in some of our better journals, managing care really means managing costs and that means limiting what doctors can do for a patient. I remember what Updike said like he was still shouting it in my ear. 'Our challenge is simply to find the right level of quality versus cost trade-off to be safe from litigation.' In other words, do just enough to stay out of court."

John asked, "What would you do if you resigned?"

"I don't know. I don't think it's very hard for an ER doctor to get a job, but I don't want just a job and I really don't want to move away from this area." After a long pause she asked, "Frankly and realistically, is there enough work to support two full-time doctors here in Cicero?"

"Probably," replied Alex.

"Probably not," interjected Peggy. "Unless, of course, they both want some normal time off and are willing to share call. They'd both have to be satisfied with less money than they could make in a city." Alex scowled at her. "Don't give me the bad eye, Dr. McKinnon. We've been discussing the subject since you returned from the hospital. I know you agree with our conclusion, you're just too stubborn to admit it."

Alex backed off. "All right, Peg, go on and tell them what we've been considering."

"Alex and I have agreed that he should back off from the practice and just see a few of his long-time patients. He would turn things over to a younger doctor as long as it didn't mean following in Peterson's steps. Alex and I will go down fighting rather than sell out to an HMO, especially a for-profit one like American Health."

Peggy refilled the wine glasses. They waited for Jenny to speak.

"It is too tough a job for too little pay and I don't know whether I could practice without the scanners and instant lab and other high tech stuff I've gotten used to."

"I guess it boils down to a choice between people or equipment," said Alex.

"What do you mean?" asked John.

"Here in Cicero we have a nice, friendly practice with adequate equipment for effective primary care. We deal well with emergencies off the ranches and roads and sometimes an oil rig. We don't have to grub around for patients and we work with people we enjoy. The fishing's some of the best in the state, the traffic is negligible and the surroundings border on idyllic. In a bigger city, you have all the sophisticated gadgets, there's competition for patients and you have to put up with a lot of political bull, especially from the bureaucrats and businessmen who are using the medical industry to get rich."

"Keep going," said Jenny

"As you know, Jen, the hours are much longer, but

we're our own bosses and to me that makes extra hours reasonable and bearable."

Jenny looked around the table. "You guys! I guess the choices are clear. Write a letter of apology to Krohl and crawl back to American Health and Hugh Drummel. If I don't do that I'll be kicked out. Or I resign and try to find a job somewhere else as an ER doc. That means moving away and starting at the bottom of the medical ladder again." She stood up. "I love each of you very much. I have a lot to think about and a stroll along the creek with Gus might help me sort things out."

It was almost dark when she returned and curled up on the porch swing with a writing pad. The letter came quite easily:

Mr. Drummel,

This will confirm my receipt of your letter and your request for an apology from me to Dr. Krohl.

Your reprimand concerns my care of a young expectant mother forced by your administration to attend Dr. Krohl's maternity clinic for the indigent where a hurried pelvic examination was performed by a medical student in a manner that caused considerable anguish and pain to the patient. The distraught young woman refused to return to Dr. Krohl's service. My intervention was based solely on the patient's needs, which I consider fundamental to the practice of sound medicine. Your intrusion into this matter is offensive.

Please include this letter in my "personnel file" since it represents my official resignation from the staff at your hospital.

Jennifer Morgan, M.D.

cc: American Health Corporation, Paducah, Kentucky.

Chapter 19

AFTER A GOOD NIGHT'S SLEEP, Jenny drove back to the hospital, changed into her OR greens and white coat and sat down at her desk in the emergency room. She prepared two handwritten copies of her letter to Drummel on hospital stationery. The extra one she addressed to American Health Corporation headquarters. She walked out to the mailbox on the street corner opposite the emergency room and mailed the letter to Paducah before heading upstairs.

Drummel hadn't arrived yet. Patricia was making coffee. "Jenny!" she exclaimed. "I wondered when we'd see you. Did you get the nasty letter? I hope you noticed that I didn't put my initials at the end. What are you going to do? Sit down, the coffee is almost ready."

"Relax, Pat, everything's fine."

"You've talked to him already?"

"No way." She pulled her letter out of the envelope and showed it to Pat, who read it and almost dropped the coffee pot.

"My God, Jenny. He'll explode."

"Good." Jenny retrieved the letter.

"And you're really going to send a copy to headquarters?"

"It's on its way."

Pat poured the coffee and sat. She glanced at her watch. "He'll be here any minute. Look, Jen, at the risk of being shot at dawn, you need to know that Hugh is in deep shit with headquarters. Peterson's practice is rapidly turning out to be a disastrous cost center. Hugh has orders from headquarters to stop patients transferring from the Simms Clinic to Dr. McKinnon's practice in Cicero. Without guaranteed patients from outlying areas the center will go belly up. They're telling Hugh that he's burnt toast if he doesn't succeed. He has to 'secure peripheral markets,' which means he has to take over Cicero for the center."

"What's he going to do? Send in the Marines?"

"Something like that. Don't forget they squelched the private pediatric group in town by opening their own reduced-rate Kiddy Klinic next door."

"I remember that. Now both the privates and the commercials are going down the tube. Too many baby doctors and not enough babies except those on welfare. It's the same story all over the country. Hostile takeovers are used to capture markets and make money. Someday the patients will wake up and rebel."

"I hope so." Pat tilted her head toward the door. "Mr. Drummel."

"Good morning, Pat. Oh hello, Jenny. I'm glad you came up. I'll be right with you. Pat, would you step in for a moment?"

Pat stood. "I won't say a word," she whispered to Jenny.

When the door to the inner office closed, Hugh said, "Does she have the letter?"

"She has an envelope in her hand."

"What a relief! How does she seem?"

"What do you mean?"

"Well, you know, is she subdued, angry, passive?"

"I've never known Dr. Morgan to be subdued or passive. If she's angry she certainly doesn't broadcast it."

"Show her in, Patricia. And bring coffee."

Pat filled a cup with coffee and topped off Jenny's. "He's all yours. Take his cup in for me. It'll make him feel loved." Jenny walked into Hugh's office, handed him his coffee and sat down.

"Thanks for coming up so promptly, Jenny. I trust your father is doing well."

"We're not quite sure yet," she replied, sipping her coffee. She pulled the letter from the pocket of her white coat and gave it to Drummel.

He smiled benevolently. "Oh, Jenny. Thank you." He opened the letter and a moment later his eyes popped and his face froze in shock. He gasped, "Is this some sort of joke?" She shook her head and sipped more coffee. "You can't just up and quit. This whole thing is an incident. We can negotiate."

"There is nothing to negotiate."

He glanced at her letter again. All color drained from his face as beads of sweat appeared in the furrows of his brow. His eyes registered alarm like an animal caught in a beam of light. "You're sending a copy of this to Paducah?"

"It's gone."

"Gone!"

Jenny stood. "Don't worry, Hugh. Your bosses are the ones who make the rules, remember? You told me your job was simply to apply them. You don't make policy, you just execute it. You may need to remind them of that if they think your efforts are less than satisfactory."

Jenny strode out of the office, pausing just long enough at Pat's desk to say, "Go into him, Patricia, dear. He needs mothering."

Chapter 20

O N SUNDAY EVENING, John and Emma walked over to Doc's cabin where Alex and Peggy sat on their porch enjoying a glass of wine.

"Jenny ordered us to come over here and stay until she comes for us," said John. "They're up to something but I don't know what." Emma winked at Peg.

An hour later, Stan and Jenny arrived to escort John, Emma, Doc and Peggy to chairs set on a hay wagon next to the open barn doors. Stan's brothers and their wives and kids had set up trestle tables in the barn and loaded them with food: barbecued meat and Dutch oven ribs and roasts swimming in gravy and vegetables, baked potatoes wrapped in tin foil and a huge pot of pork and beans. Donny and his family provided fresh sourdough rolls, biscuits and enormous bowls of home grown lettuce, fresh peppers, tomatoes and cucumbers. Shirley and Jim showed up with cherry and apple pies, brownies for the kids, and a huge chocolate cake with "Welcome Home Doc and John" traced in vanilla icing. Chocolate chip and cherry ice cream were ready to be scooped from their tubs by Wilma Thomas and her husband Joe, who ran the drugstore and the best soda fountain in three counties. Members of the Cicero Volunteer Fire Department brought an ice tub full of pop and two kegs of beer, enough to wash down the food and oil the joints for the music that would follow.

The school superintendent, portly and serious, stood with the football and basketball coaches, slightly less portly and certainly not as serious. Their wives and older kids

191

helped at the tables. John Polson and Hank Collette sat visiting on bales of hay next to the wagon. Art Bigelow joined them. Hank talked the ear off anyone with the patience to listen, and John, who was hard of hearing, said "Yup," whether he heard or not.

Ma Green had closed her café for the evening and was in attendance with Flo and Margene, her help. As the crowd gathered, the mayor, Phil Watson, who was also the local Farm Bureau agent, stood tall on a wooden box. He was attended and steadied by Deputy Moose Magoo in full regalia, the burliest man in the sheriff's department and escort to the mayor when the occasion called for a dab of officialdom. Phil and Moose clapped their hands for attention and the chatter subsided.

"My friends and neighbors, guests from beyond, family members, I have been asked by Emma and Jenny Morgan, and Peggy Strong along with Stan Cummings and his brothers to welcome you all here to celebrate the return to Cicero of two of our most stalwart and valued citizens, John and Doc. Speaking, as I do, as a friend of both men, I am sure the doctors and nurses at the center were relieved to have them leave healthier than they arrived. Taking care of such strong-minded, independent men must have presented them with a challenge. I gather from reliable sources that Jenny saw to it that her dad and Doc toed the line."

"Yeah, Jenny," shouted Donny, and others joined in the cheer.

"And now," added Phil, "Father Dave will say the blessing."

As soon as the "Amens" were said, people lined up on both sides of the food tables. They joked and poked fun at each other as they piled food high on stout paper plates. Gus sat on his haunches observing the people and food. When one of his many friends came down the line, his big tail waved in recognition and he followed them to a table, waiting politely for a pat and a morsel of meat. Hank Collette loaded his plate with spare ribs and corn, and Gus followed him back to the hay bale. John Poulson was already eating. Gus sat drooling in front of the two men. Hank tossed him a rib. "Now git, ya ol' mutt." Gus devoured the bone, sat up and howled for more.

Alex looked around, "Are you spoiling my dog, Hank?"

"He's howlin' in misery, Doc. Don't ya ever feed him?"

Women circulated with pitchers of coffee and lemonade while others laid out plates of pie and cake on a separate table. Kids chased each other until corralled by a couple of moms who sat them down with plates of food.

The deputy's brother and sister, Terry and Tilly Magoo, warmed up on the guitar and fiddle, then launched into country tunes accompanied by Moose on the base.

Stan and Jenny started the dancing, followed by Doc and Peggy. As they sashayed past Moose, Doc shouted, "Let's hear those strings."

Moose slapped and spun his base.

"What a character," said Peg.

"Yes, he is. If only I could get him to take his diabetes pills."

Soon the barn floor was crowded with John and Doc's friends. For hours they rocked to fast gymnastic rhythms for the jitterbugs, a few polkas for the energetic, genteel two-steps, sentimental waltzes and slow dreamy dances favored by the young at heart with squeaky knees. The beer flowed and the food disappeared. Gus, under a table, chewed on succulent bones. During a break in the dancing Jenny stood on a chair and Terry strummed his guitar loud and fast to announce her. "Folks, Jenny would like to say a few words, so grab a beer or a pop and have a seat." After a shuffling around, the gathering settled down.

"Thank you all for coming to this party for Dad and Doc. As most of you know, Doc has been my mentor since before medical school. He and Peggy have taught me a lot about taking care of people. We're all happy and relieved that Doc is back with us. It took a heart attack for Doc to review his lifestyle and, hopefully, live in such a way that we'll have him with us for a long time." The gathering applauded and whistled.

"My dad taught me to do what had to be done without whining. He taught me that success comes only after long, hard hours of fencing, mucking out stables and pens and checking and feeding the stock in any weather. We want to thank you again for coming. Now let's have more music."

The party broke up about 9:00 P.M. and, when the sleeping kids were lifted into trucks and the place put back to normal, the people drove off and the night stillness returned.

On the front porch, Stan and Jenny sat swinging gently on the same cushioned bench that had held them so frequently in the past when they were shyly cautious of their passion.

"Now that Doc and John are on the way to recovery I'd like to make an appointment with you for a peek into the future," said Stan. "Or futures," he added quickly.

Jenny kicked off her shoes and curled up next to him. He put his arm around her and she rested her head on his shoulder.

Jenny kissed his chin. "I hope the future has room for both of us as individuals."

"We've talked about that before and I know we have no future together if that isn't the case. In a funny way, I don't worry about how it'll work. If it's meant to be it will happen naturally."

"I feel the same way," said Jenny.

Stan kept them swinging gently—too much, he remembered, would make the chain squeak on the ceiling bolts. She looked at his strong hands and recalled the first time their friendship had been made public. In their early teens, she was tall for her age with long hair and skinny legs and he still had some growing to do for his body to catch up with his hands and feet. She was often teased, particularly by two brothers, thirteen and fifteen years old, who were bullies and the arrogant sons of the county's prosecuting attorney, himself a bully with those he considered below him. The family was an aberration in a ranching valley.

One day the younger boy, Ralph, had added pushing and poking to his constant stream of insults and attempts to denigrate Jenny, referring to her as "squaw girl" because she had braids and rode bareback. Jenny traveled on the same bus week after week and ignored him for as long as she could until one day he poked her hard in the ribs as she made her way down the aisle to the door. She turned around and, with a right hook planted squarely on his double chin, decked him. His older brother, Robert, jumped up from a back seat and advanced threateningly. Stan intercepted him and doubled him up with a hammer blow to his gut followed by a left upper cut that straightened him up and dumped him on the floor on top of his brother.

Surprised and hurt, the bigger boy whined, "Why are you stickin' up for the squaw girl? She ain't nobody."

"She is somebody, sure enough," said Stan. "She's my girl and don't you ever dare touch her again. And you said, 'Thanks for your help, but I'm not anybody's girl. I belong to myself.'"

Jenny added, "And then you said, 'That's why I like you. You're not a sissy or a Virginia creeper who wraps herself around a guy and smothers him.'"

Jenny lay on her back with her head on his leg and they savored their comfortable silence filled with so many memories. Stan lifted her head gently and leaned over to kiss her. She put her arms around his neck and kissed him firmly and passionately.

The telephone rang. Jenny sighed and hurried indoors to answer. The voice on the phone was barely audible. Children cried in the background.

"Dr. Morgan?"

"Yes. Who's this?"

"Waynona. You know, the girl you delivered in the ER. Remember?"

"Of course, Waynona. What's going on? Who's crying?"

"Melissa and the baby. They're scared. We're all scared."

"Where are you? Where are you calling from?"

"I'm at the post office in Simms. Wait. I want the kids in the booth." Jenny heard her comforting Melissa who was apparently carrying the baby. The infant's bawling increased. "Lawrence got crazy drunk and beat us up."

"Are you safe where you are? Can he get to you?"

"He's probably passed out."

"All right. Now listen. You and the kids go in the post office lobby and stay there. We'll be there shortly."

Waynona protested. "I hate to have you do that."

"I'll see you shortly."

"Dr. Morgan, listen. My mother lives in Sage City. If we can get there, we can stay with her."

"Fine, Waynona, but now just stay put. We're on our way."

Chapter 21

WAYNONA AND THE KIDS ran out to meet Stan and Jenny as they drove up. Waynona's bloody face was swollen and bruised; Melissa's lip bled down her chin onto her shirt but she held onto her screaming struggling little brother. Stan pulled his seat forward and the three climbed into the back.

"What happened?" asked Jenny.

"The son of a bitch went for the baby 'cuz he was crying. I stopped him, but he slugged me in the face and chest . . . all over. He even slugged Melissa. We ran off and he fell flat on his face trying to chase us. A man picked us up in his truck. He said he'd drive us to the clinic and I told him no, I didn't want to go there, but he insisted because I was bleeding and the kids were crying and he said he couldn't just leave us on the street. He called 911 on his car phone and I guess they called Dr. Peterson." She paused to catch her breath.

Stan started up the pass, crested it rapidly and headed down toward the tiny collection of cabins and trailers called Sage City.

Waynona rushed on. "Peterson came. He's really a shit. He was angry and shouted at Melissa to shut up. He asked me what the hell happened. I told him I got beat up. He said in his holier-than-thou way, 'You ever been with a man that didn't beat you?'" Waynona sobbed, "He looked me up and down like I was naked trash, said I was a tramp and asked me if I'd ever heard of contraception. I asked him if he'd ever heard of broke, like stone-plum-dead broke. He said to put ice on my face and that Melissa's lip didn't need anything and that I owed him forty dollars for an out-of-office-hours visit. I told him I didn't have it and he pushed us out. I didn't know who else to call, Dr. Morgan. I found the Morgan Ranch in the phone book." Her voice was high pitched, near panic: "I didn't know what else to do."

"You did the right thing to call, Waynona," said Jenny. "We'll drive you to your mom's and I'll take a look at you and Melissa."

At the bottom of the pass, along the road to Cicero, an old gas-station-store and post office and a smattering of old shacks and patched up trailers were all that remained of Sage City. Like Simms, it had been a relay station for stagecoaches and freight wagons in the days before the highway was straightened and widened for cars and trucks.

Waynona directed Stan to an ancient, battered trailer, one of three using hookups on a dirt clearing behind the store. A rusted, green Oldsmobile with a peeling black top was parked by the front door steps. It looked tired and down on its wheels.

Waynona said, "Ma doesn't know anything about what's happened and she's kinda sick herself, so I'll go in and explain. She'll understand. She had her share of beatings in Kentucky. Her name's Joyce." Waynona and the children disappeared into the trailer. A few minutes later she waved at them to come in.

Joyce Jefferson lay in a recliner with a pillow behind her head. Her puffy, pasty face showed tight lines of suffering and the long dusky look of fatigue. The skin above her swollen ankles was mottled blue. She stuck out her hand. "Thank you for taking care of Nonie. She's had a rough time over the last couple of years and I haven't been able to help much."

"She's a fighter and a good mother," Jenny replied.

"This is my friend, Stan Cummings."

"Pleased to meet you. Nonie is making coffee, so have a seat and make yourselves at home." Joyce spoke with a gentle, undulating Kentucky accent and her warm, blue eyes could have been those of a younger woman. Melissa handed the baby to her grandmother and straddled the arm of the recliner.

In the kitchen, Jenny fixed an ice bag for Waynona's swollen face then checked Melissa's lip. The tooth cut on the inside would heal rapidly. Waynona showed her the small bedroom and bath beyond the kitchen.

"Ma sleeps in her recliner, so there's plenty of room for us."

"She does look sick, Waynona. Do you know why?"

"Not really. She had a terrible time pulling this trailer with that old car all the way from Kentucky. She fell down the steps when she was visiting us and the ambulance took her to Peterson. She didn't want to go anyplace. She's almost as broke as I am."

Waynona poured coffee and served Oreos on a paper plate. They all visited and laughed and became acquainted as if nothing awful had happened to Waynona and as if Joyce was in the best of health.

Jenny said to Joyce, "I gather you've not been well. Dr. McKinnon in Cicero is a good doctor and he's gentle. He and Peggy, his nurse, live on my folks' place. Unless you'd rather I didn't, I'll talk to them about you. Maybe you and Waynona could call Peggy and make an appointment."

A truck roared up to the trailer. Waynona looked out. "Shit, it's Lawrence."

"Nonie, don't you go out there."

Stan opened the door and stepped out. Waynona and Jenny watched from the window. Lawrence stumbled and shouted, "Where's that fucking little bitch. Waynona, get your ass out here."

Stan blocked his progress. "Back off mister. You're not going in and she's not coming out."

"Who the hell are you?"

"Someone you don't want to mess with."

Blind drunk, he lunged at Stan who sidestepped and let him fall on his face. He crawled on his knees, vomited and collapsed in the dirt.

Waynona called back to her mother from the window, "He's zonked."

Joyce picked up the phone and called 911. "A drunk who almost killed my daughter is trying to break into my trailer. Joyce is my name. In Sage City behind the store. Thanks."

A short time later a sheriff's car pulled up and Moose Magoo got out. "Howya, Stan. Who's your friend?"

Lawrence focused on the bulk of Moose and let out a defeated groan.

Chapter 22

JENNY WALKED over to Alex and Peggy's for breakfast and a short planning session. She had taken ten days off to be with her father, plus four weeks of accrued vacation time, which would cover the six weeks notice for her resignation to become effective. Her future was wide open.

"I didn't know how burnt out I was with the ER until I woke up this morning and realized that I don't have to fit into a schedule," Jenny said, joining them at the kitchen table. Peggy poured her a mug of coffee.

"Make the most of it," said Peggy. "The timing is perfect for all of us."

"What I'd like to do is work with Stan during the day and cover night call for you."

"Sounds like a plan," said Alex. "Are your folks happy with it?"

"Delighted, and we're all glad Stan is here. Dad's frustrated by his own lack of stamina. I told him it would take a while before he could put in a full day, and a month or more before he could do heavy work."

"How is he, frankly?" asked Peggy.

"Depressed. Turned off by his colostomy and the chore of changing the bag. The yuck of it all, as he calls it. Mom is wonderful with him but he's quite short with her. I'm glad to be here and pitch with them."

"When does Woodhouse want to see him again?" asked Alex.

"He wants to repeat an abdominal scan at the end of the month to look for spread of his tumor."

"What does John say to that?" asked Peggy.

201

"He says he'll do it if we insist, but that any further surgery other than hooking his gut back together is out of the question."

"Does he know how lucky he is that the tumor was found by chance because of the emergency surgery?"

"Yes, he knows. He just doesn't want to lose his independence by being a patient. Even if the scan shows more tumor he won't do anything about it. He says he's never known anyone who's recovered from a cancer that's spread."

The three of them considered this in silence.

"I can understand not wanting to be a patient," mused Alex sympathetically.

"There's lots that can be done, even for metastatic cancer," said Jenny.

"Sure. More surgery, chemotherapy and the like. But that means being dependent on others, being a patient, a compliant patient."

"And compliance is the part John would hate," added Peggy.

"But he wouldn't want to suffer," said Jenny.

"No, he wouldn't," said Alex. "And we could assure him that we have the medicines to deal with his pain and most of the other symptoms he might develop. He'd probably want us to keep him pain free without knocking him out. He'd want to be able to visit with family and friends."

"So what do we do?" asked Jenny.

Alex answered, "I think we support his doing as much as he can and wants to do. We tell him the truth about follow-up exams and the options they might suggest. We give him time to ponder and ask questions. Some we'll be able to answer, others we'll guess at and some of his questions can't be answered truthfully. We'll support his decisions."

"Will you talk to Mom about the same things?"

"I'd be glad to. My guess is that she knows them already and feels the same way."

Jenny finished her coffee. "You'll be getting a call from Joyce Jefferson. She lives in Sage City. She's the mother of Waynona, the young woman I delivered in the ER. Stan and I saw them yesterday. Waynona got beat up by her man. I don't know about Joyce but she looks bad. I hope you can see her today."

Peggy said, "If she calls this morning, we'll see her this afternoon."

As Alex and Peggy drove past the "nursery pasture" on the way into town, they saw Stan and Jenny riding among the cows and their newborns. Alex tooted and waved. They waved back.

"Do you think they'll stick together?" asked Alex.

"From the few hints that Jen has dropped, I'm sure they will, if they can. It's a question of how and when."

They arrived at the clinic just as Tammy Roberts pulled up in a mud-splattered truck filled with a couple bales of hay, fencing tools, cans of oil and assorted junk. She jumped out of the cab, a stocky five-foot-four young woman with boots, jeans and shirt of a working rancher and a black wool cap with ear flaps perched on the top of her head.

"Made it," she said. "Hope you can do me fast so I can get back to calvin'."

"How are the joints?" asked Alex.

"Not too bad."

Peggy led her into the lab and moments later had drawn her blood, checked her pressure and pulse.

In her early twenties, Tammy had developed rheumatoid arthritis principally in her wrists and knuckles, ankles and feet. She'd suffered through months of stiffness and pain, thinking that she was just overworking her joints before she finally came in. After a thorough workup and lab tests her diagnosis was rheumatoid arthritis, like her grandmother. Alex had used anti-inflammatories then gold injections and some prednisone with limited success.

Tammy had continued to work her large spread, halfway up the valley. Occasionally she had some help, but most of the time she was the boss, foreman, cowboy or cowgirl, fencer, feeder and ranch manager. One winter when her joints were so painful and stiff in the morning that she could barely do her work, Alex had increased her dose of steroid. She continued to feed her stock using a sleigh pulled through deep snow by a team of four huge Percherons. She never complained, only stated the fact that such work was difficult with swollen and painful joints. A couple of years ago, with input from a senior rheumatologist in Missoula, he had started her on Methotrexate. Her response to the treatment was dramatic, even at low doses. She came in for blood and liver checks every three months.

"Any problems, Tammy?" asked Alex.

"Just need to quit goofin' off with you guys and get back to work."

"You have enough medicine?"

"Sure do. I understand you were kinda ornery when they took you to the hospital."

"Not at all. I was a pussycat. Did everything I was told eagerly, without complaint and without question. Just like you."

Waynona called about her mother, and Peggy told her to bring her right in. The young woman thanked her and added, "I hate to talk about money when my mother's so sick but I want to be up front with you. Ma doesn't have insurance or Medicare."

Peggy said, "If money's a problem we'll work things out so that you can pay small amounts over a period of time. We never refuse care to people who need it."

"That's a relief."

At the end of the morning, Joyce hobbled into the clinic helped by Waynona. Peggy showed them into Alex's exam room and let him know they'd arrived. She and Waynona settled Melissa and the baby in the kiddies' corner of the waiting room where small chairs and toys kept the children occupied.

"Thank you for seeing us so soon," said Waynona. "Ma's in real bad pain and we're kinda at the end of our rope."

"I'm glad you could make it over."

Peggy introduced Waynona and Joyce to Alex.

Joyce said, "I'm so weak, Doc, and I hurt all over. I'm almost too weak to get out of a chair and walk. My right shoulder's real sore and my back and hips ache and at night I'm soaking wet. I sleep on towels. In the morning I'm so stiff I can hardly move."

"When did all this start?"

"My memory's fuzzy. You tell him, Nonie."

Waynona reviewed her mother's fatigue, bloody urine, fractured spine and their time with Peterson.

"Did they say which vertebra?" asked Alex.

"Thoracic, I think."

"So what did they do?"

"They put her in a body cast, gave her pain pills and sent her home to lie on her back and relax."

"Did they give you a follow-up appointment?"

"We were supposed to go back in two weeks, but after a few days Ma's pain was worse and she made me cut off that stinky cast with pruning shears."

"And you saw blood in your urine?" asked Alex.

"Just that one day," replied Joyce. "The whole toilet bowl was red. Scared the hell out of me."

"Have you had blood in your urine before?"

"A coupla times, but not like this."

"Tell me about the 'coupla times.'"

"I had bladder infections a year or so ago. The visiting nurse in Kentucky told me I had blood in my urine. It couldn't have been much because I didn't see it myself. She gave me antibiotics."

"Did you have burning or pain when you passed water?"

"Sure did before but not this last time. That's what scared me. I didn't expect it."

"What about urgency, where you have to go right away?"

"No."

"What did Dr. Peterson do?"

"Nothin' except for the cast. He gave me some pills for pain and told me to call the nurse in a week if I wasn't better. Oh, and he gave me a lecture on smoking."

Waynona added, "We heard him tell someone out in the hall that he'd joined American Health, the outfit that took over the hospital, and had to fly off somewhere for a business meeting. He seemed kinda proud about that."

Alex turned to Peggy, "We need to get some lab work. We'll do a blood count and sed. rate here. If we hurry, we can catch the FedEx truck before it heads out of town and get the other studies on their way to the lab. Waynona, when Peggy gets the tubes spun down and boxed up, could you meet the FedEx truck at the gas station?"

"No problem."

Alex led Waynona into the empty waiting room.

She asked nervously, "What do you think, Doc?"

"You're right about your ma being very sick. I'm not sure why yet, but we'll get to work and find out."

In a few minutes, Peggy came with the box of blood and urine samples for the lab, and Waynona hurried over to the gas station.

Peggy had Joyce propped up with pillows on the examining table. Alex sat on a stool. He asked her about her family history and any previous illness and reviewed her living, eating and drinking habits. He quizzed her about symptoms from her heart and lungs and bowels. For a woman so sick none of his questions provided any clues to her present condition.

Peggy wrote down Joyce's vital signs, which were all normal except for excess weight. Alex examined her thoroughly. She was tender along the outer part of her right collarbone as well as in her right flank and hip. Her legs and ankles were swollen but not painful. He noted his findings in her chart.

By the time Joyce was dressed and had lowered herself into the chair in front of Alex's desk, Peg came in to say the blood count only showed anemia but that her sed. rate was at 110 with another fifteen minutes to go. Waynona returned and sat next to her mother.

Alex reviewed Joyce's history and physical and said, "There's something serious going on. The test that we just did called the sedimentation rate is very simple and rather primitive. It measures how far a column of red blood cells falls in a calibrated tube over a period of one hour. Normally, it should read about 20 or less, yours is already at 110 and still going. Something is happening in your body that calls for an inflammatory response. The inflammation can be caused by bugs or tumors or by some autoimmune diseases like inflammatory arthritis. We have to wait for your other blood work to return and we have to watch you over the next forty-eight hours. I hope you have PMR. That's a condition called polymyalgia rheumatica—translated: lots of muscle pains. We don't know what causes it, but it's not uncommon in people over sixty and we suspect it if the sed. rate is very high like yours. We will give you a low dose of prednisone to take by mouth. If you have polymyalgia you should feel better in the next couple of days. If that doesn't happen, then we need to be more aggressive about finding out why you're so sick. I'm worried about obvious blood in the urine, especially when it's not accompanied by the usual signs of a bladder infection."

"When do you want to see her again?" asked Waynona.

"I'd like you to call me tomorrow mid-morning just to check in. Let me plan to see you on Wednesday. We should have most of your blood work back by then and will know whether the prednisone has helped."

Alex wrote out a prescription for pain medication and low dose prednisone and handed it to Waynona as they prepared to leave.

Peggy handed Waynona a card for their return appointment, then helped Joyce into her car. When she returned, Alex was reviewing the charts for the afternoon patients.

Peggy asked, "What do you think?"

"I hope like hell that she's got PMR, but she may well have something far worse."

Chapter 23

PEGGY AND ALEX were finishing their sandwiches and coffee when a young man walked in and introduced himself as Dr. Lester Leavitt.

"We were expecting you to call," said Alex brusquely.

"I tried several times, but the line was busy."

"It's inclined to be that way," said Peggy. "Have you had lunch?"

"I stopped at Ma Green's and had a hamburger."

"Have a seat." Peggy poured the young doctor a mug of coffee.

Lester presented well: compact and wiry like a soccer player, he was dressed in a white shirt and tie and khaki pants. His black hair was short and neat.

Alex got up. "Peg, can I see you for a sec?"

They walked out into the hall. Alex turned on her angrily. "I don't like this guy just walking in."

"Don't blame me. He tried to call."

"Not very hard. People call us all day long. This whole idea of an outsider coming in . . . I will not be taken over by these creeps!"

Peggy led him into the empty waiting room. "Alex, you listen to me. Quit acting like a jerk. You can't do it all yourself. Jenny liked this guy and she's no fool. Give him a chance."

Alex stomped across the room like an old bear shaking bees off his head. He returned to Peggy slowly. "Do you honestly feel we should let him in?"

"Yes, I do."

"Okay, I'll give him one week."

As they walked back into the room, Gus was sniffing Lester and wagging his tail.

"You just passed your first test," said Alex.

Lester reached down and scratched Gus behind the ears. "What a neat dog. I didn't know they allowed dogs in medical offices."

"There aren't any 'theys' around here. 'They' is us," replied Alex firmly.

"What sort of dog is he?"

"He's a mutt from the pound in Bozeman. He's my fishing buddy."

Peggy added, "An old patient who drives sixty miles to get here really comes to see Gus. Once, when Doc left him at the vet for his shots and a bath, she showed up and was really upset that Gus wasn't here. She told Doc, 'I suppose you think I drive this distance to see you.'"

Alex leaned back in his chair. He was over his petulance. "Gus keeps me humble," he said with a chuckle. "He's a natural healer, old Gus. He lies behind my chair or under the desk and I've seen him get up and walk over and put his big head on a girl's lap when she's crying. Anytime you can take him for a walk, you'll make his day."

"I'd really like to go fishing with you guys," replied Lester. At the word fishing Gus' tail slapped the floor a couple of times.

"I'm sorry to hear about your wife," said Peggy. "How long does she have to wait for a kidney?"

"We're not sure. She's on the list and we're hoping for a perfect match. The sooner the better. It's tough not being together, but I have to make a living for both of us at this point."

"So welcome to our practice," said Alex.

Peggy added, "We do have a heavy load. We're actually running over five hundred patients a month."

"That many?" said Lester.

"Yes. We have most of the people in this valley and more and more from other areas—about thirty percent," Peggy replied. "We had two new patients from Simms today."

Lester added, "Well, I've heard good things about your practice from Dr. Moore at the center. I look forward to pitching with you in any way that helps."

They worked out a schedule. Lester would alternate nights on call with Jenny. He would take care of all walk-ins, sore throats, stomach aches, bladder infections, sprained ankles, school physicals, insurance physicals, Department of Transport physicals, pre-employment physicals and urine and blood checks for drugs and alcohol required by some of the companies in the area.

"It doesn't mean that you won't see some interesting patients, but we can see those together at the beginning and certainly do house calls together," said Alex.

"House calls!"

"We do a lot of them," said Peg. "In today's lingo they're called home health care or hospice care, but to us they're just house calls."

"We do them and enjoy it," added Alex. "You get to know patients and their families in a whole different way."

"When do you have time for house calls?" asked the young doctor.

"Usually before or after regular office hours."

Lester looked at Alex and Peggy with an incredulous expression on his youthful face. "I can't believe I have to come to Cicero, Montana, to find people that practice medicine the way I've always dreamed about. You thoroughly enjoy what you're doing, don't you?"

"You'd better believe it," said Alex.

During the afternoon, Lester saw a few patients with Alex and took care of some himself—always after being introduced by Peggy or Alex as "our new temporary assistant." He enjoyed himself thoroughly. After office hours, Alex helped him settle into a small apartment above the drug store while Peg fixed supper in the cabin. Lester joined them for the evening meal and met Jenny and Stan over coffee.

After the young doctor left, Alex showed Jenny the letter from Drummel and said, "I can't believe such a nice guy, who seems quite sane, would sign his life away to Hugh Drummel."

"He needs the money," said Jenny. "He told me that he graduated from medical school with a debt of over a hundred thousand dollars, then his wife went into kidney failure. American Health picked up his school debt, accepted his wife for dialysis at a reduced rate and guaranteed him a reasonable income."

"How much?" asked Peggy.

"He didn't say and I didn't ask. But it must be enough. He has a new Bronco and no expenses."

"Where do I sign up?" asked Alex. "I can just see myself taking orders from G. Hugh as the High Caliph's chichi boy."

"Forget it Doc, it's not your world," said Jenny.

On Wednesday, Joyce and Waynona returned to see Alex for a follow-up in the middle of the morning. She reported that the prednisone had not helped: the pain in her shoulder and back remained severe. The weakness in her legs and throughout her body was worse.

"We have to take the next steps in figuring out your diagnosis," said Alex.

"I guess it could be something serious if it's not what you hoped it might be," said Waynona.

"It could be," replied Alex. "That's why we need to do more studies."

"Like what?" asked Joyce.

"We need to do a bone scan and probably scans of your chest and abdomen. What I'd like to do, with your permission, is to call a colleague of mine and arrange for him to schedule the scans, then see you himself." He added gently, "A hidden infection or a tumor are the two most important things to rule in or out."

"What do we do if it's a tumor?" she asked.

"That depends on what sort it is and where it is."

"Well, I guess we'd better get with it."

Alex called Peg and gave her the plan. He dialed the number for Bill Blanford in Missoula and was put through to him right away. He arranged for the scans and a consult first thing in the morning even though it would be a Saturday and hung up.

"You'll like Dr. Blanford," said Peggy.

Alex looked up from the chart. "I know it's a push to drive up to Missoula today, but I think it's important to move fast. Because it's hard for you to get around, he may want to put you in the hospital for the studies. I'll fax him a note this afternoon and he'll call me as soon as he's seen you."

"What will you do with the children?" asked Peggy.

"They'll come with us," replied Waynona.

Joyce said, "I don't know how we're going to pay for all this."

"I'll talk to Dr. Blanford about that. I know he'll make the best arrangements possible for you," replied Alex.

On the way home, Alex and Peg stopped in on Gerald. He was half-sitting, half-lying on the sofa. The windows in the overheated living room were closed and the shades pulled down. Two oxygen concentrators hummed in the hallway, one for the nasal prongs at two liters, the other for the face mask set at five liters. The air was heavy and damp with exhaled breathing. Edna and Nichole dozed in two deep arm chairs. On the TV, basketball players ran from one end of the court to the other with the regularity of a metronome.

Edna started to rise, but Alex put his finger on his lips and made a sign she should stay put. He stood next to Gerald and watched him. Drops of moisture clung to the inside of the plastic mask that covered his face and the sparse white hairs on the top of his head stuck to an oily film of sweat on his scalp. Each breath was a whole-body effort, but the struggle and anxiety that were part of air hunger were attenuated by the Duragesic patch started three days before. Alex looked at Gerald's puffy feet. He was retaining more fluid, partly because of back pressure from his heart struggling to push blood through his scarred, chronically infected lungs, and partly from the steroid he was getting to decrease the tightness in his chest. Emphysema, especially in its terminal stages, was a hell of a way to die. Gerald stirred and opened his eyes.

"Hi. Doc. How's it going?" His voice was muffled by the mask.

"I was going to ask you the same question."

"I'm fine if I don't do anything."

"Let's look at you."

Peggy checked his pressure, which was normal, and his pulse, which was fast. She measured the oxygen saturation in his blood with her finger oximeter. "Ninety percent on six liters of oxygen."

Alex noted the dilated jugular veins in Gerald's neck, sponge-like rales in both lungs and a liver that was enlarged and tender. "Your heart is working overtime because of your lungs," he said, stuffing his stethoscope into the bag. "We'll give you another shot of Lasix to get rid of more of the fluid in your body. It'll help your breathing." Alex pulled the mask up and wiped off Gerald's face with a cool towel.

Gerald looked at Peggy and rasped through the mask, "That's a handsome nurse you have working for you, Dr. Strong. Where'd ya find him?"

"Wandering in the woods with his shaggy dog. He's learning, but it's hard to find reliable help in the boonies," she added.

Gerald chuckled and thanked them both, then lay back to resume his struggle for air.

In the kitchen with Edna and Nichole, Alex reviewed Gerald's medicines again. "The patch seems to be helping him cope," remarked Nichole. "What does it actually do?"

"It's a synthetic morphine that helps relieve pain and some of the anxiety that goes along with air hunger. We can increase the dose if we need to. Our main goal now is to keep him comfortable. He's where he wants to be, here at home with his family."

"Do you think I should call my sister and have her come?"

"Yes, I think you should, although it's impossible to say how long your dad can continue like this."

"I'll call her. She and I could alternate staying up with Mom."

Alex turned to Edna. "You don't go to bed?"

"No, I don't. I want to hear him when he calls."

He put his hands on her thin shoulders. "Are you doing all right, Edna?"

"I'm just fine, Doc." She looked up at him. "You don't know just how tough I am."

Chapter 24

LATE FRIDAY AFTERNOON, Jenny signed out for the weekend and met Stan at Paulette's for dinner. As Paulette led them to the corner table Stan had reserved they became aware of Drummel and Peterson who were finishing their meal over coffee and cognac. It was clear immediately that they had eaten well and imbibed liberally.

Drummel proclaimed loudly, with exaggerated formality, "The dragon lady herself, with escort, approaches." Hugh waved them over. "Hellooo, Jenny. Glad to see you living it up. Introduce me to the cowboy."

"The cowboy is my fiancé, Stan Cummings," stated Jenny. Stan raised his eyebrows then smiled broadly. "Stan, you know Pete. This other gentleman is Hugh Drummel, the administrator of the center."

Stan shook hands with them.

"We'd ask you to join us but we've just finished our dinner. Interesting time. Pete's got unique views on primary care and its relationship to hos . . . hosp . . . hospitalists." The word had difficulty exiting Hugh's loose lips.

"I'm sure he has," said Jenny. "Drive safely," she admonished, turning away.

"Wait, Jenny, wait," shouted Hugh. "Siddown and have a drink. We can patch up differences and tear up your resignation. How did your ol' doc like Dr. Leavitt? Bright young man. Tremendous possibilities."

Jenny waved him off and Stan led her to their table, greeting some of the other diners.

"Do you want to go somewhere else, Jen?"

"No. I like this place. They have wonderful food.

Those two will be out of here soon."

Paulette handed them menus and took their order for drinks. Stan chose a Michelob Lite and Jenny a margarita.

"I can see why Drummel turns you off. Is he always that pompous?"

"Always," replied Jenny, "drunk or sober. What are you going to have?"

They were perusing the menu when Drummel, with Peterson pulling at his sleeve, unsteadily approached their table. "Jenny, I just wanted to say that I count on you as a leader of our professional team regardless of what's happened." His voice had turned nasal and whiney. "If I could give you the big picture you'd . . ."

Jenny raised her hand to stop him. "Hugh, please. Not now."

Peterson said, "Come on, Hugh. Leave them alone."

Drummel brushed him off. "Jenny, I only want to say . . ."

Stan stood, towering over the administrator. "You heard Jenny. Not now!"

Drummel sneered up at Stan. "I was talking to Jenny, not you, cowboy."

Stan stepped around the table and grabbing Drummel by the shoulder and seat of the pants marched him smartly to the front door, which Paulette held open. With a light thrust, Stan propelled Hugh onto the sidewalk. "Out, little man." He turned to Peterson. "Can you see him safely home?"

"Oh sure. Sorry about the scene."

"Not your fault."

A scattering of applause greeted Stan as he walked back to their table. Paulette stood ready for their order as if nothing had happened. And in a moment she returned with their drinks.

Stan raised his glass. "Happy engagement party, Jen.

Were you serious?"

Jenny looked at him straight on. "I wouldn't joke about our being engaged. I was going to break all tradition and ask you to be my partner and the father of our children over dinner. Just had to rush it a little."

Stan shook his head slowly.

"Was I too early, too quick?" asked Jenny. "Should I have asked for your father's permission to marry you?" she added, half teasing, half anxious.

"No. Nothing like that."

"Then why are you shaking your head with a big grin on your face?"

"I've been sweating out day and night how to propose to you. With our two different lives I wondered if it would even be wise, and now you've made it so easy. I accept your offer with all the love I've carried in my heart for you for so long. I think we should celebrate, don't you?"

Stan caught Paulette's eye and ordered a bottle of champagne. "Hold on," he said. "We need more than one bottle." Standing up he announced proudly, "Folks, Jenny Morgan and I are about to celebrate our engagement and we'd like to offer you a glass of champagne to drink a toast to our future."

The other diners clapped and a couple who had worked for the Cummings came over to offer their congratulations. "It's been a long time coming," said the old cowboy.

Stan and Jenny pulled into the ranch just in time for the changing of the guard in the calving barn. John sat at the table in his maternity office. A sturdy cot and sleeping bag were handy for the night man. Emma herded the cows still left to deliver into the holding pen for the night.

"What's the count?" asked Stan.

"Ten calves since eleven this morning. We have a hundred and eighteen to go."

Emma came in. "Hi, you two. How's Paulette?"

"Wonderful," said Jenny.

"We have something to tell you," announced Stan.

"Shoot," said John.

"Over dinner we decided to be engaged. I've been thinking about asking you, but things happened quickly," said Stan apologetically.

John laughed. "Quickly? You've known each other for years. Emma and I have often wondered whether you would ever pop the question, Stan."

"I didn't pop the question, Jen did."

"Oh, Jenny. Did you really?" said Emma.

"Of course. Why not? Our marriage will be a partnership, not an employment contract."

John asked, "How are you going to work out your partnership when one of you is a rancher and the other a doctor?"

"We'll work things out," said Jenny.

"You might change how you practice?" asked Emma.

"I might, Mom." She put her arm around Stan. "Tell them about Drummel and Peterson."

Stan outlined what he referred to as an episode. John and Emma laughed and John said, "Good for you, Stan."

"Well, I just hope Jenny doesn't get blackballed because of tonight's incident. Somebody that stuffy could be real nasty."

"I'm sure Jenny can handle any of that," said Emma. "We'd better get you to bed, Mr. John Morgan." She turned to Jenny. "Your dad has ridden, pulled calves and is just about back to normal."

"But ready for the sack," admitted John. He stood up and gave Jenny a hug. "I'm so happy for you. Your guy has been more like a son than a neighbor over the years." He held out his hand to Stan. "Welcome to our family."

Stan and Jenny walked them back to the house.

"Let's stop in at Doc's and give them our news," said Stan.

Alex and Peggy were delighted. They offered to toast the event, but Stan said he'd better get back to the barn.

Peggy reviewed the calls that had come in during the weekend. Only one of them needed more attention. Shirley had telephoned to say that Jim had been unable to keep his pain medicine down. The one course of chemo Jim had received had aggravated his nausea with little relief of his other symptoms. He had refused a second course. Peggy had driven over and given him a shot of morphine during the afternoon and promised to check in before they turned in for the night.

"I'll go see him," said Jen. "I'm so excited I don't think I'll sleep tonight anyway."

Doc handed her his bag and she left.

An hour later, after tucking Jim in for the night with more painkiller, followed by a cup of coffee with Shirley, Jenny drove home. She climbed the steps to the porch and noticed that the outside light was on in the holding pen. She dropped the bag inside and walked over to the barn, opening the door to the "office" to peek in. Stan slept, fully dressed, stretched out with his boots hanging over the end of the cot. She sat in the stuffed chair and watched him breathing. If she bore him a son, she hoped he would have his father's strong chin.

A cow bellowed, calling her calf. Stan woke up and saw Jenny. He stretched out his hands to her. "C'mon over and keep me warm." He wrapped her in his arms and gently freed her ponytail from its scrunchie. She shook her head and her hair framed their faces. They kissed passionately.

"Umm, you smell wonderful. Jessica McClintock?"

"How did you know?"

"I stole a sniff from the bottle in your bathroom. I didn't know a feminist could be so sexy."

"There's a lot you don't know about this woman, my big macho cowboy." She reached over his head and turned off the light.

Chapter 25

ON MONDAY, the day's schedule was packed with rechecks and quickies with a few patients that would need more time and patience. Peggy had Lester scheduled for two insurance physicals and walk-ins. Alex would have him see a couple of patients with him so they could get a measure of how he worked.

Barb Tate returned for a review of her work-up. She sat in front of Alex's desk in her sweater and jeans, neat and nervous.

"Sorry it has taken so long to pull everything together," said Alex.

"That's okay, Doc. I'm just glad you're all right. I got really shook up when I heard you'd had a heart attack. And now there're rumors you're retiring."

"Don't listen to rumors, Barb. I'm not about to leave. Emma told me about your diarrhea. Did the medicine she gave you help?"

"Sure did."

Alex opened her chart. "I just need to clarify a couple of points. A year ago, you developed attacks of real panic and had trouble breathing. Tell me more about these attacks. What are they like? How often do you get them now and are there any special places or occasions when they seem to occur?"

"They come once or twice a month, real bad like I'm going to die. I can't get enough air and I get real dizzy like I'm going to pass out. My heart pounds, I can feel it in my head and I sweat like mad."

"What do you do?"

"Just curl up in a ball on my bed hugging my knees until it passes."

"How long does that take?"

"Too long. Maybe ten minutes."

"Then what happens?"

"Nothing. But I get worked up and worried, knowing the attack will come back."

"Do you have warnings before an attack hits you?"

"Not what I'd call warnings. But I know that if I walk into the shower or into a grocery store I'll get an attack."

"Are those places you have had attacks in the past?"

"Yes. That's why they scare me. That's why I bathe in the tub and do most of my shopping at Mini Mart."

Alex reviewed her physical exam, which was normal, and told her that her lab work was also fine.

"So that means there's nothing wrong with me? I'm just crazy?"

"No, Barb. It means you're having panic attacks and those are caused by a sudden release of adrenaline into your body from the adrenal glands that sit on top of your kidneys. We don't know what triggers the attacks. But after you've had a few, you dread being in a place where you had one before."

"So what do I do?"

"I'll have you take a medicine that will help prevent the attacks by blocking some of the chemical reactions that cause them. We use the same medicine for people who are depressed." Alex wrote out a prescription. "I want you to call me any time if you get another attack." He jotted down his home number. "And I'll want to check on you in one week to make sure you're getting along all right. Peggy will give you an appointment card." Alex accompanied her to the door and Peggy took over after handing him Howard Lindsey's chart. "If Lester is free ask him to join me."

Howard was perched on the end of the examining table.

"We have new temporary help, a young doctor from a doc-in-a-box outfit. I'd like him to meet you."

"Sure, Doc. Whatever."

Lester walked in. Alex introduced him and summarized Howie's history, then turned back to the patient. "How did you get on at the center?"

"Fine. Did they call you?"

"Yes. All four of your neck arteries are fine except for the internal carotid on the right that has a calcium plaque on it and they couldn't see whether you have a significant narrowing in that one artery. All the velocities of the blood flowing through the arteries were normal so it's unlikely that there is real narrowing under the plaque. The doctor suggested that we do an MRA—magnetic resonance arteriogram—to be sure. Have you had any more babbling spells?"

"No, I'm fine, Doc. Really. Do you think I need that other exam?"

"I do. I doubt it'll show a need for surgery, but we won't know until you have it. I want Lester to check your neck."

Lester carefully palpated Howie's carotids, then listened to them. "I don't hear a bruit, but there is a difference between each side."

"That's why we sent him for studies."

Howie said, "I'll get the other test sometime if that's what you want."

"If you have another spell, we'll both wish you'd done it yesterday."

"But I feel good, Doc, honest. I'll call 'em this week, but I'm much more worried about Ike. He can't hardly stand up if he's been lying around. He's stiffer'n hell."

"You should give him some Rimadyl. That's what I give Gus for his hips."

"Can you write me a prescription?"

"Sure. How much does he weigh?"

"About fifty pounds."

Alex wrote:

> **For:** *Ike, Howard Lindsey's fifty pound mutt*
>
> **Age:** *Older than Howard*
>
> **Rx:** *Rimadyl 100 mg.*
> *# 60*
>
> **Sig:** *½ tablet twice a day in a ball of fresh hamburger or Braunschweiger*
>
> **Refill:** *Whenever*
>
> **Substitutions permitted:** *No*
>
> **Signed:** *Alexander McKinnon, M.D.*

He showed it to Lester and handed it to Howard. "Take it to your favorite vet for filling."

"I go to the same one you do," said Howard.

"I know. That's why I wrote the prescription. Call me when you have the date for your MRA."

Peggy picked up sandwiches and the mail and rejoined Alex and Lester, who were discussing patients. Lester opened a manila folder with some notes Alex had made several years ago on a cowboy called T-bone—there was no other name on the chart.

"This patient dropped in just before lunch without an appointment. What a character," said Lester.

"What was he complaining of?"

"Heartburn," replied Lester, turning to the last page of the chart. Alex glanced at his note:

> **Subj.** *Patient has heartburn.*
>
> **Obj.** *Very slight epigastric tenderness.*

Assess. *Reflux esophagitis aggravated by beer and Copenhagen.*

Plan. *Cancel beer and Copenhagen. Use antacids.*

Alex put his hand on the paper. "I hate these SOAP notes. I'm sure they're useful when you're processing consumers through a gatekeeper's slot, but I'm also sure, in the long run, they miss more than they help."

Lester replied, "I've considered them sort of a shorthand statement about the patient's current complaint."

"You're right there, they are a form of shorthand, but look at it this way. Has T-bone ever had any heartburn before? Is his heartburn associated with recent weight gain or loss? Has he tried anything to relieve it? How many cans of Copenhagen does he chew in a week? What about beer? Is he doing his own cooking? Is he drinking a lot of coffee . . . eating a lot of chocolate? Is he worried about Hambone?"

"Who's Hambone?" asked Lester.

"T-bone's old buddy—his dog. Sort of a ranch mutt," said Alex. "Those questions wouldn't take more than a minute and you'd know more about him right away. You won't find much in T-bone's chart because most of the time I see him when I'm out walking or run into him at the post office. When I first started practice here, T-bone was deaf and gave the impression of being a slow thinker. A brain scan showed he had normal pressure hydrocephalus: a little more fluid in his head than most people. Maybe that's why he's always so pleasant and cheerful.

"A couple of summers ago he found this scruffy dog with his hair all matted over skinny ribs. They took to each other right away, and on the days when T-bone took a long, hot shower he brought the dog in with him and washed him and cut his hair with a sheep shear. He found out quickly that the dog was crazy for ham bones and that became his name.

"Last summer, I was up riding and saw a man and a dog sitting a long way off on the side of a steep hill. I rode over. It was T-bone and Hambone. I called out, 'What are you guys doing up there?' He shouted back, 'I'm showin' Hambone how beautiful this place is.'"

Peggy added, "T-bone won't stop drinking beer except in the winter when he's snowed in and can't buy it. Same with his snoose."

Alex continued, "I'd just keep an eye on his weight and appetite. If these are affected I'd want to be sure that he doesn't have an ulcer or even a tumor. You have time to do things properly in this practice."

"That's a relief," said Lester. "I've just gotten into the habit of going too fast. Next time I see T-bone I'll cover these points. I must say, I really liked the way you took care of Howie's dog. That will make both of them happier."

Peggy came in with the first afternoon patient, a new one, in need of a Pap and pelvic. Mary was a middle-aged woman. "Healthy as a horse," as she put it. She'd apparently had an abnormal Pap smear a year ago and "wanted to stay on top of things."

"A Pap is all you need?" asked Alex.

"That's it, at least for now, Doctor."

Following the examination, including checks of her blood pressure, breasts and nodes, Alex returned to his office. Mary came in followed by Peggy. "Mary works for the Agricultural Extension Service in Simms. She called me and said she'd like to be followed by us rather than by people in the Simms Clinic. She was starting to explain why and I thought she should tell you."

"Would you mind if we include Dr. Leavitt? He's our new assistant."

After introductions, Mary said, "Peggy wants me to tell you why I came over here. The fact is that ever since

Dr. Peterson sold his practice to the center, he's hardly ever there. There's talk he spends more and more time at the center and flies off to Kentucky for meetings. Many of his old patients are seen by new people even if they have appointments with the doctor."

"What sort of new people?" asked Peggy.

"Well, there's a new physician's assistant and a family nurse practitioner. Nice enough, but not doctors. One of them asks a lot of questions and talks a lot but doesn't do anything. They've also added a mental health worker and a social service worker to the staff. All these new people work for the center. The couple of times I've been over there it seems they have more staff than patients and you never know who you're going to see. A lot of people are turned off by their impersonal approach, and the new paint job with the fancy American Health Corporation sign seems superficial. Do you know what I mean?"

"Sure," said Peggy.

"Why don't you write a letter to Mr. Drummel?" suggested Alex. "He represents American Health in the region."

"Do you mind if I say something?" asked Lester.

"Go ahead," said Alex.

"The business types that run health care industries invented the system. Their staff jump through hoops and bring in fortunes for the CEOs and stockholders. I know, I've worked for them since I finished my residency in family practice. Our training program was paid for by American Health—we called it American Wealth. We were trained as gatekeepers, not as real physicians. I signed up with them because I needed the money, desperately. Dr. McKinnon knows all about that."

"Good for you, Lester," said Alex beaming. He turned to the patient. "We'll call you with the results of your Pap. Let us know if we can help in the future."

After the patient left Lester said, "I hope Mary doesn't repeat what I said about managed care. They'd come down on me like a ton of bricks."

"Don't worry about it. You didn't say anything that isn't widely known. People around here are suspicious about the motives that drive for-profit HMOs and they are confused by the advertising and promises made on TV."

Lester asked Alex to show him how to do a radical removal of an ingrown toenail.

"Didn't they teach you how to do that in your residency?"

"No. The most we ever did was pull out the nail. I'd like to learn how to do it properly. The patient is Agnes Hill. Emma told me her husband runs the hardware store."

"Okay, Lester. Get the toe prepped and put a rubber band around the base and infiltrate it with xylocaine, then call me."

Ten minutes later, Peggy interrupted Alex to tell him that Agnes' toe was ready. Alex marched into the treatment room.

"Hello, Agnes. This won't take a minute."

He put on a pair of gloves, grabbed a knife and held Agnes' big toe. Both sides of the nail looked inflamed— the outside maybe a little more than the inside. Alex pushed the blade into the nail on the outside of the toe, carried the incision up into the matrix where the nail was formed, then with another incision along the fleshy side of the nail he removed a wedge of tissue. The bleeding was minimal because of the tourniquet. He placed two sutures through the nail into the side of the toe, then wrapped it in a tight gauze bandage and cut through the rubber band tourniquet.

"Agnes, we'll keep you here for a bit and refresh the dressing. When the blood dries it will act like a cast. We can take the sutures out in a week."

Lester and Agnes thanked him. He stripped off his gloves and walked out.

Bill Blanford called about Joyce Jefferson. "I hope some day I can call you with better news," he said when Alex picked up the phone.

"What did you find?"

"She's riddled with cancer. Her bone scan shows tumor in her sternum, right clavicle, ribs and thoracic spine with one vertebra destroyed by tumor threatening her spinal chord. Her right flank is filled with a huge destructive mass where her kidney should be. I don't think she has lung cancer, more likely a renal cell tumor. I think we should biopsy the area in her clavicle to make a definitive diagnosis. I am worried about the collapse of her thoracic vertebras especially where there's already pressure on the spinal cord. She is very near to a full cord syndrome with paralysis of her legs, bladder and rectum. If the biopsy shows a renal cell tumor, I think we should offer her palliative radiation to deal with her back pain and hopefully delay further collapse of her spine."

"How are she and her daughter taking this?"

"It's tough for them. I had to explain to them that the reason her sternum and vertebra were fractured by her fall was because they were weakened by tumor. I get the impression that, after being warned about lung cancer and smoking, she's relieved, in a bitter sort of way, that her cancer is not in her lung. She's worried that her legs are getting weaker and, although I told her that the radiation is to prevent more damage to her vertebrae, she hopes that it will bring back her strength."

"I wish it could," said Alex.

"She's a strong person," added the oncologist. "Waynona told me that when she was a young girl in Kentucky, she rode bareback in the woods and communicated with wild animals. I can believe that. Although her body has let her down, there's a strength, sort of peaceful strength, in her blue eyes."

"Bill, you're almost poetic."

"Well, she's different."

"I'm sure she is. I haven't seen that side of her yet."

After a pause, the oncologist continued, "I have to tell you that Waynona is very angry with the first doctor they saw, the one in Simms. She feels he not only missed the diagnosis but treated her mother in an offhand way because they don't have insurance."

"No comment, my friend."

Chapter 26

THE NEXT DAY Lester called Agnes to see whether the pain medicine he'd given her for her toe was adequate.

"The pain's not too bad, but Doc operated on the wrong side. It was the inside part of the nail that was and still is killing me."

Lester hesitated, at a loss for words. "Let me call you back."

He waited until Alex stepped out of his office to speak to him. "I just called Agnes to see how her toe was doing. She said the pain wasn't a problem, but that we operated on the wrong side of her toe."

Alex leaned against the wall and stared at Lester. "How embarrassing. She's a tough lady and her husband can get real ornery on occasion. I'd better go over and see her."

"Can I come?" asked Lester.

"Why not."

They walked down to the hardware store. Alex opened the door and headed directly to the back office where Agnes sat behind her desk, her foot on a stool. Two of her clerks unpacked boxes nearby.

Standing in front of her desk, Alex said, "Agnes, I have to admit to being a damn jackass, in a hurry, with my head in the wrong place. Please accept my apology for operating on the wrong side of your toe. We obviously won't charge you and we'll do the proper side for nothing if you want us to."

Agnes smiled at him. "Thanks for coming in, Doc. We all make mistakes."

The clerks were surprised and delighted.

On the walk back to the office, Lester said, "That sure is a straightforward way of dealing with a mistake. Any other place I've worked you'd have to make a report and alert the insurance company—and you'd avoid the victim like the plague and *never* ever admit fault. Another plus for you and Cicero, Dr. McKinnon."

After office hours, Alex took Lester on a house call to meet Jim and Shirley Davis. Almost a month had elapsed since Jim's trial of chemotherapy for his wide-spread tumor. He was losing ground rapidly.

Shirley was delighted to meet Lester and welcomed him to the community. After the doctors visited with Jim and checked him over, they sat with Shirley at her kitchen table where she had a large piece of cherry pie under a mountain of fresh whipped cream set out for Lester and black coffee for Alex, according to Peggy's standing orders. They reviewed Jim's status and agreed that his pain was controlled with increasing doses of long-acting oral narcotic, which also helped ease the anxiety so often part of suffering at life's end. Over the following days, Alex and Lester alternated in seeing Jim every day. Shirley called Peggy one evening and told her how much Lester's house calls meant to her and Jim.

The young doctor spent more and more time with them. Shirley enjoyed feeding him, and Lester appreciated her cooking. Often in the evening, when the conversation lagged, he played the piano: lilting Chopin waltzes and cowboy melodies, which he sang softly with nostalgia.

A week after the x-ray treatment to her back, Joyce returned home to die. She was barely able to swallow fluids because of the irritation to her esophagus. Her legs were paralyzed from the tumor in her spine. During the day, Waynona helped her change positions in bed and fed her ice cream and cool drinks that she was able to sip. An indwelling catheter kept her free of bladder symptoms.

Alex and Gus drove over to see Joyce and Waynona on the evening after their return to Sage City. A hospital bed took up most of the space in the trailer's living room. He checked her over and assured himself that she had plenty of pain medicine and that the catheter into her bladder was draining well. Waynona made him a cup of coffee and whispered that she wanted to talk to him outside. When his visit with Joyce was through, he took his leave of her, promising to return soon. He followed Waynona outside and they sat on the steps.

"I had a couple of long talks with Dr. Blanford," she said. "He's nice and straightforward like you told us. I told him that you'd suspected something real serious with Ma because of the bleeding from her bladder without pain. He told me that painless bleeding like that is often a tumor. I asked him if he thought Peterson had missed the diagnosis and he said he didn't know enough to say. I'm sure he didn't want to get involved in any of that."

"I can't say I blame him," said Alex.

"But I have to ask you, Doc. Did Peterson miss the boat?"

Alex thought hard and answered slowly. "Yes, he did miss the diagnosis. I'm just as angry as you are." He paused. "But I think a legal battle would upset the peace your mother needs during the time she has left with you and the kids."

Waynona wiped her eyes. "Whew! You talk about angry. I could kill the pompous son of a bitch." She blew her nose. "I hadn't thought of the ruckus it would make around Ma if I went after him." She stuffed the handkerchief into her pocket. "Well, maybe you're right, but I am going to write to the paper to warn people they'd better not get involved with Peterson and his new outfit if they're real sick. I have a duty to warn other patients, don't you think?"

"That's up to you, Waynona."

"I know that. I can sympathize with a doctor who misses a diagnosis but only if he's really put out for the patient. I wouldn't be so pissed if Peterson had spent time with Ma. I get so damn mad when I think of how he treated her. He didn't even do blood tests and a decent exam like you did. He didn't do nothing except preach to her and run off to some important meeting. I have to warn people what they risk when they go to the Simms Clinic."

"You do what you must, Waynona, but remember, our most important job now is to keep your mom comfortable and peaceful." He whistled for Gus. "I'll be back tomorrow."

Alex or Peggy called on Joyce daily. These visits seemed to bring her comfort. She asked Alex every time he came, "Is there anything new, Doc?"

His reply was inevitable. "Only that we'll continue to keep you comfortable so you can enjoy your daughter and grandchildren." She'd nod her understanding and look up at him with her clear blue eyes that smiled and seemed to contradict the malignancy that had taken over the rest of her body.

Three more patients had transferred from the Simms Clinic to Cicero. Lester took care of them with Alex's continued encouragement to be thorough and take his time.

Jim Davis had stopped eating and drank only small amounts of iced tea and chicken broth that Shirley made herself, carefully spicing it with the cumin and curry he liked. But he was wasting away.

On a Saturday evening, Lester stopped in and found Shirley struggling to change the bed sheets and clean up Jim after an accident with his bowels. Shirley's sister, who had come down from Missoula to help, had driven home for the weekend to catch up with the needs of her own family. Lester carried a basin of soapy water from the bathroom and gave Jim a bed bath while Shirley rinsed him off with a warm sponge and dried him. Together they rolled him from one side to the other as they stripped the soiled sheets and replaced them with fresh ones.

Shirley sat on the edge of the bed and rubbed Jim's back with alcohol and dusted him off with talcum powder. Gently she massaged the wasted muscles along his spine and shoulders and neck remembering how strong he'd been not so long ago. His suffering and loss of substance tugged at her heart and she cried softly turning her head away from Lester. But he saw her pain and said, "Here, Shirley, I can do that. We could both use some coffee."

Jim purred like a contented tomcat and mumbled, "Didn't know docs knew how to nurse."

"I was an orderly before I went to medical school."

Jim sighed deeply and was back on a cloud. Shirley carried the soiled linen into the laundry room. She returned with a fresh stack and put them on the chair next to the dressing table under the tintype portraits of Jim's father and mother. She turned off the overhead light. The bedside lamp cast its subdued glow in the bedroom with its king-sized bed, flowered wallpaper and matching curtains and chintz covering the deep armchair in the corner. In the shadowed warmth, the room reverted to the comfortable, homey privacy she had shared with Jim for so many years. She looked at him lying on his side, his bony shoulder tenting the covers, and wiped the tears from her eyes. Lester sat on the corner of the bed wondering how long the struggle would last.

"I'll warm up some supper for you," said Shirley.

"You don't have to do that," said Lester.

"I know I don't have to. But I want to. Come on." Lester joined her in the kitchen.

"How long do you think he can go on like this?" asked Shirley.

"I don't know. He's beginning to breathe like . . . it's called Cheyne-Stokes respiration. He breathes less and less, then stops for several seconds, then starts breathing more and more, in cycles."

"What does that mean?"

"It usually means the end is near. But how near is hard to say." He didn't want to tell her that he had never sat with a dying patient for any length of time. That wasn't done in a hospital. Most of the time a doctor answered the call after the patient expired to certify the death, its time and cause by filling out forms with a black ink ballpoint pen.

She fed him and poured coffee for both of them.

"You aren't eating?" he asked.

"I had something earlier. I don't have much of an appetite."

"I understand. When does your sister come back?"

"Tomorrow, around noon."

"Good. Thanks for the supper. I'll just sit with him awhile."

"I'll be in after I get the kitchen cleaned up."

Lester walked back into the bedroom and sat in the armchair. A while later, Shirley looked in. "Thanks for all your help, Lester. I'll sit with him. You'd better go home and get some sleep."

"You get some sleep, Shirley. I'll call you if anything changes."

He sat in the armchair watching and listening as Jim's

crescendo-diminuendo breathing continued. Occasionally his body twitched and he moaned softly. What was it like to be comatose or semi-comatose or out of it? Lester wasn't sure about Jim's level of consciousness but he was certain that he was not suffering. He watched him and found he breathed along with him, following the cycles and holding his breath when Jim did. The breathing filled the room and, like rushing air against a wing, seemed the only element supporting audible life against the silence of death that grew longer as time ticked away on the bedside table. And on and on the doctor breathed with his patient, dreading the moment when it would stop. He'd only heard from others how "terminal events" presented. Would Jim just stop breathing and go quietly? Or would his body tighten in a seizure and yield life with a loud guttural, agonal groan?

Lester woke up with a start. Shirley was standing over him in her bathrobe. "Sorry to startle you."

"Gosh, I must have dozed off. Sorry. What time is it?" He pulled himself out of the chair.

"About 11:30. I just woke up myself." She stepped over to the bed and put her hand on Jim's shoulder. "He's gone."

Lester was devastated. He reached for his stethoscope and, leaning over the bed, went through the motions of listening for a heartbeat he knew was not there. "I'm so sorry, Shirley. I wanted to be with him when he died."

"You were." She hugged him as she would a son. Lester shook his head. Jim was his first dying patient. He should have been awake, holding his hand or rubbing his sore shoulder when he took his last breath and died.

Shirley said gently, "He went to sleep. A wonderful way to go."

Chapter 27

ON SUNDAY, Alex and Gus went fishing, returning with dinner. Alex pulled his boots off and tossed two nice brown trout into the sink and turned to hug Peggy.

"You look fetching, Madame, in my old shirt and cut-offs."

She kissed him. "Good day?"

"Wonderful day. Gus jumped into every hole in the river just seconds before my fly, but we did bring back two for supper. I'll clean 'em and cook 'em in butter and almonds. I stopped in to see Tad."

"How is he?"

"He's got pneumonia again, but doesn't want to go anywhere."

"I guess that's his privilege," said Peggy. "Art Bigelow called a while ago. He needs to talk to you."

"About what?"

"He didn't say."

"I'll call him." He stepped over to the sink and cleaned the fish. A Sunday afternoon call from his lawyer worried him. He dried his hands and dialed Art's home from the wall phone in the kitchen.

"Hello, Art. Alex."

"Sorry to call on the weekend. I was going to wait until tomorrow but, after some thought, I concluded we might need to act fast."

"On what?"

"On a letter intended for the *Simms Weekly Reporter* written by the daughter of one of your patients. Do you know about it?"

"All I know is that the daughter of a patient with cancer wanted to write a letter about her mother's care in another clinic."

"Is the patient's name Joyce Jefferson?"

"Yes. Her daughter's name is Waynona."

"And Joyce was a patient of Dr. Peterson's and came to you?"

"Right."

"Now we're on the same page."

"How did you get involved?" asked Alex.

"Yesterday, I received a call from an attorney in Paducah called Siberling who represents American Health Corporation. Do you know them?"

"I know the administrator at the center, but I'm not involved with them. Start from square one."

"The story, according to the company lawyer, is that Waynona, the daughter, plans to send a letter to the Simms paper this coming week warning people that if they are seriously ill they should avoid Dr. Peterson and the Simms Clinic."

"How did the lawyer get the story?" asked Alex.

"He was evasive when I asked him the same question, but when I told him not to believe small town rumors, he told me that Waynona had been overheard reading the letter to a couple in the Simms Café. The eavesdropper, a friend of Peterson's, had reported it to the doctor and I guess he called Drummel at the hospital."

"What's in the letter?" asked Alex.

"He didn't go into the details which, after all, are just hearsay, except to claim that the letter is a vicious attack against Dr. Peterson and American Health Corporation."

"That's very funny," said Alex. "What are they going to do, sue Waynona?"

"No. They're threatening to sue you. Apparently she wrote that she had to drive over to Cicero to find a doctor concerned enough by her mother's condition to see her on a Saturday."

"So?"

"She accuses Peterson of missing the diagnosis of advanced cancer and that he didn't give her mother the time of day and didn't follow up. She intimates that you told her that her mother's symptoms had to be caused by a tumor."

"The oncologist in Missoula told her that, not me," said Alex.

"That's good. But their lawyer also said that you went along with Waynona when she faulted Peterson and American Health."

"She asked me whether Peterson had missed the diagnosis and I said yes. I told her my main concern was her mother's comfort and peace of mind and that a lawsuit would upset her."

"Be that as it may, they're threatening to sue you for defamation of character of Dr. Peterson."

"You must be kidding!" shouted Alex into the phone.

"Simmer down, my friend. I'm sure this is a pressure tactic to get you to call Waynona and persuade her not to send her letter to the paper. He said as much. You stop Waynona's letter and they won't go public with a suit against you."

"Listen, Art, what Waynona does is up to her."

"Think about it, Alex. My impression is that American Health considers you an obstruction to their expansion and success. He used terms like old-fashioned, disappearing sort of country doc that wouldn't change with the times."

"Coming from them, that's a compliment."

"They see Tuesday as a deadline. The *Simms Weekly* goes to press on Thursday. Give it some thought, Alex, and call me anytime tomorrow."

That same evening, after talking things over with Peggy, Alex called Art and told him to notify the Paducah lawyer that he had no plans to interfere with Waynona's intentions and if they wanted to sue him for defamation of Peterson they were welcome to take him to court. They'd be ridiculed and run out of the county.

Art said, "You know they're very big and have lots of money for litigation."

"I know. But, unless you double your fees, we'll take them on."

"You have no intention of speaking to Waynona?"

"Not about that."

Chapter 28

EARLY MONDAY MORNING, Tim Moore called Alex. "I gather from Jenny that you're back to full schedule and having a ball."

"We are. Maybe it's because I've already lost some weight and, with Peggy's help, I'm becoming quite civilized."

Tim laughed. "I'll believe that when I see it. The other thing I called about is the uproar created by Jenny's possible resignation."

"It's not a possible resignation, Tim. It's the real thing."

"Nobody wants that, especially Drummel and his people in Kentucky."

"They shouldn't have interfered with her role as a physician. She'll never yield her responsibilities as a doctor to anyone. I wish there were more like her."

"Listen, Alex. Jenny's one of the best. She knows what she's doing, she's genuinely respected by the attendings as well as the house staff, and she's willing to give change a chance."

"Some changes. Not all changes. When people like Drummel and his hired hands start telling some of us doctors, especially people like Jenny, who they can see as patients, how long they can spend with them, and what they can and can't do with them, the shit's going to hit the fan. The battle for domination is already becoming a legal issue, and it'll become a government issue if those characters in Washington can quit gazing at their belly buttons and pay attention. The doctors will win if they fight, because the administrators and bureaucrats cannot and must not practice medicine."

"I understand all that, but I'm worried about Jenny. The HMOs have lists of ER doctors they can tap tomorrow to replace her. They don't care about an individual's personal principles or commitment to patient care. They have their own agenda and budget."

"Including million of dollars for their CEOs."

"I know, I know," said Tim. "I don't want to argue with you about the pros and cons of managed care. I want to try and persuade you to have Jenny reconsider her resignation. For her own sake, Alex."

"Did Drummel ask you to call me?"

"No, damn it, he didn't! I took this initiative on my own. I don't want to see Jenny lose out. For a young woman, she has an extraordinary chance to be a leader in our profession, she's got know-how and guts. This business about the girl she delivered in the ER is an incident. I know Krohl, he's a bit of a Prussian but not a bad guy."

"Look, Tim. What you call an incident is a major sign that the administrative managers will only settle for full control of how we practice medicine. Drummel was stupid enough to think Jenny could be bullied."

"I agree. But Drummel doesn't call the shots, his bosses in Paducah do. He may seem like a big fish here but he's a minnow in their pond. And now he's a very frightened little guppy."

"I am *so* sorry," Alex exaggerated. "Please give him my sympathies."

Tim forged on. "We had an emergency meeting of the hospital board where, as you know, I represent the attendings. Drummel told us that American Health has lowered the boom on him. Apparently, since Peterson sold his practice and went to work for them, some of his patients have deserted the Simms Clinic and are either driving over to you or somewhere else."

Alex interrupted. "Tell Drummel to set a road barrier across the top of the pass and stop all these incursions into our peaceful valley."

"Knock it off, Alex. I'm serious. Drummel was purposely vague about what he termed 'steps to correct the situation,' but I thought I should call you as a friend and colleague. My major concerns are for you and Jenny. I'm no more a company man than you are and you know it. You're ahead of the game now. You're successful and respected, but if you buck these people you'll lose. They'll defeat you. They have all the money to do it. Believe me, Drummel is trying to help you."

"That, my dear old friend, is congealed bullshit. Let me tell you what Drummel is doing. Two of his people drove over to Cicero and told our home oxygen girls that they have the choice of leaving their Missoula-based company and working for American Health or they would be replaced. Drummel is planning an annex building in collusion with our very business-oriented mayor. He plans to send in his home care agency people and take over the medical equipment business run by our local women."

"Are you sure about that, Alex?"

"Call the mayor's secretary and Shelly at Home Oxygen if you don't believe me."

"I have no reason not to believe you, but all Drummel has told us is that he's trying to help you with your practice."

"Wake up, Tim. He's a businessman. He's sweetened you with a new heart lab and tells you what you want to hear. Businessmen are taught not to reveal their hand before they move."

Both men were silent, each hoping the other would pick up the conversation. Finally, Tim asked, "Is there no way you would join forces with us over here at the center?" He added, with emphasis, "That's a question that comes from my heart, not from anyone else. I want to make that clear."

"It is clear. I trust you implicitly, otherwise we wouldn't be friends. But the answer to your question is *no*, that is impossible."

"Why, Alex?" asked the cardiologist desperately.

"The way I see it, doctors like you have to be hospital-based because of the sophisticated and expensive technology you use every day. Thank God you and all your gadgets were there for me. I wouldn't have made it otherwise. It's natural that you have different views about patient care than those of us practicing outside of hospitals. But the number of patients you process is a drop in the bucket compared to the huge number of people who need much less sophisticated care. Especially people who need a doctor's time and consideration in non-emergency situations."

"That's well put, Alex, but why can't we work together approaching the patient's needs from our different perspectives?"

"We've been doing that for years. But now, the people who run your hospital want primary care doctors to be triage officers with cheap standardized care for routine problems—read between the lines, low cost problems. That's not my idea of good medicine. If your wife got sick, would you want some modern gatekeeper to spend ten minutes with her, fitting her into a company-designed slot that was cost effective or would you want a doctor to spend time with her, listen to her, try and understand her feelings as well as her symptoms and go over her properly?"

"That's not fair. You know the answer to that. Mary comes over to you whenever she needs care." After a long pause, he added, "I guess, in my situation, I have to work with the system. I'd be sunk without our heart lab."

"I understand that and I hope you and I will always be able to talk and work together. I certainly rely on you for my own health and the health of my patients who need your services. But as far as the system is concerned, I think it stinks and I see no reason why I should join it. It's trying to make technicians and functionaries out of physicians, and product consumers out of patients. They are bastardizing medicine. They're responsible for the subversion of trust between patients and doctors. I despise that. They are trying to turn what used to be a noble profession into a corporate commodity. The whole thing makes me want to vomit."

"I knew what you were going to say before I called you. I'd be surprised if you didn't realize that American Health may employ dirty tactics to crush your independence."

"They've already started, Tim."

Later that evening, Lester called Alex. His wife, Jody, was scheduled to receive her new kidney the following day and he wanted to fly out as soon as possible. Alex backed his trip wholeheartedly, then asked him, "Has Hugh Drummel been in touch with you?"

"No. I was told that he was out of town."

Chapter 29

L ESTER TURNED THE DOORKNOB very slowly and peeked into the room. Jody sat in the Lotus position in the middle of the bed with her legs folded, her back and neck straight and her hands on her knees. With her eyes closed and her head tilted up a little bit she was focusing on a thought or a sound or a hope. A surge of love filled his heart. She had worked so hard to support them while he struggled through medical school.

He stepped into the room, closing the door without a sound. When he turned back she had not moved but her eyes were open and her face shone with a wide smile. "I was working like mad to relax and wishing so hard that you would walk through that door. And here you are."

Lester hurried to the bed. "Are you okay?"

"I am now."

"You look sixteen and gorgeous. I love you *so* much. When is the surgery scheduled?"

"In about an hour. The surgeon's been in. All the papers are signed and it looks like my new kidney will be a great match."

"Are you nervous or a little scared?"

"Of course, aren't you?"

"I am. I just want it to be over and know that you won't need to be a patient ever again."

She lay back on the pillows. "How about you? What's the new job like?"

"The new job is like the sort of practice we used to dream about."

"What are they like?"

"Doc's in his sixties and Peggy I would guess middle fifties. They're a team. They spend time with their patients, do house calls and have a great time taking care of people together. He just had a heart attack but is doing great. They're the sort of people we could work with and the patients are neat. Most of them, according to Peggy, don't come in unless they are really sick or badly hurt."

"Do you think the company will let you stay there?"

"I hope so. But I'm just one of the temporaries they use to plug a hole in staffing. I don't know, this is the first job I've had that feels like more than a job."

They spent half an hour together before Lester was chased out by a nurse who had work to do on Jody prior to her surgery. As Lester passed the nursing station, the floor clerk handed him a note. It was from a Mr. Anthony DiBico, Vice President and Personnel Director for American Health. The note expressed hopes that Jody's procedure would go well and requested that he contact the personnel office at his earliest convenience. Lester stopped at a bank of phones in the entrance hall and put in the call. Mr. DiBico came on the line.

"Dr. Leavitt, thank you for calling. I hope Mrs. Leavitt is doing well. I understand she is to have her transplant this evening. I'm sure that will be a relief to you both. Let's see, it's now almost four o'clock. Our headquarters building is just one block south of the medical center. I would be most appreciative if you could come over now."

Lester's heart skipped a beat. "I'll be right there."

The vice president's office was on the twenty-seventh floor just below the summit where the suites for the president and CEO of American Health commanded a most impressive view of the city. Lester was welcomed at the elevator by a tall blonde in a short-skirted black pinstripe suit who escorted him into the presence of Mr. Anthony DiBico. He was an enormous man, like a linebacker, wearing a black silk suit and a grey satin tie that set off his gun-metal crewcut.

"Thanks for coming so promptly, Doctor," boomed the vice president, striding around his desk to shake hands. His raptor eyes bored into Lester and cast doubt on the welcome of his smile.

Hugh Drummel detached himself from a window and turned to Lester. "A marvelous coincidence."

"Mr. Drummel, what a surprise."

"Jody's doing well I trust?"

"Yes she is, although I think she's nervous, as I am."

DiBico indicated a sofa behind a coffee table. "Please sit down, gentlemen. As Hugh says, this is a fortuitous coincidence." The VP sat in a straight-backed chair that allowed him to peer down on his two visitors.

"I won't take much of your time, Doctor, because I know you'll want to return to your wife's bedside. So let me be forthright. I understand from Hugh that you have been acting as a locum tenens for Dr. McKinnon at the Cicero Clinic following his heart attack. Originally, when Hugh came up with the idea of helping Dr. McKinnon keep the reins of the practice in his hands following his illness, I considered it a gesture of goodwill that the community of Cicero would appreciate. It won't come as a surprise to you that we are anxious to work with Dr. McKinnon and develop a productive liaison between his well-established but old-fashioned style of practice and our renovated regional center. I'm sure you know that we were delighted to have Dr. Peter Peterson of the Simms Clinic enter into a mutually profitable relationship with us. Unfortunately, for reasons of sentiment that have nothing to do with efficiency, an alarming number of Dr. Peterson's patients have elected to drive over to the Cicero Clinic." The executive paused, "Forgive me, Doctor. Would you care for a cup of coffee?"

"No thank you, sir," said Lester. "But I could sure use a glass of water."

"Hugh?"

Drummel shook his head.

DiBico reached over to his desk and buzzed his secretary who came to the door. "Cynthia, would you bring us some ice water, please?"

He turned back to the business at hand. "Now, I would obviously not want you to reveal any professional confidences, but what does Dr. McKinnon possess that Dr. Peterson lacks?"

Lester's laugh shocked both men. "I'm sorry. I know it isn't funny, but there's a world of difference between those two. In a nutshell, Peterson's out for himself and Doc's out for his patients."

Hugh snarled sarcastically, "That's so simplistic, Lester."

"I suppose it is. I guess I'm just a simple guy, but I'll tell you one thing, since I've been in Cicero I've felt more fulfilled and useful to my fellow human beings than I ever have before."

Hugh was condescending. "That's so nice." He turned to DeBico, "I told you he's an outstanding young doctor with a sense of calling to the profession."

"Yes, yes," replied DiBico. "That's all very well, but unless things are on a sound business track, sentiment will simply remain what it is, an emotion." He stood up and paced in front of the couch with his hands in his pockets, apparently in deep thought. The door opened and Cynthia brought in a tray of glasses with ice water and left. Lester reached for his glass and swallowed half of it gratefully, as DiBico, who had resumed his pacing, came to a stop in front of him.

"The most important question, Dr. . . . uhhh . . . Leavitt, is just what do you think you're worth?"

"Me?" replied Lester, caught off guard. "I haven't the foggiest idea. That's not why I went into medicine, although I do hope to make a reasonable living."

"Answer for him," DiBico ordered Drummel.

"You're worth big money, Lester. You're a doctor who's not afraid of work. That's why we continue to invest heavily in your salary which is, I believe, twenty percent above the median wage given a locum with limited experience. It's also why we've underwritten most of your wife's medical care. In return for this, you signed a contract, which, I am happy to report, you have honored to the letter. In a perverse way, honored too well perhaps, since I understand some of Dr. Peterson's patients have been attracted to your care in Cicero. I think . . . "

DiBico held up his hand. "Let me get to the point. We will be importing into Cicero a modular clinic fully equipped with the latest diagnostic equipment and treatment facilities. It will be called the Cicero Unit of American Health Corporation. The building will be slightly larger than Dr. McKinnon's clinic and infinitely more state-of-the-art. We expect you to be its doctor. Your prices will be set by Hugh according to competitive rates we apply when acquisition of a market segment is our aim."

Lester was stunned. "I can't do that. I can't betray the trust Dr. McKinnon has in me."

"What about our trust in you?" hissed Drummel.

"Trust has nothing to do with it," said DiBico impatiently. "We own part of you, Dr. Leavitt. You signed a contract and it states that you will follow orders with no breach of confidence."

"The gag clause," Lester said under his breath.

"A crude term," said Drummel, "but realistic. I must point out to you that there are five floors of lawyers in this headquarters building, and should there be a threat to your contract by anyone, including you, you would find yourself in serious legal trouble. In other words, your complete silence on company information and policy is explicit in your contract."

Lester suddenly felt a cold wave of fear in his gut. What if the patient called Mary from Simms had repeated his negatives about managed care.

"Do we understand each other?" barked DiBico.

"Yes," replied Lester. He stood. "Is there anything else?"

"No," said DiBico. "Please give my regards to your wife."

With a heavy heart and crushed spirit, Lester walked back to the hospital and rode up to the surgical floor. The clerk told him Jody was scheduled for the OR in a few minutes. He opened the door to her room. She was lying in bed and opened her eyes as he tiptoed in. He stepped over to her and kissed her. "You okay, sweetheart?"

"Couldn't be better. I'm as clean as a whistle inside and out. You could eat off me." She put her arms around his neck and returned the kiss. "I love you, Les." He sat on the edge of her bed and she held his hand to her breast. "I keep thinking that a week from now we might be together in Cicero working with your new friends at the clinic. Do you think they can use another nurse?"

"I'm sure they could use another nurse, but I haven't asked them yet. I do know Dr. McKinnon and Peggy want to meet you."

Chapter 30

WITH LESTER AWAY, Alex and Peggy were back at work in full harness. Jenny called around noon. She told Peggy that the news of her resignation had spread through the hospital like a brush fire fueled by the medical staff's frustration and resentment against Drummel and company. The staff council convened without Jenny and drafted a strike resolution which they posted on every bulletin board in the hospital requesting signatures. Two hours later the sheets, overflowing with names, were gathered and presented to Patricia for transmission to Paducah. Alarmed, she called Jenny who was packing up her apartment. Together they met with a quorum of the council. Jenny told them that even if American Health withdrew Drummel's letter and the demand for an apology, she would move on. She was almost debt free and was sure she would have no trouble finding work. Reluctantly they withdrew their action against the administration.

During the afternoon, Howard Lindsey checked in. The MRA for his carotid arteries showed that no surgery was needed. Howard had been impressed by the science and equipment involved in his care, but he was uncomfortable as a patient. The label of patient, with its expectation of compliance and a graceful acceptance of others' efforts on his behalf, ran counter to the culture of self-reliance from which he'd sprung. He was glad when Alex closed his chart and had time for a chat and a return to non-patient status.

Lester called Alex at home that evening full of the happy news that Jody had received a perfectly matched kidney. She was expected to have normal renal function for many years. He planned to be back in Cicero on Sunday, ready for work on Monday. He hoped that she would follow in a week or ten days. He almost told Alex about his time with DiBico but thought it wiser to wait until they were face to face. Administrators and lawyers scared the hell out of him.

On Friday afternoon, John and Stan drove to the center to help Jenny load her belongings into a horse trailer and move back to Cicero. John rode with Jenny in her car while Stan drove the pickup. On the way back John announced his plan to celebrate her homecoming on the following day. For the first time, the four of them—John, Emma, Stan and Jenny—would drive to the foothills and ride up to their forest allotments and meadows on Dutch Dan's and Big Indian Creek. Emma was preparing a feed they would pack with them. The weather report promised a fine summer day with the usual scattered evening thundershowers to add a touch of drama. John was as excited about the outing as Jenny had seen him in a long time.

"You know, Jen, there seems to be a divine planner up there that's looking out for us. Doc came over for a chat a couple of evenings ago after supper. He and I sat out on the porch. He puffed on his pipe and scratched his shaggy dog. We did some fine recollecting. He lived several lives before coming out West, you know. I knew some of it, like why he left New York and his feelings about the social set and what he calls man-made religion. When I hear him tell how he found himself during walks along the stream and out in the fields after the hay was cut, I realize how fortunate we are to be part of this land." He asked Jenny to pull over at the top of the pass.

They stood together and Jenny glanced at her father's pale, weather-worn face. He put his arm around her shoulders and gazed at the familiar view of their valley and pictured the memories he cherished: Jenny riding bareback on Thunder, her Morgan stallion, and whooping and hollering like an Indian. Emma packing lunches and ice tea in saddlebags, hanging out the wash, sweeping the house and gathering fresh eggs from the chicken coop. She wrangled horses, fed bum calves and the dogs, then rang the bell to feed her family around the kitchen table. After dinner and a read and tuck-in for Jenny, he and Emma visited on the porch swing. In the winter they sat by the fire each in their special chair. Emma sewed. John read his horse and cow magazines.

He turned to Jenny. "I've had a wonderful life thanks to Emma and all the work we did together to produce a fine ranch and a fine daughter. Your mom and I are proud of you, Jen, proud of the way you stick to your guns."

"Thank you, Dad. That means a lot." She was too moved to say more.

As they reached the floor of the valley and passed the ranches and home pastures of their friends and neighbors, Jenny felt a new bond with her dad that was stronger, by far, than the demands and expectations of family.

That evening, Jenny drove over to Sage City with a big box of groceries and a couple of toys for the children. Waynona was surprised and very happy to see her.

Jenny held Morgan as she visited briefly with Joyce. "I just came over to bring some fresh stuff from my mom's garden. Dad threw in some Morgan beef."

Joyce was clearly weaker than the last time Jenny had seen her, but she smiled and thanked her for coming over.

Waynona walked out to the car. Jenny reached into her shoulder bag. "Here's some cash to help tide you over."

"I don't want you to do that," said Waynona.

"It's not just for you, it's for my namesake. I take him very seriously."

Waynona took the money and stuffed it in her pocket. "You're off a special tree."

"I don't know about that. But I do know, that when you have more time, we'll sit down and figure out how to get you some training that will free you from a life of dependency on men."

"Like what?"

"Like being an emergency medical technician or an assistant in a clinic or whatever. You're smart, you're a hard worker and a wonderful mother. You just need some extra training."

"You really think I could work in a clinic?"

"Of course. You'd be good at anything you set your mind to."

Waynona took the box of food from Jenny. "Wow! What a great idea. Thanks a lot."

Just before sunrise, Stan and Jenny rode out to the horse pasture and wrangled those they would need for the day, saddled them, and led them into the horse trailer. They walked over to the main house for breakfast with John and Emma.

By 8:00 A.M., they headed up country and an hour later rode from their lower cow camp up a washed-out logging track toward the ridge that bordered the meadows called Dutch Dan's.

John led them through stands of aspen and fir and small clearings where wild iris, yellow paintbrush and pink pussytoes were freshly bloomed. He followed a game track that wound along the base of a natural sandstone castlerock whose shallow caves provided shelter for does and fawns. Above them a redtail hawk screeched to protest the invasion of his hunting ground and higher yet a golden eagle soared and circled in the deep blue sky. They rode up a narrow defile between two sandstone butresses and their sweating horses scrambled up the final steep slope to a flat projection of rock that dominated the land below. John dismounted and the others followed. He put his arm around Emma. Stan and Jenny stood next to them. A vast perspective spread silently before them. Beyond the valley, undulating blue-green hills with late patches of snow on their northern slopes gave way to lonely sculpted buttes and softer ridges whose pastel ochres faded to a grey haze where the curve of the horizon met the dome of the sky. With a sweep of his hand, John turned toward his mountain meadows, opened his mouth and sank to the ground clutching his side.

"Dad!" Jenny knelt beside him. She reached for the pulse in his neck: fast and weak. John stretched out, breathing hard; Stan peeled off his jacket and made a cushion for his head. A dark stain spread on his shirt. Jenny pulled open the snaps. The colostomy bag was full and leaking a red brown ooze.

"You're bleeding, Dad." Her mind raced back to the scan films of the ill-defined mass under the opening of the colostomy. The red in the ooze was bright red. The tumor had probably eroded an artery. She peeled off the bag and carefully stuck her index finger into the opening. She felt a hardness at the tip. "Stan, give me your handkerchief." Gently she stuffed the cloth into the bowel's opening until it formed a tight packing. Enough pressure might stop the bleeding. Emma opened a canteen of water and with paper napkins cleaned John's abdomen. In a few minutes John's pulse was slightly stronger. Stan helped remove his soiled shirt and pulled a sweater onto him, then eased him back to the ground.

Jenny said, "He'll have to ride behind you, Stan. We'll use his rope to tie him to your back. We have to make it to the trucks, then call Doc and have him meet us with the ambulance."

John passed out again when Jenny and Emma heaved him up to straddle the horse behind Stan. Stan pulled John's arms around and tied his hands together with a bandana while Jenny and Emma wrapped the rope around both men, turning John into a human back pack. Stan started down the steep narrow passage they'd so recently climbed. He leaned back as far as he could, pushing his heels down hard in the stirrups. With stiff extended front legs, the horse worked his way down hill, sliding on his haunches when the gravel gave way. They reached an apron of scree and turned left along the game track.

John mumbled, "Ride 'em cowboy," and struggled to free his hands.

"Stay put, John," ordered Stan. "It won't be long now."

Emma and Jenny, leading John's horse, caught up. They passed through the woods and glades—the magic of their earlier passage had disappeared. A short time later, John was lifted into the back of Stan's truck with his head resting on Emma's lap. Jenny followed in the other truck pulling the horse trailer. As soon as they were free from the hills, Jenny called Doc on the radio. He and Peggy would be with Donny in the ambulance and would meet them along the highway for the drive to the center.

They met at Sage City. Jenny told Alex and Peggy what had happened and what she had done as they lifted John onto the gurney. He was barely conscious, but when Alex squeezed his shoulder he opened his eyes and mumbled weakly at his friend, "Sorry."

"Sorry nothing, we'll get you fixed up," replied Alex.

They lifted the stretcher into the ambulance. Alex started an IV and oxygen while Jenny called the hospital and was patched through to Joe Woodhouse at home. Jenny briefed him.

"He seems to be stable for the moment," she added. "We'll head for the hospital."

John pulled the plastic mask away from his face. "No hospital."

Jenny replaced the mask.

Joe's voice came over the speaker. "What are his vitals now?"

"Hold on," said Jenny.

Peggy inflated the cuff. "100/50 and 120 pulse."

Jenny repeated the reading into the mike. Relieved, she patted her dad on the shoulder.

He frowned and shook his head. His voice was muffled by the mask, but he was adamant. "No hospital."

Jenny held his hand. "We have to stop the bleeding, Dad."

"You have."

"I just put in a plug. As soon as it's pulled out you'll start bleeding again."

He squeezed her hand. "No!"

She said with authority, "Joe will use a scope to find the bleeder and deal with it directly."

Joe's voice came over the speaker again. "When will you be at the hospital?"

Alex took the mike from Jenny. "Stand by, Joe." To John he said, "Work with us. We know what we're doing."

John replied with hoarse urgency, "Have Joe come to the ranch."

Alex glanced at Jenny. She nodded. He keyed the mike, "Joe, are you still there?"

"Go ahead, Alex."

"John refuses to go to the hospital. He wants to know

if you can take care of him at home?"

A long silence followed.

"Joe, are we still connected?"

"Yes. I was just thinking and getting used to the idea. I don't see why not, but it might be better to see him in your clinic. Do you have a cauterizing unit and suction and the rest of the stuff?"

"Sure do. Bring a universal adapter if you have one," replied Alex. "How soon can you leave?"

"I'll pick up my stuff and be on my way."

"Thanks. Just drive into Cicero and you'll see a blue highway sign that says Clinic. Thanks, Joe. See you soon." He handed the mike back to Donny.

Alex leaned over John. "We'll take you to my office and watch you there until Joe can check you out. If the bleeding can't be stopped you are going to the hospital whether you want to or not. Is that clear, Mr. Morgan?"

John sighed. "It's clear. But I'm sure the bleeding has already stopped. I hope you doctors won't start it up again."

Alex glanced at Jenny. "I can see where you get your stubborn streak."

In the treatment room, Peggy checked John's hematocrit. He'd bled down to thirty percent. His pressure was stable at 100/70 but his pulse was 120, reflecting his loss of blood. She replaced the oxygen mask with nasal prongs.

John spoke to Emma, "Would you mind running out to the house and bringing that document we wrote a couple of days ago? Art called it a codicil. It's time to show it to Alex and Peggy and the kids so they're reassured I've done some thinking about these things and that you and I have come to our own conclusions."

When Emma returned she gathered everyone around John and opened a manila folder. "A few days ago, John and I sat down and talked about the medical options he'd been given at the hospital. He told me how he felt and what he wanted to do. When Art came I gave him the notes we'd made and he turned them into an official part of John's will." She picked up the paper. "This is what your father said. I'll just read it to you."

I understand that during the course of emergency surgery, a cancer was found in my bowel and removed. I also understand that my most recent x-rays show that I may very well have more tumor in my bowel and in my liver. I am grateful for all the care I have received, but I do not want to follow the path of additional x-rays, additional scans and more surgery. If everything turned out to be benign, I would still be expected to have periodic rechecks. The fear and anxiety of something more showing up would cast a shadow on my life. I would rather live with reality than speculation. I do not want the questions of malignancy or not, further treatment or not, to haunt my mind. There is no way of knowing if some other condition is lurking in my body as I write. In my work as a rancher fatal accidents are not uncommon, but their possibility is not a haunting specter. If I have more cancer in me, so be it. I am neither apprehensive nor frightened. I would not consider any further treatment, surgical or otherwise, as an acceptable alternative to letting nature take its course. I assume Dr. McKinnon can deal with the pain. Personally I think that our current abilities to preserve life at any cost border on the unnatural and color our later lives with fear and bankruptcy. I will never want artificial life support or extreme medical efforts to extend my life.

I deeply appreciate my family, my friends and my doctors for allowing me to remain in control of my life and for thoroughly explaining everything and continuing to treat me. When my time comes to die, I want the funeral to be a celebration of the wonderful life we have lived together.

Emma rested her hand on John's shoulder.

"Thanks, Emma," said John. "There's one more thing I'd like. I know that in today's world, especially with your generation, Jenny and Stan, marriage sometimes brings with it baggage that becomes negative. But Emma and I have always appreciated the friendship and respect you two have developed. I hope you'll have kids, and I'm self-ish enough to hope that one of them will be called John Morgan Cummings. If this ambition of mine accords with your plans, I want to be around when you get married." He paused. "Now that's the longest speech I've ever given in my life."

Stan put his arm around Jenny. "I'll call Father Dave," he said.

John added, "He'll rustle up the JP for the license, I'm sure."

The door of the clinic flew open and Dr. Woodhouse strode in. "What a fantastic valley!" He looked around. "And what a nice place you have, Alex. No wonder you hold your own over here. I almost brought Hugh along, but decided not to. Hi, Jenny and everybody. Where's our patient?"

Alex said, "He's in the treatment room and seems stable."

Jenny added, "He may have lost some blood, but he sure hasn't lost any of his feistiness. His hematocrit is down to thirty percent. I think the bleeding has stopped. Come on in."

"Hi, Joe," said John. "I appreciate you coming all this way."

"After driving over that pass into this gorgeous country, I'm glad I did. Sure is different from the farmlands around the city." He stepped up to the gurney and rested his hand gently on John's abdomen. "His vitals steady?"

Alex replied, "Around 100/60+, and his pulse is down to 100. If I know this old bird, I'd say he'll make up his blood loss in a couple of days with some red meat and a shot of bourbon."

"That's my Doc," said John. "Always up on the best treatments."

Joe examined John's abdomen and carefully lifted the gauze pad off the colostomy. Four inches of red kerchief protruded from the stoma.

"Let me get my stuff set up and we'll take a look."

In short order, Joe had his colonoscope hooked up, and checked the light, suction and water.

"John, please roll over to your right side."

Jenny fixed the pillow under his head and put another one up against his back.

Very slowly Joe pulled the kerchief out of the colostomy and dropped it into a basin Peggy produced. A small amount of bloodstained mucous and liquid stool escaped from the open bowel. He wiped it away and inserted the tip of his scope, advancing carefully. At the six centimeter marker on the surface of the long flexible tube, he stopped and carefully rotated the instrument.

"Take a look."

Jenny, then Alex, looked into the eyepiece.

"What do you see, Joe?" asked John.

"We have an irregular raw area in your bowel with some seeping from under a blood clot. I'll inject it with epinephrine to shrink things down and then cauterize it to stop any further bleeding."

Jenny handed him the injector, followed by a long probe to cauterize what was clearly more tumor. Joe was tempted to explore further but fearful of provoking more bleeding. Slowly he withdrew the instrument, unplugged the cords and tubes from its base and gave it to Peggy.

"That should do it, John," said the surgeon. "Jenny saved your life by putting that plug in far enough to put pressure on the bleeders. I think we've done as much as we can or should for now."

"Thanks for coming," said John.

Peggy washed off the scope, dried it and put it back in its case. Jenny, Alex and Joe walked out to the front of the building.

Joe said, "Between Jenny's pack and my cautery we've stopped the bleeding, at least for the moment. After that, we'll have to see. I don't have to tell you he could bleed again anytime. Does he still insist on no further treatment?"

"Yes," replied Alex. "He had Emma read us a document he wrote a few days ago detailing his decision to let nature take its course, hoping that we can keep him comfortable."

Joe gave Jenny a hug. "He's quite a guy, your old man. It's a privilege to come over here to help in a small way."

Chapter 31

THE EVENING SUN filtered through the cottonwoods, each warm ray supporting mini-constellations of gnats suspended among shiny specks in the warm evening air. John lay on the swing with his head resting in Emma's lap. With rhythmic prodding of her foot she kept the swing in motion like a mother rocking a cradle. Jenny and Stan sat nearby on the porch steps.

John chuckled. "I'll bet that's the fastest anybody's ever gotten married around here without it being a shotgun wedding."

Stan replied, "That's the best wedding I've ever attended—short and sweet."

They were all exhausted but relieved to be together on this porch that had been such a refuge to them over the years. The swing was part of the family, however silent and inanimate it might be. Its gentle rocking had comforted them when the pain of growth kept them awake and anxious. Each of them, in their own particular way, wished their reunion in this familiar place could last forever. Each hesitated to say good night.

Emma opened her eyes and lay listening to a whispering breeze in the cottonwoods. She glanced at the clock: 5:30 A.M. Listening again, more focused, she snapped on the light. "John?" Then, more of a command, "John." She touched his shoulder and his head fell toward her, lifeless.

Alex opened the back door and let Gus out. He stretched and drew in a lung-full of dawn air.

Stan ran toward him. "John died. Emma woke up a few minutes ago and John died in his sleep."

"We'll be right there."

Jenny was in the kitchen making coffee and crying softly. Alex and Peg hugged her, then walked into the bedroom. Peggy pulled over a chair and sat next to Emma.

"I woke up and he was gone," said Emma. "Didn't make a sound, didn't cry out or move. Just let go in his sleep."

Peggy held her. "It's the way he wanted it."

Emma wept, "Oh yes, he would have been miserable if he couldn't work and take care of us. I know this is for the best, but I'm sure going to miss him."

From the door Jenny said, "Coffee's ready."

"We'll come," said Peggy.

Alex stood at the foot of the big bed and gazed at his friend and whispered, "I'm sure going to miss you, old buddy." He brought his hand up slowly, saluted and walked away with tears streaming down his cheeks.

That afternoon, Alex and Peggy stayed with Jenny and Emma to receive the stream of people who came calling. Each visitor brought freshly prepared food: roast turkeys or chickens, ham, casseroles, pans of scalloped potatoes, salads, cakes and rolls. People stayed long enough to show their sympathy—none stayed too long.

Alex took a call from Lester. He had just heard about John's death.

"Where are you?"

"In my apartment. I just got back. What can I do to help?"

"I'd be grateful if you'd take calls for the rest of the day. I'll be around if you need me."

"I'll do it. By the way . . . "

"Yes? What?"

"Nothing. It can keep." Again, Lester wanted to tell him about his talk with DiBico and Drummel, but this was clearly not the moment.

Chapter 32

IT SEEMED as if the whole valley gathered for John's church service. The inside of the modest building was packed and many stood outside listening through the open doors and windows. In the middle of the service, Lester was called away to the clinic. A kid had crashed his bike and needed attention.

The service was short, at John's request, with Father Dave announcing that Jenny and Stan would have some remarks to make after the burial when the family hoped that all those inside and outside the church would gather on the lawn where the ladies of the valley were serving dinner. A long line of cars escorted John to his final resting place in the Hilltop Cemetery. After the brief interment service, people returned to their cars for the short drive back to town, leaving the family together for a moment of privacy.

In the clinic, Lester was applying a cast to a kid with a greenstick fracture of his forearm when the telephone rang. He asked the boy's mother to take a message. She told him the man on the other end wanted him to call back—it was urgent. She showed him the number. He recognized Paducah's area code. His mind raced, thinking of what could have gone wrong with Jody's operation. What complications: embolus, infection, kidney rejection? With conscientious effort he finished the cast, molding it and holding its position until it hardened. He washed off the extra plaster on the kids fingers and washed his own hands. After arranging for a follow-up appointment he sat at the desk worried sick about Jody—hardly daring to dial the number.

The phone was answered after the first ring.

"Paul Siberling."

"This is Dr. Lester Leavitt, Dr. Siberling. Is there something wrong with Jody?"

"Jody?" A pause, then, "Oh, yes, Dr. Leavitt. No, no, I'm not a doctor. I'm an attorney for American Health. I'm calling at the request of Mr. DiBico. I believe you know him."

"Yes, I do," replied Lester anxiously. "We had a talk a few days ago. I hope everything is all right."

"Everything is fine. I'm calling to ask you to intervene in a small misunderstanding, miscommunication you could call it, with Dr. McKinnon, the medical director of the Cicero Clinic. You've been working with him, I understand."

"Yes."

"Well, Mr. Drummel has been under the impression that Cicero, and indeed Dr. McKinnon himself, would welcome an annex to his clinic to expand our services to him. We are quite clear now that this is not the case."

"Well, that makes sense," said Lester, wondering where this was heading.

"Unfortunately, two modular units were dispatched to Cicero and we gather from the trucking company that they should be showing up sometime today."

"Today! Really?"

"I am authorizing and requesting that you apologize to Dr. McKinnon for this misunderstanding and order the drivers to return the units where they came from. A faxed order is on its way to you. Is this clear?"

"Yes. Very clear," said Lester.

"Good-bye then doctor."

"Good-bye, Mister . . . " The receiver was dead.

Lester quickly mopped the plaster off the floor and

pulled fresh paper over the treatment table. The fax stuttered by the front desk. He retrieved the message and headed out.

By the time the Morgans rejoined their friends, the dinner was ready to serve. Father Dave gave the blessing and soon the tables were crowded with people tucking into plates piled high with food.

At the head table, Jenny clapped her hands. The chatter of voices calmed.

"I just want to say a couple of things. First, I want to thank all of you for coming to John's funeral to celebrate his life as a husband, father, cowboy, rancher and friend. Two days ago he told us he'd put all his affairs in order except for one thing. He wanted to be present when Stan and I got married. He wanted to do his duty as my father. Stan, you tell the rest."

"Jenny and I were married on Saturday."

The crowd clapped and Hank Collette hollered, "Lucky man!"

Ma Green shouted "Lucky woman!" Everyone laughed.

Stan continued, "My brother, Rick, was my best man. Peggy was Jenny's matron of honor and Doc and Emma witnesses. John took Jenny's hand and gave her to me. He made all of us promise that when it came time for his funeral, he wanted a brief service and, to put it in his own words, that we'd have a hell of a party to thank all of you for being such true friends and making his life what it was. He also wanted the party to celebrate our marriage and the continuation of ranching with Emma at the M Bar." Stan put one arm around Jenny and the other around Emma. "The Magoos are here with their music so we can all do what John asked." The gathering whooped and hollered.

As the music started, two big trucks loaded with modular units pulled up in front of the church. A sign on one of the structures read, "American Health Corporation—Cicero Unit." The music stopped. Moose rested his bass fiddle on a chair and walked over to the trucks, then returned to the head table. "The driver says they were ordered to deliver the prefabs to Cicero in care of the mayor. Do you know about this, Doc?"

"No," replied Alex.

"Wait a minute," shouted Phil Watson.

Jenny jumped up. "You wait a minute, Phil." She addressed the crowd. "Let me ask you, is there anybody aside from our mayor who wants to support a second clinic run by the regional center whose aim is to close down Doc and the Cicero Clinic?"

A voice from the crowd shouted, "Hell no!" and was joined by others.

Watson jumped to his feet. "That's not fair, Jenny. I don't want to see our clinic shut down. I want to see Doc get help." He stepped up on a chair to be better seen and heard. "As your mayor I'm concerned that the people of our community have the assurance of medical coverage, especially emergency coverage after Doc retires. A facility supplied and operated by the center will be a big addition to the community. It will allow Doc to slow down and enjoy the life he so richly deserves. I was assured by the center's administrator that everything would be done with the collaboration of Dr. McKinnon."

A man asked, "Did you speak to Dr. McKinnon yourself about this, Phil?"

"No. I was planning to do just that in the days ahead."

"What did the hospital people promise you, Phil?" asked Ma Green.

"They asked me to be on their community advisory committee. They didn't promise me anything."

A woman from another table shouted, "I'll bet they'll contribute to your next election campaign."

"That would be up to them, of course," was the mayor's answer. He stepped down.

Lester drove up, screeching to a halt. He ran toward Alex waving the fax. "Maybe I can explain." He stopped, suddenly aware that he was the center of attention. "I just got a phone call from American Health headquarters. I was asked to pass on to Dr. McKinnon their apology for a misunderstanding and to send the modular buildings back where they came from. The request and authorization is on this fax." The crowd roared its approval.

Hank Collette stood up waving his hand for silence and attention. "Doc McKinnon has been my doc forever and I want it to stay that way. But I've got one great big question, ya might even call it a worry. I know you well enough, Doc, to ask this straight out. Now that you've had that heart attack, we all know you should slow down whether you recognize it or not. Ya told me that yourself. What're we gonna do for a doc to help you or to take over when you do decide to retire?"

"I'll answer that," announced Jenny. "I've resigned my hospital job at the center. Now that Stan and I are married, he'll run the ranch along with Emma and I'll be your new full-time doctor here in Cicero working with Doc and Peggy so we can all have some time off and be with our families. Believe me, you don't want outsiders taking over your medical care."

"Now you're talking," shouted Donny. "Yeah, Jenny!" In seconds, everybody was cheering, and Gus joined in with a happy howl.

Jenny turned to Lester. "What are you going to do?"

"I'll send those trucks back. After that . . . I just don't know." He turned and headed out of the churchyard.

Shirley Davis stood in his way. "You will come back, won't you?"

He looked at her and shrugged his shoulders, shaking his head, "Oh, God. I hope so, but I don't know if I can."

As the party broke up, people came to the family to thank them for an extraordinary celebration. "One of the best funerals we've ever attended," said Ma Green.

Milly Hastings gave Jenny a hug and handed Alex two packages in a plastic bag. "These are from Tad."

"Thanks. How's he doing?"

"I'm surprised he's still alive," said Jenny.

"Oh, he's alive," replied Milly. "His friend Beak came for a visit, slept under the wagon rolled up in a blanket. Tad asked me to explain that two of the lamb chops are for you, Alex, and three are for Jenny. In his own words, 'Da lady doc who'll take care of Dog.'"

They laughed, and Jenny promised to run out and thank Tad personally.

At sunset, as they so often did, Peggy and Alex sat on their back porch relaxing after the full day of sadness and joy.

"What a party," said Peggy, as she poured coffee.

"People won't believe a small town like Cicero stood up to the city and that a rural practice like ours told American Health Corporation to go to hell. What do you suppose happened?"

"I guess the people ran them out," replied Peggy. "Maybe the reaction against American Health and what it represents will gain momentum and snowball through the country. But what do you think will happen to Lester?"

"I don't know," Alex replied. "I'm sure American Health has him by the short hairs." He looked up as a car turned into the ranch and drove past the big house. "It's Lester."

Alex walked out to meet him. "We were just talking about you. You ready for a cup of coffee?"

"No thanks. I hope I'm not interrupting or coming too late."

"Of course not," said Peggy. "Come and sit down. It's been quite a day, hasn't it?"

Lester put his elbows on the table and covered his face with his hands. "Drummel called me to check that the trucks and buildings were on their way back. He told me that I was to report to him in two days for a new assignment. He's pulling me out of your clinic." He pulled a handkerchief out of his pocket and held it to his eyes. "He had the nerve to go over all the arithmetic of Jody's kidney operation and the cost of her long-term follow-up. I've spent the last hour checking over my possibilities and there's no way I can leave the company. There's just no way Jody and I can be in private practice."

Peggy put her arm around his shoulders. "We understand, Lester. You'd be a wonderful asset to our practice, but you'll be a wonderful doctor wherever you practice and you have to take care of Jody."

"I know, but I had such great hopes of being free to practice the way you guys do and not as a flunky in some medical business."

"We'll miss you," said Alex. "But I think these HMOs are shooting themselves in the foot. You just hang in there wherever you are. We'll stay in touch. You and Jody can come visit for your holidays or anytime."

"Thanks," said Lester. "Well, I feel better having talked to you directly instead of over the phone. You'll tell Jenny, won't you?"

"No, Lester," said Alex firmly. "You'll tell her yourself. Remember, you're a friend, not some rent-a-doc. I'll tell you what. I'll bet you a hundred bucks that within the next few years the crass, ugly, nasty, greedy, for-profit

HMOs will be things of the past."

Lester stood. "Well, I'll tell you something. The time I've spent with you all will be a foundation for the way I practice wherever I go. So, good-bye for the moment." He stuck out his hand and Alex shook it.

Peggy gave him a hug and they watched him drive away.

"Poor guy," said Peggy.

"He'll be all right. He's well-trained and his heart's in the right place. But I do worry about all the young doctors who have been trained as gatekeepers and Instacare operators who are stuck in a system they hate."

"More coffee?" asked Peggy.

"No, thank you. I'm for the sack."

"Speaking of the sack," said Peggy, "do you know if Jenny and Stan are planning a honeymoon and, if so, where?"

"He told me this afternoon that he would like to take Jenny up to an old cabin above the Cummings ranch for three or four days. He's apparently fixed it up as a surprise."

Chapter 33

ALEX LET GUS out for the last time before bed. He stood at the door and took in the night air scented lightly with pine. In the starlight, Gus made the rounds of his favorite sniffing trees. Alex thought with relief and gratitude about Jenny and Stan and the fun that he and Peggy now had before them. Gus returned and Alex closed the door.

From the bed, Peggy held out her arms. "Come here, old bear. I want to hold you."

He kissed her and rolled into her arms and rested his head on her breast. "My favorite place," he mumbled.

"Question?"

The phone rang.

"Shit," said Alex and sat up. "I'm sure there's a hidden camera in this room that triggers something every time we lie down together." He grabbed the receiver and barked, "Hello. . . . Oh, Waynona, it's you. . . No bother. What's up?" He listened and looked at Peggy. "We're on our way. . . . It's all right, Waynona, we want to come." He put the receiver back. "Joyce just took a turn for the worse. She's not responding and her breathing is irregular."

Waynona met them at the door. Joyce was clearly in a coma.

"Coffee?" asked Waynona.

"Sure," said Peg. "I'll help."

"It's all ready."

The three of them squeezed in around the bed. They'd

had many visits like this in the past, talking about all sorts of things. Sometimes they'd read juicy tidbits or pontificating editorials from the local paper. Other times, they just sat sipping coffee.

Father Dave had been out earlier. They'd visited and prayed. Joyce liked him. He never tried to ram his beliefs down her throat. He was an older man who was gentle with people's views of the afterlife.

Waynona held her mother's hand and spoke softly of the sacrifices her ma had made to raise her by herself after Waynona's father had run off with another woman.

Alex watched Joyce's breathing wax and wane. He looked over at Waynona and said, "This reminds me of another lifetime, when I sat with dying people in a whole other culture. They believe that when a person becomes unconscious, the body continues to function and the spirit hovers nearby and communicates with the person's shadow. When breathing ceases, the spirit is welcomed to the ancestral village and the shadow divides among those close to the one who died."

"I bet Ma's ancestral village is in a meadow filled with wildflowers in her Kentucky hills. How long can she go on this way?"

"She has a strong heart," said Alex. "She could go on for a while."

They sat together, visiting quietly.

Waynona stood, "Thanks for coming out. I'll be fine with her now."

They walked out to the car. Waynona put her arms around Peggy, then Alex.

"What happened to that letter for the paper?" asked Alex, almost as an afterthought.

"I'll get it." She ran back to the trailer and returned with an envelope.

Waynona explained. "Peterson found out about it

through some gossip, then it was all over town. The only person who knows about the letter officially is some lawyer in Paducah who called me to check on the gossip. I read it to him over the phone the day before John Morgan's funeral. I told him I knew a lot more about Peterson and American Health that, at least for now, I left out. I also told him that if they mess with you and Peggy in any way whatsoever, I'd blow their whole fucking operation out of the water."

Waynona handed Alex the envelope. He turned on the headlights and read what she had written, then handed it to Peggy. They returned the letter to Waynona.

"You saved our clinic, Waynona," said Alex. "I'm glad we're on the same team."

On the way home, Peggy said, "That was quite a letter."

Alex agreed. "She's quite a woman."

Alex wearily pulled on his pajamas. "Have you searched the room for that camera?"

"I'll do it in the morning," Peggy replied, buttoning her nightshirt.

"Let's try lying down one more time."

"Shall I pull the phone lines out of the wall?"

"Not yet."

He kissed her and crawled under the quilt to lie beside her.

"This is where we came in," said Peggy. "Question?"

"Ask it before the phone rings."

"You've always been the boss. Aren't you going to miss that?"

"No. I can give Jen my ideas and she can do what she wants with them. If she likes them, putting them into effect will be her responsibility."

"Aren't you going to miss being *the* Doc?"

"No."

"But medicine has been your life, your habit, your mistress. Aren't you going to miss her?"

"No, my love." He kissed her softly on each eye, each corner of her mouth, then a long soft kiss on her lips. "I have a wiser and more exciting mistress called Peggy. She knows all about the old one and how to handle her. He crooned softly, "Peg o' my heart, I've loved you . . . right from the start, or something like that."

Epilogue

THE RANCH FLOURISHED under Stan and Emma's careful management in spite of serious depressions in cattle prices. Within a year, Hugh Drummel was fired and the regional center reverted to a free-standing hospital under the aegis of a non-profit Catholic group of community hospitals.

Lester and Jody could never afford to break free from the world of HMOs even when the company was fragmented, then swallowed up by a huge insurance company. Peterson retired from clinical medicine to work for a pharmaceutical company.

Tim Moore took early retirement from cardiology and occasionally covered for Jenny and Alex when the need arose—his need as well as theirs.

Over a period of four years Jenny expanded their work in Cicero and took over the Simms Clinic.

Alex and Peggy enjoyed a gentle practice with their older patients and, before the year was out, took an open-ended vacation to France so he could introduce her to his friends who'd saved him from his missionary mentors in Africa so many years before.

Waynona moved her ma's trailer to a small lot behind the Cicero Clinic and, after passing her GED, finished a correspondence course for medical office aides and became part of Jenny's team. She kept the following letter in a safe place.

The Simms Weekly Reporter
Letter to the Editor

Dear Sir,

When I think about the past few weeks, when my ma got real sick, I think about two kinds of doctors. One like Dr. Peterson at the Simms Clinic and the other like Dr. McKinnon in Cicero.

Dr. Peterson was rough and rude and really didn't give a damn. Dr. McKinnon was gentle and considerate. Dr. Peterson was rushed and more interested in his business than his patient. He kept looking at his watch. Dr. McKinnon took his time. Dr. Peterson missed Ma's diagnosis, lectured to us and pissed us off. Dr. McKinnon, with help from his friend, a doctor in Missoula, found out that Ma had advanced cancer of the kidney. He gave her what she needed for pain and saw both of us many times at home. We trust him.

I know there are many kinds of doctors working in different ways. What I don't understand is why American Health Company that took over the regional center allows a bad doctor like Dr. Peterson to even be in their Simms Clinic. I also don't understand why the same medical business would want to kick out Dr. McKinnon and take over his practice. We patients should not stand for that. I've got plenty more facts for anyone who wants them.

I consider it my responsibility as a daughter and a mother to warn people who are real sick that if they want to be treated right instead of being pissed off they should go to Dr. McKinnon, not Dr. Peterson.

Respectfully,
Waynona Jefferson

About the Author

WILLIAM T. CLOSE is a Fellow of the American College of Surgeons and a Fellow of the American Academy of Family Physicians. He is the recipient of an honorary degree, Doctor of Humane Letters, from the University of Utah. Prior to settling in Big Piney, Wyoming, he spent 16 years in Africa, arriving in the Congo just before independence and just in time for the mutinies, coup d'états, and rebellions that have marked the history of that unhappy country. He became the chief doctor for the Congolese Army and the president's personal physician.

Dr. Close, now in his 50th year of medical practice, continues to see patients in what he calls "a gentle, limited practice." He speaks frequently around the country on the disparity in care between the haves and the have-nots and the overriding challenge of bridging the gaps in a shrinking globe.

William T. Close is also the author of *Ebola: Through the Eyes of the People* and *A Doctor's Life: Unique Stories*. *Subversion of Trust* is Dr. Close's first novel.

Acknowledgments

Thanks to the many patients, far and near, who have taught me to listen and try to understand the depth of feeling in people who are sick, and frightened, and hoping for the best.

Thanks to my trusted colleagues over the years without whom my practice would have been of a lesser quality and unfulfilled.

Thanks to my wife, Bettine, who put up with my stares into space as scenes and dialogue insulated my mind from immediate company and surroundings.

And finally, thanks to our publishing team, all professionals of the highest order:

Susan Lehr, long-time assistant, inspirer, perceptive editor, and archivist extraordinaire.

Gail Kearns, Editor and Managing Editor.

Christine Nolt, Book Designer.

Peri Poloni, Cover Designer.